BLACK BLOOD

A Frankie Black Thriller

J.D. WESTON

BLACK BLOOD

"The essence of a man lies within the choices he makes. Those moments of decision that will, for better or worse, impact a lifetime. "

"Some choices should never have to be made at all."

"What will it be, Frankie?" said Carter. His cruel words echoed off the bare concrete walls and seemed to Frankie, that they would echo for eternity. "It's time to decide who dies."

The handgun was heavy in Frankie's hand and burdensome on his heart.

Despite the lies, the deceit, and that the man who was sitting in the chair besides where he stood was nothing but an old criminal, full of evil greed, and hatred, still, deep inside, Frankie felt the blood connection and the lost time.

The regret.

The muzzle of the gun touched his father's temple.

A dizzying haze of emotions, memories, and bitterness sang through his mind in a swirl of anger, tears, and love. One day the apartment would have smooth plastered walls painted white, expensive wooden floors and soft furnishing that made the place a home. Frankie imagined the owners toasting themselves with fine wine on the balcony, looking down at the River Thames as if they'd just bought a slice of heaven.

For Frankie, it was anything but heaven. It was just a dusty, concrete shell and the next time his feet touched the earth, his world would be a very different place.

"Do it now," Carter shouted. His voice was deep and commanding above the high-pitched squeals and cries of Frankie's son. "Do it now or the boy dies."

"Dad," cried Jake from the shadows. "Dad, he's hurting me."

The boy's plea for help was cut short with a whimper.

At the sound of his son's anguished cries, Frankie exhaled as if he'd taken a blow to his gut. Then he sucked a deep breath of warm stale air. He panted as if it were the first breath he'd ever taken, or maybe the last he'd ever take. Heavy footsteps rumbled in the shadows at the edge of his blurred vision. Carter approached, dragging Jake by the scruff of his neck. The boy's feet scrambled for purchase on the bare, concrete floor. Frankie startled, blinked away the tears, then turned to face Carter as the man raised his son into the air and held him with one hand over two-hundred metres of nothing but biting cold air.

"All you have to do is pull the trigger," said Carter. His voice boomed like a drum in the empty space.

A wave of pressure pulsed through Frankie. He hung his head, and let his eyes refocus on the bare and broken feet of his father who sat, stripped to the waist, on a small wooden chair beside him, with his arms bound and with a smear of dark red blood across his torso. Angry blue bruises lay beneath the blood from the brutal beatings the men had delivered.

Frankie met his father's eyes, but the man who had raised him cast his head down, shame weighing heavily on his mind.

"I'm sorry, Dad," he said, his voice thick with emotion.

"Don't be sorry, Son," came his father's broken reply. He raised his head to meet Frankie's sorrowful stare. "It's your turn for life now. So live." A sudden passion grew in his tone, unfamiliar yet endearing. It would be the last words Frankie heard from his father, they had to count. "Just promise me you won't make the same mistakes I did. Be there for Jake. Watch him grow. Be a father, Frankie. Be a better father than I ever was."

"But, Dad-"

"Don't," said his father. "Just don't say it."

A silence fell, thick and impenetrable like being lost in a fog.

Jake struggled. Carter tightened his grip, holding him further out above the drop. The biting wind seemed to suck at Jake's hair and clothes. The rain that fell in sheets washed away his tears. But that face, that tortured expression could never be washed away. He stared at his father with hope, and with fright; his eyes pleading for help.

"Pull the trigger, Son," Frankie's father whispered. "Pull the trigger and start over."

"This is all most touching," said Carter. "You've said your goodbyes. Now get on with it."

Through the haze of Frankie's muddled mind, he held Jake's eyes. Carter's fat hands held the boy tight.

"Don't look, Jake," called Frankie. "Close your eyes."

Frankie raised the gun once more and returned his gaze to his father.

"I love you, Dad."

His father tore his eyes away ashamed of the tears that ran free. His face contorted as he fought the battle inside him to remain strong for his son, and grandson. The choices he had made so long ago had finally come full circle.

"I love you too, Son," he croaked.

"Finish him," Carter screamed.

"On three, Dad," said Frankie and he raised his left hand, extending three fingers.

His father closed his eyes, braced himself and nodded once in confirmation.

"Three," said Frankie. His voice wavered.

His father's head rocked forward once as if counting along in silence.

"Two."

His father took a deep breath through his nose, leaned his head back and, for the briefest of seconds, seemed at peace with the world. Frankie withdrew a single digit.

"One."

CHAPTER ONE

HIGH-PITCHED SQUEALS, PLAYFUL BELLS, AND LOUD MUSIC emerged from the living room as Frankie pulled a tray of frozen chips and breaded fish from the oven. He placed the tray on the oven top, set the microwave to two minutes then closed the door as his phone vibrated on the kitchen work surface.

Another '*call me*' message pinged on his phone. It was the third one that day, but Frankie hadn't had a chance to reply since picking Jake up from school, emailing clients, and getting dinner ready. It wasn't as if he was avoiding her. He wanted to sit and compose a nice message, or even call her, and he would do, but maybe later.

"Jake, can you turn that off? Dinner's ready," Frankie called into the living room.

He slid the phone along the granite worktop and pulled two plates from the cupboard. He pushed the fries and fish from the baking tray onto the plates in proportion to his and Jake's respective sizes, dropped the tray in the sink, and pulled the door to the microwave open just before it pinged.

"Jake, now, buddy."

"I'm not hungry. I'm going to stay in here," came the reply.

Frankie held the door to the microwave, closed his eyes and let his head fall back. He stayed that way and called back to his son, reluctantly beginning the nightly rigmarole of getting Jake to eat.

"It's not an offer. It's an order. And what do we do when we're ordered to do something?"

Silence.

"Come on. What do we do?" said Frankie.

His persistence was answered with Jake's footsteps as he pattered into the kitchen.

"But, Dad, I'm watching telly. Can't I take dinner in there to eat it?"

"You could do, Jake, if that's what you want."

"Honest?" Jake's eyes lit with hope.

"Yeah, you could. Mind you," said Frankie, "you'd better make the most of whatever you're watching because if you do take your dinner in there, the telly will be gone by the time you get home from school tomorrow."

"Eh?"

"Not eh, pardon."

"Pardon?"

"You heard. I'd prefer to sell it than have you become a slob."

"But Mum used to let me-"

"Don't lie to me, Jake."

"You wouldn't know. You were never here. We used to sit and watch the cartoons together, we'd eat dinner on the sofa before I went to bed."

"How old are you, Jake?"

"Eleven."

"Right. So that means you're a big boy now, right?"

Jake shrugged.

"It does, trust me," said Frankie. "And big boys do as they're told."

"That's not fair."

"Life isn't fair. Now go and turn the TV off, and get back in here to eat dinner. It'll be cold by now."

Frankie watched his boy traipse off to the living room, then sighed with relief when the squeals, bells and music fell silent. Frankie didn't mind if his son watched TV while he ate. Frankie had done the same when he was young. But dinner time had proved to be the most effective time to engage with the boy, which was becoming more of a challenge as each week passed.

He pulled the beans from the microwave and spooned them from the bowl onto the two plates, which he then set on the table. Jake dragged the high stool back from the table, then clambered onto it, waiting for Frankie to hand him his favourite Disney cutlery.

Frankie pulled his own stool out and sat opposite his son.

"Why don't you tell me about school?"

"Like what?" Jake replied, without looking up from his food.

"Like what you're learning. Tell me what lessons you had today."

"We did PE, music, and spelling," mumbled Jake.

"PE?" said Frankie, trying to bring a little enthusiasm into the conversation. "I used to love PE. What games did you play?"

"They played rounders."

"What do you mean, *they* played rounders? Didn't you?"

Jake shook his head and spooned another mouthful of beans into his mouth.

"No? Why not? You love games, don't you?"

"I didn't have my PE kit, Dad. Mr Forsythe said we can't play unless we have our shorts and running shoes."

"Why didn't you have your kit?" asked Frankie.

"I didn't take it. It wasn't in my bag."

"Your school bag?"

Jake nodded his head, as he pulled the layer of breadcrumbs from his fish, tipped his head back and stuffed it all in his mouth.

"So, it's *my* fault," said Frankie. "I'm sorry, Jake, but you need to tell me when you have PE so I can make sure you're ready. Maybe you could give me a timetable or something, and I'll make sure you have what you need, okay?"

"It's okay, Dad. I can pack my bag, but I couldn't this morning."

"Why not? Why didn't you ask me for help?"

"Because it's all still dirty from when I used it last week."

Frankie's eyes closed as he realised he'd been neglecting the simple things, the things that Jacqui had done that he'd taken for granted.

"I'm sorry, Jake," said Frankie. "I'll do the laundry this weekend."

"You're working this weekend, aren't you? You said I have to go to Nan and Granddad's house because you have a job."

The boy was right. Frankie offered him an apologetic smile across the table, then reached across and ruffled his hair.

"You're a smart kid, Jake. I don't know what I'd do without you."

Jake recoiled at the touch, then stopped as soon he saw the hurt look on Frankie's face. A moment of silence held them both.

"I'm sorry, Jake," said Frankie, his voice quiet. "I'm still learning how to do this without your mum. But you know what?"

Jake looked up at his dad, his eyes wide.

"We're a team, mate. You and me. It might be tough now, but things will get easier, I promise. Just bear with me, yeah?"

A little tear formed in the corner of Jake's eye. Frankie bit his bottom lip. He wanted to say more, but the words just weren't there. The Disney cutlery fell to the plate.

"Jake? It's okay to cry you know?"

The little boy bowed his head.

"Can I get down now, Dad?"

Fighting the urge to say more, to get the tears rolling, Frankie just sat in silence and wonder.

"Go on then. But no telly. You need to clean your teeth and get to bed."

The stool scraped back as Jake pushed away from the table. He dropped to the floor and trotted through the kitchen to the living room. His bare feet slapped the floor tiles. Frankie waited for the usual banging as Jake ran up the thirteen old wooden stairs, but not this time. There was no sound, no excitement, no rush, and no stamping of heavy feet on the stairs.

CHAPTER TWO

"Did you see the new guy over there?" asked Shorty. "Bruno, his name is. The screws reckon he's one to watch out for. He's done time in every category A prison in Britain, he has, and quite often leaves a trail of blood wherever he's been."

"So what's he doing here on A-wing?" asked Smiler. "It's two to a cell already. What's he going to do, bunk on the floor?"

"He's in the admin wing until there's room for him," replied Shorty, as he shovelled a forkful of questionable mash potato into his mouth.

"What did he do?" asked Smiler.

"Jenkins the screw said he signed him in and checked his scorecard. Reckons he's a right nasty piece of work," said Shorty. "He also said old Bruno there was originally sent down for rape and aggravated assault, and landed himself in solitary pretty much straight away. He sliced some paedo's face open. So, they added three years for grievous bodily harm to his time, and since then, it's just been building up."

"And they've put a scumbag like that in with *us*?"

Shorty laughed. His mouth was wide open for the rest of the mess hall to see his half-chewed sausage.

"What? Are you scared, Smiler?" he said. "You worried he'll come and keep you company at night?"

Smiler turned to his food.

"You are, aren't you?" said Shorty. "You're worried about him. Well, don't worry too much. I heard it only hurts the first time."

Shorty burst into laughter at his own joke, and the other prisoners beside him laughed. But it was more to stay on the right side of Shorty than due to the actual humour itself.

"You can laugh, boys," said Smiler. "But old man Issac over there is getting out in a couple of days."

"So?" said Shorty, wiping gravy from his mouth with the back of his hand.

"So that'll leave a bunk free, won't it?" said Smiler. "More to the point, it'll leave a bunk free in my bleeding cell."

"Well, Bruno will bring a smile to your face, won't he?" said Shorty, creating another wave of laughs among the men.

Isaac's stare caught Shorty's attention.

"What's up, old man?" said Shorty. "Is there something you'd like to add?"

Isaac shook his head and returned to his own sausage and mash.

"So, you're getting out, are you?" Shorty said.

Isaac knew it was pointless ignoring him. He'd learnt over the years to be polite and to think before he spoke. He nodded in reply and averted his eyes.

"So," Shorty continued, "now you're leaving, you can tell us."

The question caught Isaac off guard. He raised an inquisitive eyebrow.

"Come on, old man," said Shorty. "Did you actually do it then?"

Isaac placed his cutlery down beside his dinner tray. He may not run the wing, but his age and experience inside commanded a certain respect.

"Now, now, Shorty. You know that isn't a polite question to ask."

The table had fallen silent as the eight prisoners all waited to hear if Isaac had served twenty-three years for a crime he didn't commit.

"Well, that's not strictly true, is it, Isaac? There is one exception to the rule, isn't there?"

"There's an exception?"

"Yeah. When you're you, and I'm me, and you have two days left to keep your nose clean. I mean, they can bolt a couple of weeks onto my sentence and I'd be none the wiser. But you, old man, have a lot more to lose, don't you? In fact, I'd go as far as to say that if you stayed inside, my friend here would have a much nicer time of it."

Isaac dragged his heavy arms to the table, linked his fingers and rested his chin on his hands.

"Listen, Shorty, I've done my share of stir. I was in here when you were still nicking chocolate bars from the corner shop, and in my time I've seen many people come and go. Fat men, skinny men, tall men, short men, black men, white men. You name it, and I've seen one. I've got less than forty-eight hours left here, and as much as I respect you, Shorty-" He held an index finger out to support his statement. "As much as I respect you, there's nothing you can say to get a rise out of me, and nothing you can do that'll stop me from walking past those big ugly screws, through those big ugly doors, and waving goodbye to a big ugly chapter in my life. So, if you want to know, if you really must know, and if it'll shut you up and give me two days of peace and quiet, then yes. I did it. I pulled the trigger. It was me who robbed that bank. It was me that pulled the trigger, and it was me who killed those men. I ain't proud of it, son. In fact, it's what keeps me up at nights. But life goes on. I've served my time. And now it's time for me to go outside into the big beautiful world and see if I can do a bit of good with whatever time I've got left."

Shorty clapped, quiet enough that the screws wouldn't hear. "Nice speech, old man. Nice speech."

"We've shared a wing for over ten years, Shorty. We've eaten dinner in the same room, slept beneath the same roof, and listened to the same haunted, junkie cries night after night. Are you really going to make this hard work now after all this time?"

"Oh, Isaac," said Shorty, turning to face the old man, "when you put it like that. Who am I to stop you leaving and living the rest of your life? But mark my words, before you leave, you need to swing by my cell for a little chat. A word in your ear, as they say."

"Is that right? And why would I do that?"

The bell on the wall rang, announcing the end of dinner. The quiet room became a hustle of scraping chairs and low murmurs. Shorty smiled as he collected his tray, and stood. He leaned over to Isaac who stood his ground and didn't recoil.

"Because what I have to tell you, you soppy old bastard, might just save your life."

CHAPTER THREE

Weaving through the back streets of Essex, a Greater London suburb, on her Vespa motorcycle, Penelope Pike enjoyed the late evening and the warm, summer breeze running across her skin and lifting her long, curly auburn hair from her nape.

Summertime in London, for her, was worth enduring the cold and miserable winters. Her spirits were lifted as were those of the people she passed. Kids played in the parks. Beer gardens were packed full of smiles. And, for just a few short weeks, life seemed wonderful. She approached a set of traffic lights and smiled to herself as she passed a line of black cabs, each with the driver's browning right arm resting on their open windows.

Upminster Station passed by on her right-hand-side, and soon she had left any semblance of commuting behind with nothing but open roads ahead. She pulled into The Fairway, passed three houses on her left, then stopped her motorcycle in the driveway beside a familiar, shiny, black Range Rover.

Dressed in a cute, knee-length, floaty, floral dress, and flip-flops, she pulled her helmet off and checked her make-up in the bike's tiny mirror before stepping off and locking the helmet in the seat compartment. A quick glance at the four-bedroom house told her that her arrival had gone unnoticed. So she pulled her handbag from over her shoulders, retrieved her phone and checked for emails.

Her boss, the editor of the Express newspaper, had sent her a new assignment by email. The email was brief, so she scanned through it, got the gist, then closed her email app, making a mental note of what time she'd need to meet the media team in the morning.

Penelope dropped her phone back into her bag, checked the mirror one last time, then bounced up to the front door. She gave two light taps on the small glass window as she always did, not loud but distinct.

A silhouette approached from inside, its form obscured by the opaque glass panel. More out of habit than anything else, Penelope gave the surrounding street a quick glance, then, happy her presence was unobserved, she returned her attention to the house to find a friendly but tired-looking figure framed in the open doorway.

A pained smile crept across his face, curling at the edges as a newspaper might succumb to the heat of a fire.

"Are you going to leave this girl to stand out here?" she asked, pulling her mass of hair across one shoulder.

He stepped to one side and let her pass into the wood-panelled hallway, then closed the door behind. As if the house was oblivious to the summer feeling of the outside world, the tension inside was claustrophobic. With open arms, she coaxed him into a welcoming hug, to which he responded with a peck on the cheek and a quick squeeze. He then pulled away and padded into the kitchen.

Bright sunlight filled the south-facing kitchen. But it failed to quell the heavy and oppressive mood. Penelope placed her bag on the worktop and watched as he filled a glass of wine and handed it to her. She took it and continued to watch his methodical mannerisms. He put the wine back in the fridge, pulled out a bottle of beer and cracked the lid with the opener he'd used on the wine.

Propped with one elbow on the granite, Penelope waited for him to talk. She knew him well enough that any avenue of questioning she tried would just block the information. It was always better to let him find the words in his own time.

Turning to look through the window into the south-facing garden, she sipped at her wine and wondered where he found the time to keep it so neat and tidy. Thick hedges lined both sides of the grass all the way down to the large, brick-built outbuilding at the bottom of the garden. Outside the back door, a paved patio area with a large, glass-topped wicker table and chairs provided outside seating. A brick barbecue and smoker sat to one side, with a small shed on the other.

Without ever looking inside the shed, Penelope knew it would be neat and tidy. Anything he needed would be to hand, ready to grab with minimal fuss. It was just his way.

The back door opened, and he stepped outside. Penelope followed him into the garden, where, ever the gentleman, he pulled a chair from its place beneath the table. He gave it a wipe with a cloth and set it to one side for her to sit on, facing the sun.

Remembering her manners, Penelope nodded her thanks, sat down, crossed her legs, and placed her wine on the table. Then, just as she knew he would, he ducked inside to fetch some coasters.

At first, his mannerisms and compulsive behaviour had irritated Penelope. But the longer she knew him, the more she found she loved them.

He returned a moment later, wiped the circle of residue from the glass top, and set the glass back down on a little wooden coaster, before wiping his own seat, dropping onto it and closing his eyes as if the weight of the world hung heavily on his shoulders.

He set his own beer on another coaster, rested his elbows on his thighs and let his head fall into his hands. His fingers created channels in his short shaved hair like forest rivers meeting at an estuary.

The silence for some may have been intimidating, irritating, or even rude. But for Penelope to sit and watch the sun go down in peace, with a glass of wine and the man she'd grown to adore, was the perfect end to a beautiful summer day.

Beyond the manicured garden far away on the horizon, Penelope watched as small, white clouds teased their way across the sky. She imagined them escaping with the hues of blues and reds, and running from the night sky that approached from the east. They would continue their unending journey, bringing sunshine and life across the world, and spreading joy wherever they roamed in their constant quest to evade the relentless and tenacious darkness that was ever on their tails.

"I'm not sure I can do this much longer," he said at last.

Dreamlike visions of an evil nighttime sky in an everlasting pursuit of the glorious army of sunshine washed away, leaving reality to snap back into place.

"I thought I'd moved on," he continued. "But I know everything could change at any time, everything I've worked for, the progress we've made."

Penelope touched his knee, then allowed her hand, warm and soft, to rest on his leg.

"I'm here," she said. "Let's take it one day at a time, Frankie."

CHAPTER FOUR

The vicious gurgling of boiling water broke the silence of the morning as the kettle came to a boil.

Dressed in shorts that had been cut down from a pair of old army issue, olive green combat pants, and a black Norwegian army shirt with the sleeves rolled up, Frankie stood barefoot at his kitchen breakfast bar with two empty mugs and a coffee press full of fresh ground beans ready to go. The kettle clicked off just as Frankie reached for it, and the aroma of the coffee as the water poured into the press teased his taste buds, reminding him just how thirsty he was.

"You didn't sleep?" asked Penelope from the doorway. She was wearing one of her long flowing dress with her mass of curly damp hair pulled onto one shoulder. She leaned on the door frame in her usual relaxed manner.

Frankie shook his head.

"Not much," he mumbled. "Coffee?"

Pity filled her eyes, followed by a look that said, '*I'd love to stay, but...*'

"Rain check?" she offered.

Frankie nodded and let the weight of his hand push the coffee press down nice and slow.

"I don't want Jake to see–"

"No, you're right," said Frankie, as the press reached the end of its journey. He tried to say more, but words somehow failed him.

"Can I get a hug at least?" asked Penelope. She stepped into the kitchen and brought with her a smile that seemed to search his eyes for a companion.

That was when words found him. But only in his mind. He felt grateful to have her. He felt lucky they'd met. But most of all, no matter how nice it felt to hold her, to smell her hair and to just touch someone, he still felt very alone.

"Not much of a hug," she said, her face buried in his shirt.

This time, a slither of a smile reached his face. He pulled his arms in tight around her shoulders, kissed her on the top of her head, then with surprising reluctance, he let her go.

Her arms slid from around him. Her fingers found his pockets and hung there, clinging as if she too experienced the momentary sense of denial. She bit her lower lip in thought, then released him, letting her arms fall to her sides in defeat.

"Keep smiling, soldier," she said. Then she stood on tiptoes to kiss him, before turning on her heels. Her soft footsteps carried her away to the front door. Frankie watched with admiration at the way she moved. Each step she took was like a dance that set off a trail of motion as the hem of her dress swayed, and her long, thick mane of wild, red hair caught the rhythm and joined in the dance.

As if she sensed being surveyed, Penelope turned at the front door, letting one slender hand hang from the brass door handle.

His unconscious smile met her wild green eyes from the next room.

"Thanks," he said.

"For what?" she whispered. Her eyes darted to the stairs to make sure Jake wasn't awake and standing there.

"It won't always be like this," he told her.

She pulled the door open and glanced up to the sky. Then she once more turned back to him, sending her hair from one shoulder to the other in a wave of life.

"I know," she said. "See you tonight."

She winked then pulled the door closed. The little knocker rattled once then silenced, leaving Frankie alone with just the empty peace and the sweet fresh smell of Penelope's hair.

The smell of the shampoo carried Frankie off to distant memories of a weekend break in Paris before Jake was born. It had been early morning when Jacqui, wearing just a thin negligee, had pulled open the double doors to their hotel room balcony that overlooked the Rue de la Paix and bathed in the glorious spring morning light. Her body was dark and sensual against the almost transparent veil of her lingerie.

Captivated in a rare moment of utter perfection, Frankie had reached for his Nikon and snapped just one photo, before ditching his camera on the over-sized bed. He stepped across the room, slid his arms around her waist, and kissed along her neck. He felt her face tighten against his own as she smiled in reply and turned towards him in his arms. But her smooth and straight, dark hair curled before his dreaming eyes. It thickened as Jacqui turned to face him, growing in mass and lightening in colour to a rich, sunburst auburn. Even the familiar scent of Jacqui's hair turned foreign yet familiar to Frankie's nose. He felt himself leaning in to kiss her, to kiss Penelope. Even though his heart pounded heavily in his chest, and he knew it was wrong, he kissed her. His hands slid up the smooth contours of her body, found her neck, then buried deep into her hair pulling her closer into him, to kiss her harder.

He pulled away once more to admire her. But it was Jacqui

who stood there before him glowing with pleasure, not Penelope. Her smile faded. Her bright blue eyes narrowed.

"What's wrong?" she asked, her voice soft and childlike.

Frankie shook his head, not wanting the moment to pass, but pushing the sense of betrayal as far as it would go.

"Tell me what's wrong," she asked again.

He answered her question with another kiss, high above the early morning Paris traffic with nothing but the cool European air, and distant morning sun to spy them.

"Daddy, what's wrong?"

Reality emerged through a cloud of morning fog as the Parisian rooftops melted into the granite work surfaces, and the smell of crisp morning air mixed with the scent of Jacqui's hair became an earthly aroma of fresh coffee and the fading smell of Penelope's shampoo.

"Daddy?"

She was gone.

His eyes focused and found Jake stood at the entrance to the kitchen.

"What's wrong?" the boy asked.

"Nothing," lied Frankie. "I was just thinking about something."

"I'm leaving now," said Jake, and turned towards the front door.

"Already?" said Frankie. "Don't you want breakfast?"

"No," he replied.

"Well..." Frankie fought for words. He longed for a conversation with his son. "What about PE? Do you need your kit?"

"That was yesterday, Dad," Jake replied, reaching for the door.

"Well, what about lunch?" Frankie approached him, dizzied from his daydream but concerned for his son. "Surely you need lunch?"

"She stayed, didn't she?" said Jake, with one foot on the front step, and his face resting on the door's edge.

"Who?" said Frankie.

A look of disappointment washed across his son's face as he turned away and left the house.

Frankie ran to the door and pulled it open wide.

"Jake?" he called.

But the boy didn't reply. He didn't even look back. He hoisted his backpack onto both shoulders, left the driveway, and disappeared behind the neighbour's overgrown hedges.

<hr>

CHAPTER FIVE

<hr>

THE ANGRY, MECHANICAL BUZZ OF FORTY-TWO STEEL DOORS being released chorused throughout A-wing. Isaac had been sitting on the edge of his bed for an hour.

"One more time, Isaac," said Smiler as he pulled himself off his bunk and dropped to the floor. "The next time you hear that god-awful sound, you'll be getting out. How does it feel, old man?"

With a huff, Isaac pushed himself up off the hard mattress, gave the cell a habitual quick look around to make sure nothing worth stealing was on view, then made towards the door.

"Petrifying," he mumbled to Smiler as he passed him. "Absolutely bleeding petrifying."

He fell in with the line of prisoners who rattled across the steel-grated mezzanine floor and headed towards the mess for breakfast. Around him, the others spoke with hushed tones; some harmless taunts, some inevitable threats. Years of stir had taught Isaac to keep his head low.

The mood in the mess varied from day to day. It was most often dictated by the officer on duty; some were stricter than others.

Two steps into the mess and Isaac felt the oppressive weight of Prison Officer Shepherd. He didn't even need to look for him; the officer's presence commanded a ring of fear and silence. The circle of peace dissipated in concentric rings the further from the guard the prisoners sat. But as Shepherd performed his perpetual and eagle-eyed stroll along the centre alley between tables, a wave of verbal restraint followed him.

On any other day, having Shepherd on duty would have suited Isaac down to the ground. Most arguments and ill-feelings took root in the mess or in association. But following what Shorty had said the previous evening, Isaac needed a quiet word. If he missed the opportunity, the only other chance would be during association at six o'clock that evening.

The queue at the servery was sullen. The prison offered few choices of food, of which the prisoners selected their dinners at the beginning of each week. None of the choices particularly enticed Isaac, but the sausages and mash were bearable and filling, so Isaac always chose it whenever it was being served. Breakfast, however, involved a process of elimination that began with the unidentifiable through to the least unbearable, which forced the prisoner to elect for either runny porridge or what Isaac deemed to be a poor attempt at a fried breakfast.

Taking a step up to second in line, Isaac surveyed the room for Shorty, who sat in his usual spot with his usual cronies. He noted that, instead of engaging in their usual hushed banter, they all sat eating in rare silence. But a trained eye such as Isaac's could spot the communication. Shorty chewed with his mouth open and his eye on Shepherd. Patmore, to his right, replied as he lowered his head to take a mouthful of cereal.

"You eating or what?"

The man behind roused Isaac from his surveillance.

"Yeah," replied Isaac. He held out his tray to the prisoner behind the servery, who dished out spoonfuls of sorry-looking scrambled egg.

"Some might call this the last supper, Black."

As if black clouds formed above him, Isaac's world fell into shadow. He received his tray from the server and acknowledged Shepherd with a nod before averting his eyes and stepping towards the pile of cold toast.

"Well?" said Shepherd, signifying that Isaac was to reply.

Responding with a polite nod often displayed enough courtesy for Shepherd to shift his focus onto some other prisoner. But every now and again, he issued a second comment, and, if it failed to elicit a response, a higher degree of questioning would begin. It was just a power trip. Isaac knew that. All the prisoners knew it, and as long as it was somebody else on the receiving end, the display offered a level of welcome entertainment to break up the monotony of daily prison life.

The already silent room somehow dropped a discernible decibel.

"Mr Shepherd?" said Isaac, unable to think of a response to the prison officer's original question.

"It's your last breakfast here. What do you have to say about that?"

Eighty pairs of eyes fell on Isaac. Some pitied his position. Some longed for the interaction to escalate to something much more.

"I'd say that there are about eighty men in this room that might betray me, and about nine billion outside these walls that will deny knowing me, sir."

The comment was neither meant as humour or as a vindictive retort. But Isaac knew that Shepherd, being an educated man would recognise the biblical reference, and could take it as either.

To Isaac's surprise, the officer seemed to mull the comment over. He nodded once.

"Keep your nose clean, Black. I don't hear the jangling of keys just yet."

It was a warning that most of the prisoners had seen before.

Equality between the guard and the prisoner was imminent when the prisoner was being released. In a matter of hours, they would be equals, which questioned Shepherd's authority over him. Isaac could handle that. But a final jab or two with Shepherd's provocative tongue could rattle the cage of a sensitive prisoner, which would provide ample opportunity for Shepherd to delay the release.

The tactic mostly applied to prisoners that were in Shepherd's pocket. A favour here and a benefit there gave the prisoner a little additional comfort, but when the time came for Shepherd to seek information, the prisoner would have little room for manoeuvre. Shepherd's grasses were well-known throughout the wing. Shorty and his crew had invited a few to transfer to the medical wing occasionally. But as fast as the prisoners' methods for punishing a grass evolved, as did the guards' enthusiasm for recruiting more.

Fortune had favoured Isaac from day one on the wing. He'd spent the first week, as did most prisoners, on the admin wing. He'd spent that time working out who was who, and who he might know either directly or through reputation. Then, with a few well-placed words in a few well-selected ears, he'd forewarned the wing of his arrival, allowing his own reputation to pave the way.

Doing hard time for holding a bank up with a shotgun was admirable among prisoners, but it wouldn't elevate Isaac to the lofty and secure heights of the untouchables. Isaac had made sure that the rumours he had planted conveyed that his armed robbery charge was merely secondary to the multiple accounts of murder. It had taken twenty-four hours for Shorty to appear in the doorway to his cell on the first A-wing association night, deeming Isaac unworthy of the privilege of being labelled one of Shepherd's grasses.

"I will, sir," he replied. "Is that all?"

Shepherd replied with another of his authoritative nods and a twitch of his Hitler-esque moustache, leaving Isaac free to slot himself into the one unoccupied seat on Shorty's table.

"Nicely swerved," muttered Shorty.

Keeping his head down, and knowing full well that he would still be under Shepherd's sensory radar, at least for the rest of breakfast, Isaac said nothing.

"Find me at association," said Shorty. "We'll break bread."

<hr>

CHAPTER SIX

<hr>

"How did it go?" asked Casey, a fat, greasy-looking man who had climbed the rank to editor and had apparently taken every chocolate biscuit and cream tea on the way. He had a sharp mind that never seemed to dwell on a subject for long. He would often cut people off mid-sentence with a curve-ball. "Did you get what we need?"

Not waiting for Penelope's response, he reached for his desk phone, digging his swollen gut into the edge of the oak-panelled desk.

"Tammy, order me some lunch. Something meaty." He slammed the phone down and moved a pile of papers from one side of his desk to the other, presumably so he could see more of Penelope's figure.

"Another football player up in court for assault," said Penelope. "It wasn't a tough assignment. I could have just changed the names in the last two cases."

"Beggars can't be choosers, Pikey."

"I'm not begging, and I've asked you not to call me Pikey."

"What did he get?"

"Six months," replied Penelope. "He'll be out in three."

"Is it written up?"

"You'll have it in an hour."

"I want half a page."

She had expected the demand. Penelope didn't react.

"Talking of tough assignments," said Casey. "When is the next big one coming my way? Sit. Tell me about it." He extended a hand, directing her to the guest chair.

"You won't mind if I decline the offer," she replied. She knew how to play his game. She'd fallen for the subservient seat trick the first few times like a naive fly might fall prey to a web. "I'm getting close. Leave it with me. Keep feeding me the small fry, and when the time is right, I'll bring you the catch of the year."

The desk phone rang again. Casey glanced at the number that displayed on the handset, then returned his attention to Penelope.

"I don't pay you for small fry, Pikey."

His answer was almost verbatim to the response she had envisaged.

"No, but you keep feeding me them, and I'll grow them into stories worthy of a double spread."

"Meanwhile?"

"Meanwhile, Casey," said Penelope, "I've got a lead on another domestic abuse case. It's early doors, but if it goes somewhere, you'll be the first to know."

Casey was visibly displeased. But whether his displeasure was rooted in Penelope's response or in her ability to assume control of the conversation, Penelope couldn't be sure.

"One week," said Casey. "Then you're back on the dirty foot-ballers unless it goes somewhere."

He closed off the conversation by answering his phone, but his words loitered in the air, delivered with the finality of a death sentence.

Casey continued to demand a barrage of unachievable dead-lines to whoever it was he was talking to. He stopped mid-sentence, placed a hand over the mouthpiece and raised a questioning eyebrow at Penelope as if inviting her to retort or get out. But underlying the conceited gesture was the deadline being set in stone.

One week.

Taking the hint, Penelope turned and exited the room, leaving the door wide open. A disinterested and resentful look from Tammy, Casey's Personal Assistant, greeted Penelope on her exit. The charmless sneer faded to brief panic as the contemptuous little bitch realised Penelope had left Casey's door wide open, and she scrambled to her feet.

Somewhere in the distance, just as Penelope was reaching her desk, she heard the angry bellow of a wild pot-bellied editor calling for the door to be closed, and she smiled to herself.

Little victories.

It was a game Penelope enjoyed, and one that surprised her every time. Tammy had yet to cotton on to Penelope's self-indulgent amusement. But even antagonising Tammy and Casey wasn't enough of a distraction. One week to close a case she hadn't even begun was ludicrous and would mean time away from Frankie when she felt he needed her.

She searched her phone for the message and reread it.

'*I saw the Crown article. I need your help,*' was all the message had said. There was something in the word *your*. A person in distress would omit the word if they were in that much trouble. They'd need help and help from anyone. But '*I need your help*' seemed to insinuate that only Penelope could help.

Penelope dropped the phone on her desk, logged into her computer and scanned through her emails. Gone were the days when messages were left on her desk and swept into the bin.

She picked up her desk phone, tucked the handset in the crook of her neck, dialled a three-digit extension, and then began working through emails while she listened to the ring tone. After four rings, an irritated voice answered.

"King?"

"Yep. Who's this?" came the reply.

"Pike."

"Oh, hi, Penelope," said King. "I have some news for you."

"Is it good news?"

"That depends on your perspective."

"Go on."

"Well, if you're looking for the investigation of the year, you might have found it."

"Right," said Penelope, very aware of the negative connotations.

"But," continued King, "if you're looking to get your hands cut off, then you also found it."

"Too cryptic, King."

"Okay, you want to come to my lab to discuss it?"

Penelope couldn't think of anything worse than visiting Jason King's basement laboratory. Each time she'd been there in the past, he'd made a move on her, as if his skillset and efforts were worthy of a reward much more than a verbal *thank you*.

"No time, King."

"You never seem to have much time for me anymore, but I still get the requests."

"Oh, come on, you know I'm a busy girl."

King fell silent.

"Are you there?"

"I'm here," he said. He sounded as if he was trying to believe Penelope's lie. "One drink, that's all I ask."

"King, come on."

"Do you want the case?"

It was Penelope's turn to do the thinking.

"You know I want the case."

"One drink."

"Okay, one drink. Next weekend. At a bar of my choosing, and only if Casey gives me a double spread from your efforts."

"It's a date," he replied.

"It's a *drink*, King." Penelope couldn't help but raise a little smile at his tenacity.

"Carter."

"Excuse me?" said Penelope.

"Carter."

"Carter who?"

"The guy that owns the phone number that sent you the message," said King.

"I know about a dozen Carters, King."

"Ever heard of Bobby Carter?" said King. His smile seemed somehow audible over the line.

CHAPTER SEVEN

Narrow lanes that cut through trees, wound around large private estates, and scaled the rising land, brought an element of calm into Frankie's busy mind. The evening sunlight flickered through the trees above and danced across the windscreen of his Range Rover. The stereo was off. He couldn't remember the last time he'd turned it on. When Jake was in the back seat, the boy would occupy himself with the little screen in the passenger headrest and a set of headphones. Frankie would enjoy the silence.

At the forefront of Frankie's mind was a new strategy he'd been planning to try with Jake. Since Jacqui had died, the connection between father and son hadn't strengthened. It had been slipping. It had been all too easy to put it down to the boy's grieving process, or his age, but the fact was that Frankie was the boy's father, and they only had each other. The task of making it work, of raising the child, belonged to Frankie and nobody else.

Deep down, Frankie was looking forward to trying new methods. As he eased the large SUV around the long sweeping curves in the narrow country lane, he even smiled as his imagination offered images of the father and son laughing together while play wrestling, and having a little water fight in the garden. In reality, that was a long way off.

Pairs of golfers dressed in brightly-coloured shorts, white shoes, and snug-fitting polo shirts dotted the manicured landscape to Frankie's right. To his left, set back behind large driveways, were modest Victorian houses, hidden by rows of conifers with oak and elm trees lining the lanes, creating an avenue of cool shadows on the road surface below.

The Fairway, Frankie's street, approached on his left-hand side. The familiar feeling of his stomach tightening a little came and went, as it had for a year now. Once more, the memory of when he and Jacqui had first driven to see their house together in her little convertible sports car flashed across his mind like an old friend. The memory faded by the time he'd reversed onto their drive and stopped the car, as it did most days. Frankie liked to reverse onto the drive; it made unloading his camera equipment easier. It also gave him the advantage of getting away quicker if ever there was an emergency. Another emergency.

Frankie's camera equipment comprised of a large holdall with a discreet tripod and mono-pod attached to the side. Inside the holdall were his lenses, tucked into an array of cushioned, internal compartments, and Frankie's laptop, which lived in a narrow slot within the bag's lid. It was all he took from the luggage space of the car before hitting the little button that closed the rear door.

The front door to the house had two locks. The first was a standard Yale lock, and the second was a heavier duty Chubb lock for when the house was empty, and in the evenings. If the Chubb lock was unlocked when Frankie got home, it meant that Jake was already home. Trying the lower key first, Frankie found the Chubb lock to be engaged.

The house was empty.

He checked his watch. It was close to five pm, two hours after school finishes.

Inside the house, Frankie dropped his camera bag in his home office to the left of the front door and called out to the house.

"Jake? I'm home, buddy."

No reply.

In the kitchen, pinned to the fridge with little magnets was the timetable Jake had given Frankie the previous day. There were no after-school activities on.

Jake's bedroom was tidy, an attribute he'd inherited from Frankie himself. His school bag was missing, which meant he hadn't been home yet. The boy had a few friends, but only one close friend. So Frankie pulled his phone from his pocket, found the number of the boy's parents, and hit dial.

His search of the house continued while he listened to the hollow dialling tone until the call was answered by a woman.

"Hello?"

"Hi, is that Cheryl?"

"Hi, yes it is. Who's this please?' She sounded busy. The background noise of loud TV cartoons and the hustle and bustle of a family life filled the empty spaces.

"It's Frankie, Jake's dad."

"Oh, hi," she said. Her tone became a little friendlier as she recognised his voice. Then her voice turned edgy, which Frankie knew to be mindfulness at what she said, with respect to Jacqui's death. Many people just didn't know what to say to him. "Is everything okay?"

"Yes, of course," he said. "Well, no. I don't know. I can't find Jake, and well, I wondered if-"

"Sammy's here," she said. "Hold on, I'll ask him if he saw Jake. They usually walk home together."

"No, please don't make a fuss," he said. But he already heard her heels loud on a wooden floor, followed by a mumbled conversation. He pictured her with her hand over the phone leaning into her living room, with her three children all happily watching cartoons, maybe even lying on the floor doing homework at the same time.

"I'm sorry, Frankie. Sammy said they usually wait at the school gates for each other, but Jake didn't show today."

Frankie's heart sank.

"Have you tried the school? Or maybe he has other friends? You know what boys are like."

"Yeah, I do," replied Frankie, aware of his sounding distant. "I'll give the school a call. Maybe they'll be able to help. Thanks, Cheryl. Sorry to have bothered you."

"Oh, don't apologise," she replied. "And please let me know when you find him. He's such a lovely boy."

"I'm sure he's around somewhere, I'll let you know. Thanks a lot."

He ended the call before Cheryl could ask him how he was, a question he could never find the answer to. He had a range of responses that seemed to alternate by the hour. He flicked through his contacts for the school's number, then sat on the edge of Jake's bed while he waited for the call to be answered.

The call rang out, offering Frankie the chance to hit one for the reception, and two for something else. He disconnected.

Figuring that the school should still be open at five o'clock for some kind of after-school activities, Frankie shoved off the bed, took the stairs two at a time, and locked the front door behind him. A little Vespa pulled onto the drive just as Frankie was pulling out. He lowered the window.

"You off out?" asked Penelope. "I know I'm early, but-"

Not wanting to sound emotional or irrational, Frankie tried to sound cool. He offered her the house keys with an extended arm.

"I'm just off to get Jake from school. Let yourself in. I shouldn't be too long."

Before she could reply, Frankie had slipped the car into drive and pulled out into the quiet road. The school sat at the end of the road with large, iron gates that were painted green. A sign at the entrance directed visitors to a small guest car park. But, as it was out of hours, Frankie continued straight to bring him closer to the reception.

Two glazed front doors welcomed him to the small reception area. The walls were dotted with artwork, certificates, and all things the school was proud to show off to prospective parents. The reception counter was empty, but two more double doors led into the system of corridors.

It wasn't the first time Frankie had been there, and he knew Jake's classroom to be the third on the right-hand side, so he tried the door. It was locked. With two hands against the frosted glass, he peered inside, squinting to see signs of movement or a human form.

Nothing.

"Excuse me. Can I help you?"

Frankie closed his eyes at the indignant, soprano tone of Mrs Dilworth, then pulled away from the glass to face her.

"You can't just wander around inside the school, you know. Do you have an appointment?" she said, with her head tilted back allowing her to study Frankie through the half-framed spectacles perched on the end of her nose.

"I'm looking for my son," said Frankie. "He didn't come home from school."

"Well, it's Thursday. There are no extra-curricular activities on a Thursday, you know."

"Yes, but-"

"You're Jake's dad, aren't you?" she asked.

Frankie nodded and waited for the inevitable.

"How are you?"

There it was.

"I'm fine, thank you. I just-"

"He's such a lovely boy."

"Yes-"

"You know, we all look out for Jake here. He's had quite a time of it."

Taking a deep breath, Frankie made to move off.

"Thank you, Mrs Dilworth, but I really must-"

"I'm sure he's just with his friend, Sammy Little. Those two are thick as thieves, they are. Have you tried calling Sammy's parents?"

Instinctively, Frankie made a move for his phone in his pocket.

"No, I'll call them now," he lied. "I'm sure you're right. Our house is a few streets away, so I'm sure they can't be far."

Mrs Dilworth offered him a pitiful smile.

"I'm sure," she said and moved to one side to allow Frankie room to pass. As soon as he stepped through the reception's double doors, he began to run. Pulling the car fob from his pocket, he unlocked the doors as he drew close. Within moments, he'd reversed into an empty space, slammed the car into drive, and tore from the car park with the wheels spinning.

All manner of scenarios began to race through Frankie's mind. He'd spent his life watching people and forged a career finding people who didn't want to be found. But this was his own son. It was a scenario every parent prays never comes true. Once he was free of the school premises, he sank his right foot lower onto the pedal. The acceleration dropped for a split second as the automatic gearbox dropped to second gear, then hammered on the acceleration again, causing the front of the car to lift slightly with the torque and weight shift.

As the end of the road grew closer, Frankie was already looking right to check for oncoming cars. The road was free so he coasted out. He turned and checked to his left, just as three boys on BMX bikes darted in front of his car. He slammed on the brakes. The seat belt snapped into place. The boys, who had carried on riding, all turned back to see Frankie, shocked and clinging to the steering wheel.

"Watch it, mister," one of them yelled, his voice prepubescent and shrill.

"Bloody idiot," another called. This one was slightly further on in his maturity, with a robotic, monotone and nasal voice.

Frankie sat back in his seat, let his hands drop from the wheel, and took a deep breath.

A loud honking from behind roused him. His hand shot up to the mirror, signalling his apology. Once more, he checked both ways before pulling out into the road.

Calling the police was the last thing he wanted to do. The very thought of doing so stirred all kinds of memories that he'd fought hard to contain, to segregate, and to mentally archive. He even wondered exactly how much help they'd actually be once he told them his name, and what kind of questions he'd need to answer, the hurdles he'd need to jump to get answers.

The small LCD screen on the dashboard suddenly lit up with an incoming call. Penelope's name scrolled across in green letters.

The controls to answer or reject an oncoming call were beside his left thumb on the steering wheel. He hovered over the red *'reject'* button, then sighed and hit the green *'Accept'* button.

"Hey," he said, trying hard to sound upbeat. Frankie took his foot off the accelerator, let the car roll on of its own accord, and checked his mirror to make sure no cars were behind him on the quiet back street. Rows of three and four-bedroom houses either side of the street offered little in the way of views. But ahead, there was a small park that sat behind Frankie's house. "I'm just heading to one of his friend's houses to pick him up. Apparently, they went there after school."

"Hey, you don't need to explain yourself. I just wanted to make sure you were okay," said Penelope.

"Help yourself to wine. You know where everything is. I'll be as quick as I can," said Frankie, scanning the pavements as he steered. The local park came into view as the car crept along the tarmac.

"Sure, take your time. I'll see you in half an hour?" she asked.

Frankie hit the brakes.

"Less," he said, and hit disconnect. He let his head fall back onto the seat and let out a long sigh of relief.

Four-hundred yards away, all alone in the distant children's playpark, rocking back and forth on a swing, was Jake.

CHAPTER EIGHT

Association time was on a Thursday for house block one, A-wing, second-floor landing. At six o'clock, the cell doors were unlocked, allowing the prisoners the freedom to walk the steel grate mezzanine and interact with other prisoners. Most men simply took the chance to stretch their legs to burn off the energy that had been building during lock-up. Others lay on their bunks, content to have the door open even if was just for ninety minutes. A keen eye could spot the deviants and most prison officers had a keen eye. They knew that a prisoner who emerged from their cell too casually, who made a conscious effort to look bored and nonchalant, but then sidled up to another prisoner for a quiet chat, would typically be discussing something they shouldn't.

Isaac had nothing to hide, and he had one chance to talk to Shorty.

Although his neighbours were all hardened criminals and murderers, a very British sense of common courtesy defined particular rules with regards to a prisoner's cell. To go into another man's cell without being invited was considered a breach, and likely to raise eyebrows, then fists. To enter another man's cell without the owner being in there would raise a lot more than eyebrows. It would likely result in two outcomes, a visit to the infirmary for the offender, and a short stay in solitary for the man defending his turf. Solitary was a small price to pay in comparison to a man not defending his cell. The weakness would be seen by all and liberties would be taken.

The rules were simple. Isaac had followed them for the past twenty-three years, and seen many men fall foul of deviation from the unspoken rules.

He knocked on Shorty's door.

"Have you come to break bread?" Shorty's voice was dry and relaxed.

"Something like that."

"Well, don't stand out there then. Wipe your feet and come on in."

Prison rules stipulated that no more than three prisoners should congregate in a cell at any one time. Shorty, a lifer with violent tendencies, occupied one of only a handful of single cells on the wing. The TV was off. An arrangement of green teas stood beside it along with a varied selection of snacks. Shorty was laid on his bunk reading a book with one knee up and resting against the painted brick wall, the other outstretched. His bare toes flexed as if the man's subconscious programming was running a perpetual exercise regime in the background. The window, though frosted and covered with wire mesh was south-facing, allowing maximum daylight through its two-by-three-feet opening. All the room lacked was a generic landscape photo on the wall in a cheap frame, and Isaac could have sworn he was visiting an old acquaintance in a cheap hotel room.

A cheap plastic chair was tucked beneath the small desk opposite the bed. Isaac pulled it out, turned it to face Shorty, and sat down.

"Sit down, why don't you?"

"No games, Shorty," said Isaac. "We're both too long in the tooth for all that."

Making a show of using a photograph of his wife and children as a bookmark, Shorty closed his book, set it down beneath his pillow, and pushed himself up to lean into the corner.

"When did you get here?" he asked.

Isaac leaned on his knees, a strong posture for a conversation that could easily go south.

"Eight years ago," replied Isaac.

"Eight years? Longer than many, shorter than some."

Isaac shrugged. He couldn't hurry Shorty for the information he needed, but he knew it would come eventually. Probably after a barrage of questions designed to land him into someones else's bother.

"Think you deserve it?" asked Shorty.

"Deserve being sent down, or deserve being released?"

A peaceful smile crept onto Shorty's face.

"Both," he replied.

"No."

"You don't deserve to be sent down?" said Shorty.

"You're not questioning my innocence, are you, Shorty? We spoke about this already."

"So you don't deserve to be released then?"

"Probably not, considering the things I've had to do in here to survive."

"Fair point. Any regrets?"

"We've got six minutes left, Shorty. If I've got regrets I'll write a book about them and send it to you. No charge."

"You should have regrets, Isaac, my old mate. You should have." Shorty pushed himself to the edge of his bunk, collected a bottle of water from his small writing table, and stood in front of the frosted window with his back to Isaac. "We should all have them really, shouldn't we?"

"I don't think we can summarise the general conscience of Britain's prisoner community right now, Shorty," said Isaac. "But yeah, I have regrets."

"Are they strong enough to change you?"

"In what way would they change me?"

Shorty leaned against the wall, giving Isaac a simple silhouette to talk to. A halo of light bordered the dark shape.

"What are you going to do when you get out?" asked Shorty.

"Find somewhere to die," replied Isaac. It was a question he'd asked himself many times over the last few years as his sentence drew to a close.

"You don't think that would be a sin, Isaac, no?"

"Not a sin, no."

"You don't think that the last few years of your life should be wholesome? Full of life, laughter and happiness?"

"Given the choice, yeah. But given the circumstance, I'll have more luck finding somewhere peaceful to die."

"What if I told you that you wouldn't need to look very far?"

The message played on repeat is Isaac's mind. He replayed it once more to ensure he understood the question.

"You saw him," said Shorty. "The new fella."

"I saw him, yeah. Bruno, right?"

"Do you know who he works for?"

Isaac stayed silent. The information was coming now. Shorty's mouth was like a wound opening wider and wider, spilling out secrets and poison.

"Carter," said Isaac. It wasn't a question. It was a realisation.

"Carter," said Shorty, in confirmation. "Well, when I use the term, works for, loosely. He lives on favours. It makes his time a little easier in whatever prison he happens to be in. Right now he's doing favours for Carter."

Blurred pieces of a mental jigsaw that Isaac had been working on suddenly fell into place. The pieces became clearer as they did.

"Carter has pulled some strings, Isaac. Smiler thought the new guy had come to replace you, to fill his cell with fresh blood. But no, my old mucker. He hasn't come to *replace* you. He's come to *finish* you."

Suddenly aware that his back was to the door, Isaac span. There was nobody there.

"See, word has it that Carter knows you're getting out. And while he might have been content in the knowledge that you were safely locked behind bars, enduring a less than satisfying existence, he's left you alone all these years, but-"

"But now I'm getting out-"

"Right," said Shorty. "Now you're getting out, he wants you out of the way."

"So he sent Bruno?"

"As I said, Carter has pulled some very long and fragile strings to get him here. Even for someone as despicable as him, some heavy favours have been called in."

"It's association time," said Isaac. "Bruno will be loose."

"And that's why I invited you here, Isaac. As much as it would have been fun to sit, read my book and listen to the dying screams of a man who, let's face it, cheats at pretty much every game he plays, and who has the life expectancy of a blind train driver, I do still think you could be useful."

There it was.

"Useful?"

"You're no spring chicken, Isaac, but you can walk and you're still pretty handy so you meet all my requirements."

"What are you talking about?"

Slowly, Shorty began to turn. A slice of light rolled across his features, then dropped his face into darkness.

"I reckon I just saved your life," said Shorty. "Or, at the very least, saved your legs from being broken into multiple pieces."

Isaac nodded. There was no point in denying it, even it hadn't been true. Knowing that Bruno was sent for him was all Isaac needed to know to avoid him.

"The screws watch my cell day and night," continued Shorty. "They're just waiting for me to do something, so they can add a few more pointless years onto my sentence. I know I'll never see the light of day again. It's a fact I've come to terms with. But you, old man, are getting out."

Isaac nodded again. He understood the gesture. He also understood the implied conditions. Years of stir hardens a man to monotony, and it's the monotony that the guards strive to maintain. But rooted deep within the calm exterior of prison routine is an ecosystem so delicate and fragile, that should one man snap, the walls of fear, shame and frustration that hide the men inside could come crashing down with severe consequences.

Standing, and craning his neck for a glance through the open cell door, Isaac saw the huge form of Carter's man leaning on the handrail on the opposite landing. As if the hulk of a man felt his stare, he turned to face him and met Isaac's gaze.

"What do you need me to do, Shorty?"

CHAPTER NINE

TO STAND ON THE THRESHOLD OF HIS OFFICE AND TAKE IN THE
immaculate desk, the organised shelves of books, and the array of
photography equipment, of which each item had been perfectly
placed, was to stare into Frankie's mind. His heart was equally
distributed throughout the house through the medium of memories and photographs, of that there could be no question. But his
mind was a mystery. From the tokens of travel that were hanging
on the walls and stuck to the fridge, to the memories of times
gone by that adorned the walls. His photographs were impressive
by any standards, naturally framed, perfectly focused, with no
question as to the essence of each image. A visitor unaware of
Frankie's skills might consider each one an expensive piece of art.
But for someone who truly knew the man, the symbolism of each
photo was evident in the placement.

Above the old fireplace in the living room was a large, monochrome canvass of a rainy day in London. A caterpillar of legs, all
shapes and sizes, dressed in dark business attire marched, as if
they were one, towards an out-of-focus tube station. Above them,
carried by the hurrying swathe of legs, sat a protective shell of
black umbrellas, shiny and wet and unique in their own right, but

as one in the heavily contrasted monochrome image; a well-paid and over-worked insect. Much as a river might split before an impenetrable rock, the mass of blended human form broke left and right before a stationary woman dressed in white. Her head tilted to an acute angle to allow her hair, lank with rain, to hang freely. She'd turned to stare back at the voyeuristic photographer with a look that Penelope could only describe as peace.

The girl in the photo was the same in all of the images that brought an ironic sense of life to an otherwise soulless residence.

Jealousy crawled forward a little more to hold the hand of envy as Penelope stepped into Frankie's office.

Perhaps most disturbing for Penelope was the image of the eye that took pride of place across the fifteen-foot-long wall. Thick lashes, heavy and tear-laden, laced with beads of mascara, provided a frame from which ran tiny, thin, red veins. They carved their way through the soft, impeccable white and led the observer's eyes to the focus of the image: an otherworldly blue iris, electric in colour, and almost magical in shape and form.

"Jacqui," uttered Penelope to the imposing image, before taking a step further.

An immediate sense of broken trust stabbed at her, but intrigue, cunning and remorseless drew her further as if leading her by the hand. She stepped up to the image of the eye to see closer the perfect focus and the clarity that somehow eludes everyday life. But in doing so, Penelope leaned against the desk, and almost immediately, the computer screen lit up. Her attention was removed from the image.

A career in investigative journalism had taught her a few things about computer espionage. The first place she checked was the computer's recycle bin. She double-clicked the icon on the desktop and was presented with a space to enter a user name.

She considered what that might be, ignoring the little voice in her head that told her she should leave.

FBlack.

An error popped up, invited her to retry.

She entered Frankie's email address.

The same error appeared. She was just about to give up and listen to the voice in her head when she had an idea.

She entered Frankie's military ID.

A window for the password appeared.

She sat back in the chair, wondering what the password might be. She entered Frankie's date of birth.

Incorrect Password.

She tried a series of Jake's name and birthday but received a the *Incorrect Password* error each time.

But it was the eye that was staring at her from the wall above that gave her the answer. She ran into the kitchen and flicked through the calendar on the wall.

And there it was. Jacqui's birthday was marked in clear printed letters on February 29.

She ran back to the office, and after several variations of the date, and several incorrect guesses at the year, she was in.

Fear, wonder, and self-loathing now battled for first place.

Wonder prevailed.

Within seconds, Penelope was browsing through files, most of which meant nothing to her. But a hidden folder named *'Old'*, which was hidden deep with a cloud-based storage system caught her attention.

Even in the deepest roots of Frankie's files, his organised personality shone through. Folders were named by place and date. There were folders full of pictures of holidays with Jacqui, and others of Frankie when he was a child with who Penelope presumed to be his parents. She opened an image of a child on a beach in swimming trunks, squinting in the bright sunlight and wielding a plastic spade. There was no mistaking the piercing blue eyes even at that young age; it was Frankie. Frankie's father was sat behind him with one hand on Frankie's chest and a watchful eye on the boy. It was a look of adoration that somehow humanised Frankie from his silent and resilient exterior. He was loved, just like any other child. And he looked happy. Another photo of the same man with the same boy in an old sports car. The roof was down, and although the photo was black and white, it had clearly been taken on a hot summers' day.

Clicking further into the folder structure, Penelope found a folder marked 'X'. She knew she shouldn't open it. She knew it was wrong. Every part of her moral senses screamed at her to stop.

But she opened the folder.

Inside was perhaps the least organised of all she had seen. Photos were taken with different cameras, some black and white, some scuffed, and some with people's eyes covered with a black strip. Just like the family photos, they had been scanned in from a physical photo into an ever-present digital image. Penelope wondered if Frankie still had the originals and if the faces were intact.

A group of men, all wearing various forms of army fatigues and each of them holding a rifle, stood before an aircraft that Penelope thought to be a Hercules. The men appeared to be happy and confident, but a sense of trepidation shone from one man's eyes. He was kneeling on one knee, unsmiling as if he'd been forced to pose for the photo.

Another image showed Frankie cleaning a rifle while sitting on a bunk. He wore the same army issue shorts he wore most mornings but smiled as if the photographer had caught him off guard. Even from a snapshot of time, recorded in black and white more than eight years ago, Penelope could see the attention to detail. She could see the love and care he was putting into cleaning the weapon. Frankie was running a well-used but neatly folded cloth soaked in gun oil along the barrel. Behind him, slightly out of focus, the man who had been unsmiling in the previous photo lay on his bunk with a book.

The last photo Penelope opened was of Frankie in full combat attire. His face was camouflaged, his rifle decorated with strips of green cloth and even Frankie's pack formed part of the forest background. His piercing blue eyes were the only identifier.

"Who are you really, Frankie?" Penelope asked. The eye loomed above her. "I bet *you* know," she said to the photo.

With a few clicks of the mouse, Penelope had closed down the folders and switched off the monitor. Stepping back to the doorway, she glanced back at the room to make sure nothing was out of place, then tiptoed into the kitchen. She walked quietly not because she was trying to be quiet, but the house gave her a feeling of being watched. She knew why. The photos of Jacqui all over the walls, brilliant as they were, made her uneasy.

The wine was South African, not her favourite. But it was wine, and it was chilled. She poured a glass quickly, replaced the bottle in the fridge, and leaned back on the breakfast bar, just in time to hear the gentle rap on the frosted glass window.

Realising that she had Frankie's keys, she tiptoed through the hallway to let him in. A sorry-looking Jake with his head hung low stood before her.

"Hey Jake," she said. "How was school today?"

No response came. The boy simply stepped past her and crept up the stairs.

"Is everything okay?" she asked, as Frankie stepped into the hallway and pushed the door closed.

"It'll be fine," he said, as he continued into the kitchen. "You found the wine then." Suddenly, like a heavy cloak had fallen over the house, Penelope felt like an intruder in their lives. There were clearly issues to be dealt with between Frankie and Jake.

"I did but-" she started.

"But what?" he replied from the kitchen, sounding busy.

With slight trepidation, Penelope approached the kitchen doorway.

"I should go," she said. "Give you boys some time to talk."

In the short time Frankie had been in the kitchen, he'd

managed to open a beer, lay some chicken on a tray, and was now rubbing some herbs into the meat. He washed his hands, dried them on a small kitchen towel, then set the temperature on the oven.

He folded the towel into quarters, dropped it on the work surface, then picked up his beer.

"Do you see us talking?" he asked, his brow raised as if high-lighting the obvious.

"Well, no-"

"Are you hungry?"

"A little," she replied.

"So chop some carrots, drink some wine, and relax," said Frankie. Then he stepped across to where she leaned, almost hugging the door-frame. "You haven't even kissed me hello yet."

"Well-"

But before she could explain the whole Jake entrance and moody atmosphere, Frankie had stepped in. He planted a kiss on her forehead and then moved on into the hallway.

"Carrots are in the fridge. Knives are in the block. Jake likes them diced," he called out, as he began to climb the stairs.

Two-minutes later, Penelope found herself peeling carrots, dicing them and leaving them in water ready to boil. Two sets of footsteps came down the stairs, one heavy, one light. More to give her hands something to do than through thirst, she collected her wine glass before spinning around to find Jake standing by the door.

"Dad says I have to be nice to you," he said after a pause, then gave a loud sniff.

"Well, if you don't want to be nice to me, Jake, then you don't have to be," she offered. "In fact, if you don't even want to talk to me just yet, then that's fine. But I'll be nice to you. I'll always be nice to you, and one day, when you're ready to talk, I'll be ready for you. How does that sound?"

The little boy digested the information. Then he turned, and with bright, red eyes from his earlier tears, he looked up at Frankie who stood behind him.

"What's for dinner?" he asked.

"Toads," said Frankie, reaching for his beer.

"Toads?" replied the little boy in disgust, his voice thick with his emotion.

"Yep, toad and snails. You did find the snails in the garden, Penelope, didn't you?" he asked, his expression deadly serious.

"Some really big ones," she replied. "They're quite slimy at this time of year."

Jake's head switched back and forth between Frankie and Penelope, who had to drink from her wine to stop her smile broadening and giving the game away.

"You want to watch TV with dinner?" asked Frankie.

"Really?"

"Yeah, go on," said Frankie, and ruffled his son's hair. "But not too loud, buddy, or you won't get many snails."

CHAPTER TEN

THE EMOTIONS OF THE DAY HAD TAKEN THEIR TOLL ON JAKE. As Frankie pulled the covers over him, the little boy, keeping his eyes closed, pulled the duvet up beneath his chin.

"Is Penelope staying with us now?" he asked.

"No, of course not," said Frankie. "She has a house of her own."

The news seemed to settle Jake. His eyes opened a fraction. A glint of a tear rolled to his nose, then dripped onto the pillow.

"Hey," said Frankie, wiping the tear mark from Jake's face, "what's all this for?"

But Jake didn't reply. He rolled over and turned his back to Frankie.

Smoothing his son's soft hair with his hand, Frankie leaned in to kiss his forehead, but Jake covered his face. The silence grew awkward. Frankie could hear that Jake wasn't asleep just yet, his breathing sounded congested. Eventually, the boy sniffed.

"Hey, Jake," said Frankie, resting his hand on the boy's shoulder.

"Mmm," came the reply, high in pitch.

Allowing a moment to swallow, and control his own voice, Frankie spoke softly.

"I miss her too, you know?"

The boy suddenly sat up, flung his arms around his dad, and buried his hot face in Frankie's shirt. A tear of his own escaped Frankie's eye. He blinked it away, and wiped his eye with his shoulder, then lowered Jake back to bed. Beside him, on a bedside table, was a framed photo of the three of them together, a rare shot that wasn't taken by Frankie himself. He placed it beside Jake, then moved his little hand onto the edge. The photo showed Jacqui, Jake and Frankie on a beach in the South of France. Frankie recalled asking a lady who was sitting nearby to take the photo. Jake was in the centre and his arms were wrapped around his parents. Happiness glowed from Jacqui. Wonder was written all over Frankie's face as he stared at his boy, and the only person looking at the camera was a much younger Jake, with a look of utter content, as if he had everything he needed right there in his arms.

A few minutes later, Frankie stepped onto the patio, slid the French glass door shut, and joined Penelope, who sat with her bare feet up on a chair, swirling the wine in her glass around and around.

"Penny for them?" said Frankie.

"Save your money. They're not worth a penny," she replied.

Dragging his chair closer to Penelope's, Frankie sat, rested his glass on a coaster that Penelope must have brought from inside, and lay his arm across her shoulders.

"I feel like an intruder," she said finally as if she was confessing. Frankie let her continue. "I feel like I'm in the way, that he won't accept me, and that I'm somehow making this harder for the pair of you."

The conversation that Frankie had been expecting had begun.

"He doesn't hate you," he said.

"He doesn't particularly like me either. He didn't even say goodnight."

"He's eleven, Penelope. Give the kid some time."

"That's what I keep telling myself," replied Penelope. "I've never had to do this before."

A subconscious laugh emitted from Frankie's throat.

"Neither have I." He gave her shoulder a squeeze. "He needs memories, and he needs to know that you're not a threat."

"Why would I be a threat?"

"Because he lost his mum. Because I'm all he has."

"Did he tell you that?"

"Not in words," said Frankie. "When you arrived earlier, he was actually missing. I didn't tell you. I was trying to wrap my head around it myself."

"*Missing?*"

"I phoned his friend's house, phoned the school, and even went down there, but they weren't much help."

"I thought that was your job," said Penelope. "That's what you're good at, right?"

"I find other people's missing people," said Frankie. "I've never had to find my own son before."

"Did he run away?"

"No," said Frankie, a little too abrupt in his tone. "He just needed some time to himself."

"I can relate."

"I found him over the park nearby, sitting on a swing."

"Did he tell you what was wrong?"

"No, but I made sure he knows that when he's ready, he can come to me."

"Do *you* know what's wrong?" asked Penelope, knowing the answer would bring up the subject of Jacqui before she'd even finished the sentence.

Taking a deep breath and letting go of Penelope's shoulder to reach for his wine, Frankie leaned forward in his chair and rested his arms on his thighs. His eyes wandered, following the crack between the paving slabs and the small weeds that had begun to peer out, searching for light.

"He misses his mum, Penelope." No reply came back his way, but he felt the tension at the mention of Jacqui. "I can't even empathise," Frankie continued. "How hard must it be for an eleven-year-old to be without his mum?"

"That's why I feel like I'm in the way," said Penelope. "Maybe he needs more time."

"I lost my dad, you know. I was much older than Jake is, but I still felt like I'd lost a limb."

Turning in her seat to face him, Penelope put her arm on his shoulder.

"You never said."

"It hardly came up, did it?"

"I guess," she replied. "You want to tell me about it? How did he die?"

Frankie sank back his wine, placed the glass on the table and reached up to squeeze her hand.

"He just wasn't my dad anymore."

Before she could respond with an awkward question that Frankie would rather not answer, he livened up.

"Hey, are you around on Saturday?" he asked.

With a shrug, Penelope nodded.

"I've got an idea, and it could be a fun day out. What do you say?"

CHAPTER ELEVEN

"There it is," said Smiler. "That's the last time you'll hear that god awful buzzer, and the last time you'll have to sleep in that rotten old bed."

Staring at the ceiling as he had a thousand times before, Isaac barely heard the words.

"Did you hear me, Isaac? Cheer up, mate. Today's the big day," said Smiler, pulling his laces tight on his runners.

Isaac nodded.

"Today's a day for firsts, mate," said Smiler. "First taste of freedom. First pint of beer-"

"Give me a break, Smiler. Have you got any idea what it's like out there? Have you got any idea of the changes that have happened in the last eight bleeding years?"

"You're actually nervous?"

"If you only knew the half of it, Smiler."

"Listen, Isaac," said Smiler. He sat down on the bed beside Isaac. "Mate to mate. We've gotten to be mates, right?"

"If you mean, have we been forced to share an eight-by-ten room for the past God knows how many years, and haven't torn each other's throats out? Then yeah, I guess we've have become mates, Smiler."

"So, listen to me. There are two types of people in this world, my old mate. Survivors and quitters. Which one are you?"

"Can we not do the whole pep-talk thing? I need to get my head in place."

"Humour me, Isaac," said Smiler. "Which one?"

Knowing that Smiler wouldn't be letting up, Isaac sucked in a lungful of air, let his head fall back and prepared for the rest of the pep talk.

"Well I haven't quit yet," he said.

"Exactly," said Smiler. He shoved off the bed, somehow energised by the chat. "You've managed to survive eight years in here. Think of all the men you've seen come and go. Think of the men that didn't last a week. You know what I mean, mate? You've seen it as much as I have. They come in here, realise they can't handle it, and that's it. They end it. They didn't even try. They don't last a week, Isaac. You've done about four-hundred weeks. Four-hundred bleeding weeks, mate. You're a survivor."

"Leave off, Smiler."

"No, Isaac. Listen. You're going to get out of here, breathe the fresh air, go and get yourself a brass if you have to. But if you bleeding quit now, it would have all been for nothing. Nothing, Isaac. I'm not saying those years have been easy, in fact, I know they haven't. But, mate, it would have all been for nothing if you don't go out there, and live the rest of your life to its fullest."

The clang of the steel mesh landing rattled as prisoners began to amble past on their way to breakfast.

"I, for one, will be disappointed, Isaac."

Isaac gave a soft laugh.

"Are you going to disappoint me?"

Isaac remained silent.

"Well? Don't disappoint me. Because if you aren't going to make the most of your freedom, you might as well stay in here, and if you do that, Isaac, I'll have a word with Shorty myself, and I'm sure he can make your life even more of a misery."

"You're right, Smiler," said Isaac, more to quieten his cellmate than anything. "You're right."

"So, you're going to do it? You're going to get out there and show them what Isaac Black is all about?"

Isaac nodded.

"Good man. Come on. I'll buy you breakfast."

"I'll see you down there, mate," said Isaac. "Just give me a minute, will you?"

"I'll save you a seat. I'm sure the boys will want to wish you all the best."

A weak smile seemed to appease Smiler, and soon, Isaac was on his own, trying to control his breathing. Smiler was right. Isaac knew he was. The terrible fact of the matter was that even if Isaac had wanted to stay, he couldn't. Terror gripped him, but the only way through the fear, the only way to overcome the overwhelming doubt that shrouded Isaac, was to man up and face his fears.

He stood, closed his eyes, and sucked in one last deep breath, before turning to leave.

But the doorway was blocked.

Filling the entire width of the door, from shoulder to shoulder, was Bruno, Carter's man.

"You must be Bruno," said Isaac. He gave a quick glance around for something to use as a weapon, but there was nothing within reach.

Bruno stepped forward.

"Did Carter send you?"

"Does it matter?" replied the behemoth, taking another step forward.

"If you're going to kill me, I want to know who it was," replied Isaac, matching Bruno's forward step with a backward pace of his own.

"He's been after you for a long time," grumbled Bruno.

"It's taken him eight years. Why now?" said Isaac, backing off some more. The desk was now within reach. A ball-point pen was all he could grab.

Bruno's eyebrows raised as if to question how serious Isaac was about using a measly pen against a man of his size.

"Because you're getting out," said Bruno. "Nobody expected you to ever get out. And Mr Carter can't have you walking the streets. What would people think?"

Bruno stepped forward once more.

Isaac widened his stance and gripped the pen like a knife.

"If you're going to kill me, then make you sure you do it right, son."

A hearty laugh rumbled from somewhere deep inside the huge man.

Then Bruno stepped forward and, quick as a flash, jabbed Isaac in the gut with his fist. Isaac doubled over with instinct, fighting to suck in air, but saw the uppercut coming his way. Bruno's fat arm swung like a wrecking ball with his over-sized fist fixed to the end.

The punch connected. Isaac slammed back into the wall behind him. Every piece of his face felt like it had shattered. He reached up. Every morsel of sense screamed at him to escape, to get out, to fight back. But he was trapped.

Isaac stood tall with his back against the wall. If he was going to die right there, he'd die fighting.

Quick as lightning, Bruno's left hand lunged for Isaac's neck. His iron grip clamped down, and slowly, Isaac felt the air being squeezed from him. Three more blows to his gut forced the remaining air from his body, and the chokehold blocked his supply.

Darkness crept in from the sides of Isaac's vision. Bright lights danced their way across his last few memories. His son. His wife. The wasted time.

But something inside him refused to go down, knowing that

to do so would be fatal. The same carnal instinct that fought for air despite the futility gave sudden strength to Isaac's limbs. He kicked out at what felt like legs of rock. He jammed his knee out, but the big man turned away to defend his groin.

The grip tightened.

His starved lungs screamed. His airways were fully blocked. Isaac's pulse boomed like two bass drums, not just loud, but with a thudding that seemed to reverberate through his entire body.

He stabbed at last with the pen into the big man's side. Bruno's face twitched once, then smiled. His other arm swung back, ready to deliver the killer blow.

Isaac became frantic. He lunged with more stabs into the giant's side, but the pen became slippery with Bruno's warm, sticky blood, and the giant barely reacted to the pain.

He turned the bloodied pen in his sticky hand, and with his last remaining strength, as black veils fell across what remained of his vision, he aimed for Bruno's neck.

The attempt was weak. Bruno simply moved away, brushing the attack off as he might deter a fly.

Then, without reason, the vice-like grip weakened just a fraction.

Hope crept from its hiding place as air channelled through to his lungs.

Bruno's eyes widened.

The darkness began to lift.

Bruno's huge body leaned over him. He staggered once, then fell against Isaac, convulsing as if a seizure ran through his huge body.

As the remnants of the iron grip released, the weight of the giant man hung on Isaac. Dizzied and pained, Isaac's legs gave way, and he slid to the floor.

Through a kaleidoscopic haze of blurred confusion, Shorty's shiny head gleamed bright against the dull, painted, concrete ceiling. His arm became a blur of movement. The squelch and suck of blood was loud and in time with his grunts, each of which was in perfect time with Shorty's wild swinging arm. Bruno fell to his knees before Isaac. Then, as all men do, no matter the size, he fell forwards with his final gasp of breath whistling through his pierced lungs.

CHAPTER TWELVE

As usual, Frankie had already woke and left the bedroom to make coffee before Penelope had opened her eyes. The memories of the previous day had subsided, but the monochrome canvas image of Jacqui standing in a negligee at the open doors of what looked to be a Parisian balcony was a stark reminder. The photograph was fixed to the wall opposite and perfectly centralised to the bed between the built-in wardrobes and the en-suite.

She pulled the covers over her head, knowing that her deadline loomed and that Jake would be up soon. She didn't need for him to see her this morning, not when they'd made a little progress the previous day.

The shower ran hot and hard on her skin, but for too brief a time. She could have stood there all day, letting the water wash away her thoughts of Casey's deadline.

There was no time to wash her hair, so she pulled it back, tied it up, and swept it across her shoulder in a thick single bunch, before pulling on a clean dress, slipping into her flats, and throwing the rest of her clothes into her overnight pack.

Knowing that Frankie would want her to stay for coffee, she

sat on the bed, pulled her phone out and messaged Casey to tell him she'd be out all morning on the case.

Then, just as she was packing her things away, she recorded a voice note to remind her to talk to the tech guys about the locked cloud folder on Frankie's computer.

Opening the door without making a sound was an art that she'd learnt the first time she'd stayed at Frankie's house. Stepping out and pulling it closed behind her, she turned and gasped out loud.

Jake was standing in his bedroom doorway in his pyjamas and with a look of pure resentment in his eyes.

"Good morning, Jake," she said, catching her breath. She reached out to smooth his hair, but he flinched away, turned and slammed the door.

"Coffee?" said Frankie, as she reached the bottom of the stairs.

Waiting until she had reached the kitchen, Penelope declined.

"I'll get something on the way to work. I think it's best if I leave."

"And so it begins," said Frankie with a smile, trying to bring some humour into the already tense atmosphere.

"You heard?"

"I think the whole street heard him slam the door," he replied.

"Sorry," she said. "He was just standing–"

"Don't worry. Hopefully, tomorrow will make things a little easier."

She took the few short steps to him, reached up and gave him a kiss on the cheek. Then hovered.

"I won't stay tonight. Get some boys time."

Taking Frankie's nod accompanied by an acute smile for a reply, she left the room, pulled the front door open, then turned and blew him a kiss before leaving.

A weight lifted from her when she stepped down to the driveway as if a shroud had hung from her shoulders inside the house, which the fresh air and cool breeze somehow whisked away.

Ten minutes into her journey towards London, she felt the vibration of her phone alerting her that a message had arrived. Finding a safe place to stop, she pulled her phone out and saw the message displayed on the screen. The message was a location pin accompanied by a simple message. *'Coffee?'*

CHAPTER THIRTEEN

ANY PROGRESS THEY'D MADE THE PREVIOUS NIGHT SEEMED TO have been washed away with the dishes. Jake entered the kitchen in silence, not to collect his lunch or eat breakfast, but more to tell his father he was leaving for school.

"But you haven't eaten yet, buddy," said Frankie. "What do you want, cereal or toast?"

"Nothing. I'm not hungry," he replied.

"Again? You've got to eat, mate."

"Bye, Dad," said Jake, and started for the door.

"No." Frankie raised his voice a little too high, then calmed. "You're not going to school without something inside you. So sit."

The boy looked back at his dad in silent dispute.

"Sit," said Frankie, pulling a bowl from the cupboard. He fetched a box of cereal from another cupboard and tipped some out. Then he grabbed the milk from the fridge and poured some into the cereal.

Jake hadn't moved.

"Sit," said Frankie again. Then he leaned on the breakfast bar to make sure Jake knew he wasn't going to school hungry.

Jake reluctantly dropped his school bag on the floor and slid onto the high chair. He pulled his breakfast towards him and looked up expectantly at Frankie.

From behind his back, Frankie produced a spoon and offered it to Jake. But when Jake reached for it, Frankie pulled it away.

"Smile?" he said.

"Dad," Jake whined.

"Are you late for something? School doesn't start for another hour."

Jake shook his head.

"So why are you leaving so early?"

His question was met with a shrug of Jake's shoulders.

"Do you know what tomorrow is?" asked Frankie. He held out the spoon and this time let Jake take it. "So? Do you know what tomorrow is?"

Jake shook his head and began to mix his milk and cereal exactly how Jacqui used to.

Folding a dish towel into quarters and then placing it on the breakfast bar, Frankie stepped around and stood directly behind Jake. He dropped his hands onto his son's shoulders.

"Tomorrow is a special day, Jake," he began. "Do you want to know why?"

Another shrug of Jake's shoulders.

"Jake, verbalise, mate. Talk to me."

"No, Dad, I don't know." Jake's tone had slipped from despondence to irritation.

Frankie moved around to face Jake. He dropped into the stool opposite.

"I know it's been hard recently, mate," he said. He stretched his finger out and began to stroke a soft circle on the back of Jake's hand, an affectionate gesture that had worked in the past. But Jake retracted his hand and spooned in a mouthful of cereal.

"So, tomorrow, I've decided, is all about you and me. Us."

"Us?" said Jake, spilling milk down his chin. He wiped it with the back of his hand and continued to eat.

"Yeah, us," said Frankie. "You know, people will come into our lives, some will stay with us a long time, some a little less, and some will only be in our lives a short while. But I want you to know that no matter who they are, or how long they stay, the most important person in my life is you. And the most important person in your life is me. We're all we have, mate. You and me. We're a team, yeah?"

Jake spooned another mouthful of cereal into his mouth.

"Yeah?" Frankie repeated.

Eventually, Jake nodded.

"So tomorrow, we're going to get up, and we're going to the zoo," said Frankie.

"The zoo?" said Jake, his spirits lifting a little.

"Yep, and then after that, we're going for pizza."

Greed overshadowed Jake's determined sullen disposition. His eyes widened just enough to let Frankie know that he'd struck a chord.

"Sound good?" said Frankie.

This time his reply was a nod of his head, rather than a negative shake.

"And if the weather's nice and there's time, maybe we can hit the beach too. What do you say to that?"

"The beach?" said Jake, excitement now etched in his face and eyes.

"Yep," said Frankie. "And pizza, and the zoo. Do you want to invite Sammy?"

"Am I allowed?"

"Of course, you should bring a friend. See if his mum will let him come."

Suddenly, the excited eyes and beaming smile dropped as if weights pulled on Jake's face. Lastly, his head dropped to stare at his cereal.

"Does that mean that she's coming too?" the boy asked.

"She?" said Frankie. He wanted to hear Jake say Penelope's

name.

"Penelope," Jake said, his voice quiet.

"I thought it'd be a nice chance for you to get to know her, Jake. She really is lovely, you know. And she thinks the world of you."

Silence.

"Come on, Jake. We're going to have a great day. And how about this, if you don't enjoy yourself, you can watch TV with your dinner all next week?"

Sliding off his chair and dropping to the floor, Jake picked up his bag.

"I'm going to school now," he said.

"Jake? Come on."

But the boy had already begun to leave.

"How about I drive you?"

"I can walk. It's only five minutes away."

"Yeah, but I'd like to," said Frankie. He too slid off his stool and reached for his keys. But the front door had already opened. A cool breeze found Frankie's bare feet. The little, brass knocker on the front door rapped once as Jake pulled it closed behind him.

From the kitchen, Frankie could see into the living room. Jacqui stared back at him from their day in London. She was dressed in white and surrounded by a flow of commuters, each holding an umbrella. But Jacqui, who had still been ecstatic from Frankie's proposal, stood amidst a river of suits, defiant of the rain, and seemingly carefree to anyone but Frankie.

"What do I do, Jacqui?" he asked.

But much like Jake, Jacqui gave no reply. She just offered her perpetual and brazen smile, letting the busy the world roll by as if she were merely a rock in a river.

CHAPTER FOURTEEN

"Get out, Isaac." Warm, stale breath in his face confirmed that the man was indeed Shorty. "I've got this," he rasped, his breathing short and sharp. "I'll take the hit. Just get up and get out."

Reaching up from beneath Bruno, Isaac's bloodied hands slid on the painted brick wall as he tried to pull himself free from the big man on top of him. Strong hands grabbed at his arms, and as if he were weightless, he lurched to his unsteady feet.

The clanging of the landing floor began to grow louder with a depth that only a prison officer's hard-soled shoes could produce. It was a noise Isaac had grown attuned to over the past eight years.

"It's too late," said Shorty, turning to the doorway.

The clanging grew louder still.

"Isaac, I'm doing this for your own good. And just remember, whatever happens, when you get out of here, you take Carter out. Or the rest of my days here are numbered pal, and I'll come and haunt you."

A momentary lapse of reality set in before Shorty's strong

hand snapped up, took hold of Isaac's neck, then slammed him back into the wall. Searing pain shot out from the back of Isaac's skull as it crashed into the concrete.

"You there, stop." The voice called out from somewhere close, but still distant in the hazy cell. "Put him down now."

Shorty sucked in a lungful of air as if it would be his last then lunged at Isaac.

A warm, dull sensation began to grow in Isaac's shoulder. The feeling was wrong, alien somehow, but flooded with relief like years of built-up pressure had been released. The sensation was short-lived. His flesh came alive with the screams of torn sinew as Shorty snatched the tool from his body. The muscles of Isaac's arm tensed, twitched, then eased as violent pain spread across his shoulder, and warm, sticky blood meandered down his skin.

He exhaled, but the movement of his chest stabbed at the fresh wound. He felt a light, one, two, three taps of his heart. A peculiar sensation he'd never felt before.

The steady stream of blood began to form drops that dripped from his fingers. He looked down and stared at his own blood in disbelief.

Shorty gave a little wink before the charade began.

Then, as if the whole scene had played out in half-speed, real-time suddenly kicked in with frenzied violence.

A cloud of pungent, oily gas engulfed the two men. Shorty spun, planted his feet, and held his knife ready to take the guards on. But the cloud of pepper spray swallowed him whole. Then fists broke through the mist. Jarring blows knocked Shorty's head from side to side. He fell to the floor clutching at his face.

"I'm coming for you, Black."

Isaac heard the words as if they were spoken underwater.

Three large dark shapes filled the blurry void in his stinging vision, and the sound of heavy boots connecting with Shorty's ribs filled the cell. But through the violent beating, Shorty managed to roll to one side. He stared up at Isaac.

"Did you hear me, Black?" said Shorty. "You won't have your minder with you next time."

CHAPTER FIFTEEN

TUCKED INTO THE FURTHEST CORNER OF THE FRESH GRIND House coffee shop in Stratford's Westfield Shopping Centre, Mrs Carter sat alone, and as far from conspicuous as Penelope could imagine. Appearing to busy herself with the fold-out menu, her short, furtive glances from the sides of her over-sized sunglasses at nearby customers and shoppers that passed by the large glass-fronted cafe told Penelope that out of the three women that sat alone, she was the one who had messaged her.

Even as Penelope strode past her and approached the counter to order a coffee, she felt the woman's eyes burning into her back.

The mirrored wall behind the counter offered Penelope a good, wide view of the coffee shop behind her. Mrs Carter sat to one side furthest from the door without a coffee. Two couples occupied a table for four, each with a wide, white coffee cup in front of them, and they exchanged tired but friendly conversation.

Two tables hosted the other two ladies who each sat alone with either a coffee or a tea, and two more tables were occupied with shop workers from the mall, who may have been waiting for their workplace to open.

"I'll take a hazelnut latte, plus whatever my friend is having," said Penelope to the barista.

"What's she having?" came the teenage boy's reply, indicating clearly that table service wasn't an option, at least until she'd paid.

"Get her a latte as well, please."

"I'll bring it right over," the barista replied and turned the cash register readout for Penelope to see, instead of reading out the amount which would have been far too much effort.

She paid, dropped her purse into her handbag and clicked the record button on her Dictaphone, then casually strolled over to Mrs Carter, sliding her legs beneath the table before she offered a greeting.

"Mrs Carter," she began. "I'm Penelope Pike. We spoke on the phone."

The woman opposite Penelope suddenly looked frightful. Her eyes widened, and she began yet another scan of the coffee shop. The thick and ever-present aroma of coffee almost complimented Mrs Carter's expensive perfume. But as her head darted to one side, a darkened shadow was evident from her cheekbone to somewhere behind her glasses.

"Relax," said Penelope. "Just look casual. There's nothing to worry about. I'm here to help." Mrs Carter sank back into the corner. "Mrs Carter, *you* called *me*, remember?"

The barista stepped over, and without an exchange of words, placed a latte in front of each of the women.

"Thank you," said Mrs Carter. The first words she'd spoken. Her voice was local. Articulate, but not middle class. Her clothes suggested affluence.

"You're welcome."

"Who else knows you're here?" asked Mrs Carter.

Replying with an air of honesty, Penelope shrugged her shoulders.

"No-one. Why would they?"

"I thought you might have told someone, that's all."

"What's to tell, Mrs Carter?" said Penelope. "You called me to meet for a coffee. That's all there is to it."

"Call me Debbie," she said.

"Okay, Debbie. So we're two women sat in a coffee shop. What do you want to talk about?"

"Are you wearing a wire?"

Penelope gave a laugh. The sentiment was accurate, but the cliche was misguided.

"This isn't Hollywood, Debbie. Nobody wears a wire. Nobody is going to follow us, or you, and jump out. We're just two women having a chat about a problem you have. Am I right?"

Debbie's head dropped, allowing Penelope a view over the top of her glasses to see the full extent of the bruise around her eye.

"Would you like *me* to start?" said Penelope. "Maybe it'll be easier if you have a prompt?"

With one hand clamped around the collar of her long, designer coat and the other flat against her stomach, Debbie suddenly looked up at Penelope.

"I need help," she said. Her voice had suddenly aged. She sounded like a heavy smoker, but more likely, she was simply a scared lady who hadn't been sleeping well.

"And what is it you need help with?" Penelope asked.

Debbie opened her mouth to talk, but her jaw hung open, revealing perfect, white teeth.

"Is it your husband?" asked Penelope.

The words seem to knock Debbie back a little. She exhaled in three sharp jagged breaths then sucked in one long slow breath as if to calm herself.

"Hey, relax, Debbie." Penelope reached across and placed her and on Debbie's clenched fist. Her skin was soft and smooth. She took care of herself. But her hands were cold to the touch, colder than they should have been in a long thick coat inside the warm coffee shop.

"I've got to escape."

There it was, plain as day. The goal, no matter what happened, was for Debbie to get away. There were thousands of women who needed to escape from abusive relationships, but what set Debbie apart from the rest was that she'd made the first move and sought help. That was a fact that Penelope could only put down to an article she'd written a few months ago. It had exposed a man who had imprisoned his children and their au pair and had forced his wife to feed them like dogs in purpose-built cages in the cellar of a house in the woods.

Through a series of letters that the mother had discreetly smuggled from the house and posted to Penelope at the Express, the story had been put together. Penelope had enlisted outside help to track the family down and pinpoint the house. The family had been saved. Penelope had since taken the case further to bring to light other cases of domestic abuse in its worst possible form. She was now pigeonholed as the reporter who helps abused women. It was a trait that Casey adored.

"Why?"

"He's a killer."

The words came like a blind stab in the dark with Debbie seeking a visual reaction from Penelope to steer her next comment.

"You know this for a fact, Debbie? If you do, we can get you away no problem. But we'll need proof."

"There's too many secrets," she replied.

"It's those secrets that I need to know. If we can get something on him and prove it, you have nothing to worry about."

But Debbie didn't reply immediately. She seemed to waver. Her head rocked gently to and fro.

"Debbie?"

Through the dark lenses of her sunglasses, Penelope caught the slow movement of the whites of Debbie's eyes. They locked onto Penelope's.

"He rapes me," she said. Then she let go of her collar to dab at her eyes with a used tissue that must have been bunched up inside her fist all along. Penelope pulled a pack of fresh tissues from her bag and slid them across the table.

"Why don't we start at the beginning?" she said. "Take your time."

CHAPTER SIXTEEN

SETTLING INTO HIS HOME OFFICE, FRANKIE PLACED A FRESH coffee on the coaster on his desk, pulled his camera bag close and dropped down into his office chair. He pulled a cable from beneath his desk, plugged his camera into the computer, and began copying images across ready to edit. He created a new folder named '*Mr & Mrs Goldsborough*' and placed the images inside. Photographing weddings was a core part of his monthly income. One wedding each month paid the bills and more, although those couples fortunate enough to be accepted by Frankie were heavily investigated prior to him accepting the gig. He preferred smaller weddings, close to his home, and as such, Frankie often found himself turning away more work than he took on.

The files finished copying, so Frankie unplugged his camera, clipped the case shut and slid it into a space beside his desk. Eighteen hundred wedding photos stared back at him from the screen. His workflow was simple. He'd scan through the images in his editing suite, colour code the best shots, then copy those into a new folder named '*Unedited.*' Then, he'd scan through once more, selecting one or two shots from each scene that would cover the typical wedding photos married couples typically wanted. A shot of the bride and groom at the altar. A shot of them at the doors of the church. Them walking through the shower of confetti. The speeches. The cake cutting. The first dance. They were all on the list of must-haves. But after that, the selection process was purely down to Frankie's own impeccable taste, and it was often the candid shots that people preferred. The selection of photos were all edited and placed in yet another new folder named *'Edited,'* which he would copy to a USB drive for his clients.

A career in military surveillance had taught Frankie how to blend in and learn who's who. He used those same skills to spot opportune moments and find angles that his clients were overjoyed with. The military had spared no expense with his training. From being immersed in a jungle for three weeks, avoiding capture, to wining and dining at dinner parties, Frankie could blend in, identify a target, and come away with the required intelligence. Photography had only been a small aspect of his military career but had seemed the obvious choice for him when his military career had ended.

Many of his army colleagues still served. Some trained the next generation of special forces. Some sat behind desks. Others had gone into private security or even the fire service. Frankie hadn't had the same opportunities. He had taken his photographic abilities, and along with the insurance from Jacqui's death, had managed to do the minimal amount of work for the maximum amount of free time.

He opened another window, browsed to his cloud folder, and sorted the results by last modified to find the previous wedding he had done. But instead of the wedding folder appearing at the top of the results as it should have, his personal folder did. His personal folder was a folder he rarely touched.

Hairs prickled on the back of his neck. Instinct began to kick in.

He opened the folder and sorted the folders inside in the same fashion, with the last modified at the top of the search results.

The folder named, 'X' showed at the top of the results.

Someone had been on his computer.

Without needing to delve into the folder itself, Frankie closed the window and shut down all the applications. A shortcut on his desktop disguised as a wastebasket opened another application. A window popped up on the screen requesting his credentials. After that, Frankie was presented with six images: live feeds from the cameras inside his house and around his property.

There was one camera in the back garden, one at the front of the house, one inside his garage, one inside the hallway disguised as a light fitting, one on the upstairs landing focused on Jake's bedroom door, and one inside his office. The office camera was hidden inside a real camera, an ancient Pentax his father had given him, which sat on a shelf alongside more of his earlier cameras. There were no lights flashing, no visible signs at all that the unit was connected to a security network other than a tiny cable that ran along the back of the shelf, which was completely hidden.

Selecting the office footage, Frankie played the video in reverse at high speed. He saw himself in a series of very quick frames darting in and out of the office, placing his camera case down and leaving again. Then disappointment gripped his chest as he knew it would. The kind of tight sickly feeling that occurs when trust is broken. Penelope had wandered into his office, looked around, and then sat at his desk. From what Frankie saw, she didn't head directly for his computer but seemed only to wake the sleeping machine with an accidental bump of her leg.

He watched with growing disappointment as the recording clearly showed Penelope running from the room only to return a few moments later. She sat back with an expression of success, then leaned forward and began browsing Frankie's personal files.

"Are you spying on me?" he said aloud.

He tagged the marker of the footage, saved it, and closed the security application.

Penelope was one of the few people who knew Frankie's story. She knew about his military career but didn't know enough details to land herself in trouble. He was obliged never to speak about his career. He had signed the official secrets act when he signed up to the special forces, but even if he hadn't, the journalist in her had always made him wary of what he said.

She had seen his career end. She had watched from afar when Jacqui had died and had seen him try to salvage a career in photography while trying to raise his son.

She also knew about his, less legitimate work.

He'd assumed that Penelope had been satisfied that he was a mere photographer who had a knack for finding people. No further questions had been asked. Until now.

"You stupid girl," he muttered to himself.

A surge of anger coursed through Frankie, violent like white water. In a moment of frustration, he slammed his hand on his desk. But as quickly as he had lost his temper, he calmed himself, at least physically. His mind was still rattled by his own stupidity.

Other than Frankie himself, only one other person knew his true identity. But if Penelope had discovered something that she ought not to have found, she'd have questions. Questions were fine. Frankie could deal with questions. But it was the answers that perhaps she wouldn't be ready for; that and the consequences.

Frankie ran an Internet search for Penelope. He found several recent articles. A footballer who'd been found guilty of assaulting some other guy who probably deserved it and been issued a standard six-month prison sentence.

"He'll be out in under three," said Frankie.

The next search result was a link to the article Penelope had written on the Harry Crown investigation. Frankie had been there when the police had opened the house up and walked out with the children who had to shield their eyes from the sunlight. Harry Crown had been dragged out of the house, naked as the day he was born. By the time the officers had reached the waiting squad car, the skin across Crown's knees and toes had all but been torn off from the rough concrete.

The scene had reminded Frankie of his Gulf tour. Covert ops had taken him and his team further inside Iraq than the government had stated. Much further. They sat atop a mountain two-kilometres out from a village, calling shots for the US strike force. The jets' pilots listened, fired their missiles, banked and were likely back at base in under five minutes. But for Frankie and his partner, the action had only just begun. When what you see is through the magnification of a rifle scope or a spotting scope, it's difficult to focus on the rest of the world. And that scope's glass is filled with the confused and terrified eyes of children whose lives had been dependent on men that Frankie had just killed. Now, they stared in wonder at the burning wreckage of a car their daddy used to drive.

It didn't matter that daddy was a terrorist. It didn't matter that he'd killed. The only thing that mattered right there and then on the top of that mountain were those eyes.

When the Crown children emerged from their house, elated with freedom, embarrassed by their nudity, and frightened for their father's future, they'd carried that same look of hatred, relief, and bewilderment.

It had been during the Harry Crown investigation that Frankie had first noticed Penelope's heart. She helped walk the children out with a female police officer while Crown sat in the police car. Frankie had stood as far away as he could, snapping candid shots of Harry Crown's journey. Anger as he was wrenched from the house. Pain as he was brutally dragged across the concrete. The realisation that his life was over. Prison would destroy him in a heartbeat.

Frankie had caught the entire cycle of emotions on his Nikon.

Then, as the children were being led from the house along with Mrs Crown, Penelope had emerged carrying a young girl in one arm, whose little face was buried in Penelope's floaty, floral dress. A young boy walked beside her with his hand inside Penelope's.

Penelope had worn a look of both pride and triumph. She'd risked everything to free the children and was just about holding herself together. Frankie had looked on in astonishment. As they broke free of the long shadow the house cast on the concrete driveway, Frankie had raised his camera to his eye. The frame was perfect. The house in the background was slightly out of focus with its steel bars across the windows and doors. In the foreground was the corner of a flashing blue light that sat atop a waiting police car, inside which sat Harry Crown. The main focus of the image bore Penelope and the female officer leading the victims to safety. The entire scene in one image.

Frankie clicked once.

That one shot told the entire story and had cemented his and Penelope's relationship.

But now she knew about Frankie's past and had seen the members of his team.

And there were rules against that; very strict rules.

CHAPTER SEVENTEEN

BURNING SKIN, STINGING EYES, AND A POUNDING HEAD brought Isaac back to consciousness. His shoulder ached but had been numbed by anaesthetic.

He was laid out in the infirmary, a place he recognised from only three previous visits during his time behind bars.

He opened his eyes but saw nothing. His numb face and frozen shoulder returned memories, and though they were vague, a clear underlying truth ran through the images as he pieced the morning together.

A damp cloth lay across his open eyes. With his good arm, he reached up and pulled it free, but the bright light above him was too much. Kind hands took the cloth from his and placed it over his eyes once more.

"You were lucky," said the voice that accompanied the kind but firm hands.

"I don't feel lucky," he replied without thinking.

"Well, you were. If Officer Shepherd hadn't stepped in, who knows what might have happened. But as it stands, your shoulder just needed a few stitches, and your eyes will be better tomorrow."

"Tomorrow?" he said. "But I'm supposed to be-"

"You won't be going anywhere, Black. Not until tomorrow, that is."

"Shorty?" he said. He was unsure himself if it was meant as a question or just a word. A memory.

"Edgar Short?" said the doctor with a laugh that resembled a sharp exhale. "He won't be going anywhere full stop. You're lucky the officers got to you when they did. You should have seen what he did to your mate."

"My mate?"

"Bruno Young," the doctor said. He had a faint Scottish accent and a kind, welcoming tone that sounded somehow too soft for prison life. "It's okay. Short confessed to it all. He said he came for you, said there was an old score that needed settling before you got out. Is there anything you want to add to that story?"

"Am I still getting out?"

"So the warden says."

"I don't know what happened."

"I wouldn't trouble yourself too much with it. You'll put it behind you tomorrow. Bruno Young stepped in to save you."

"To save me?"

"Short killed him to get at you. Stabbed him to death. He confessed to it all."

"Stabbed him to death?" Isaac repeated the words, falling in with the story and Shorty's plan. There was no escaping it now. If Isaac didn't kill Carter, Carter would go for Shorty, and then Isaac would be running from them both.

"What a mess," he said aloud.

"Take it easy, Black. You've served your time. We're just keeping you here for the night. Tomorrow you'll be a free man again."

A free man. The words rolled around Isaac's head, intertwined with memories of death as Bruno had been so close to squeezing the life from him. Then had been the haze, which he guessed was his internal organs shutting down through lack of oxygen. And then the dull stab. The warm blood. And the fog.

"A free man," he mumbled. A laugh nearly found its way through his damaged throat but stopped.

"Easy now," said the doctor, taking hold of his good arm. "I'll give you something to send you off. Just relax and count down from ten."

"Ten."

A pinprick.

"Nine."

That warm feeling returned to his arm.

"Eight."

The fog.

CHAPTER EIGHTEEN

"It started as soon as we were married," said Debbie. "He'd take me whenever he wanted. I tried playing hard to get at first, but he'd take me anyway. Gradually, the level of force increased."

"Why didn't you get out early?" asked Penelope.

"I thought about it. Back then, I probably could have too. But now-" She sighed and seemed to finish the sentence in the confines of her mind, then started afresh. "He's always nice afterwards, you know? He's always sorry. He says something comes over him."

"What about the eye?"

Debbie ran a finger across her swollen cheekbone.

"This was different," said Debbie. "This was my mistake."

"Fall down the stairs?'

To Penelope's surprise, Debbie reached up and removed her sunglasses, revealing, for the first time, the shiner in all its glory.

"You wouldn't understand," said Debbie.

"Try me?"

With an almost seductive lick of her lips, Debbie narrowed her eyes and swallowed.

"Do you have a husband?" she asked.

Penelope shook her head in reply.

"Boyfriend maybe?"

"I'm seeing someone," said Penelope. It was enough information, and she closed the thread of conversation.

"And if you spoke your mind?"

The question stopped Penelope's trail of thought in its tracks.

"Spoke my mind?" she asked. "About what?"

Debbie gave a shrug and fixed her gaze on Penelope. "Anything. What to eat. What to drink. Where to go and when to go."

"I've never really thought about it," said Penelope.

"Because you've never had to."

"Right. I guess."

"Men like my Bobby need full control. It's how they function. You can't take that away from them."

"He hit you for suggesting dinner?"

"No," said Debbie with a shake of her head slight enough to maintain eye contact. "But it started like that. You see men like my Bobby get agitated. They have this energy that needs to be released. That's why they're successful. They have drive. But when that drive is suppressed for any reason, the slightest thing can set them off."

"Go on," said Penelope. "I think I'm getting the picture now."

"It doesn't really matter what I said, suffice to say, it was a minor thing that aggravated him and I should have just kept my mouth shut."

"No," said Penelope. "You shouldn't have–"

"Yes, Miss Pike," said Debbie, for the first time taking control of the dialogue. "Yes, I should have. I should have shut up and let him have his way."

"Please call me Penelope. Let's get you out of there, Debbie." Penelope's tone softened.

Debbie replied with a nod as slight as before, and replace her sunglasses with a quick embarrassed glance around her to make sure nobody was staring.

"I know people, police who can get you out in a heartbeat. You can be put in protective custody."

"No," said Debbie. "Not that."

"But, Debbie-"

"He'll find me. He has men. He has money. I have nothing. I've suffered for more than twenty-years, Penelope. If we do this, he goes away behind bars. That's the only way I'll keep the money. Not all of it, I know. But I have a little nest egg I've been squirrelling away. It's enough for me to live off for however long I have."

"What are you saying, Debbie?"

"I'm saying-" She stopped, lowered her voice, and once more checked around her. She leaned across the table. "I'm saying that my husband is a murderer, a drug dealer, a bank robber, and a rapist. I've got enough on him over the past two decades to put him away for the rest of his life. Him and his cronies."

The statement was bold, but sincere, and supported the information King had supplied on Bobby Carter.

"You want to expose him?" asked Penelope. "How do you see this panning out?"

"If I go to the police, Miss Pike, Bobby will get a phone call while I'm being interviewed and he'll be outside ready to pick me up and give me a hiding."

"He has the police paid off?"

"Only the ones that count. Police, prison guards, jury members. If he can't pay them off, he'll do whatever it takes to stop them testifying."

"So you came to me."

"I read your article. I think it can work."

"And you'd be happy to give me the dirt on him?"

"Anonymously."

"Everything?"

"Enough that someone higher up in the police force will have to take action. None of the local boys."

"Can you wear a wire?" asked Penelope.

"He'd find it. All it would take is for him to get horny and drag me to the bedroom. He'd kill me, Penelope. I know he would."

The two women locked eyes, and suddenly for Penelope, it was no longer about the exclusive. Or Casey's deadline. Seated in front of her, in a coffee shop, wearing over-sized sunglasses to hide her ongoing rape and abuse ordeal was a woman just like her. With the same flesh and blood, and the same vulnerabilities.

"Can you get me inside the house?" asked Penelope. "Does he have a schedule?"

"No schedule," said Debbie. "That's how he's survived this long. But he does go out. Sometimes for an hour. Sometimes he's gone for days. I never know which until he returns, and he usually has his cronies there. He says it's to keep me safe, but we all know the truth."

A plan began to formulate in Penelope's head as she spoke. "Do you know his accomplices? We need the whole crew. If anyone is left on the outside, he could still get at you."

"Yeah, I know them. But they see it all. He's got two men who are close, both armed. Bobby doesn't always drag me into the bedroom. Sometimes it's wherever he feels like doing it. Could be the kitchen, or beside the pool. And if the boys are there, then so be it."

"He rapes you in front of his friends?"

"I wouldn't call them friends, Penelope. They're paid, but paid well."

"But still-"

"A few of them turn away. I'm not sure if they do that for my own modesty or for their own consciences. But one guy, in partic-ular, likes to watch. He's a real creep."

"His name?"

"Jammo," replied Debbie, without hesitation.

"Do you have photos of all these men?"

Subconsciously, Debbie glanced at her designer handbag and then back to Penelope.

"You have them with you?'

Debbie pulled a padded envelope from her bag. From inside, she retrieved a pile of four-by-six photos bound with a rubber band. She handed them to Penelope but held on for a split second, long enough to convey an unspoken message with her eyes.

Penelope understood.

"Who do we have here?" asked Penelope, recognising Bobby in the first photo. But she let Debbie point him out to avoid her knowing about her prior research.

"That's Bobby in the middle. Rick is the tall one, and that's his brother on the right, Billy."

"His brother?"

Debbie nodded.

Penelope flicked through to the next photo. It was the same men, sitting in a booth in a West End club.

"These aren't enough to put him away, Debbie," said Penelope.

"Keep going."

A few shots later was an image of a much younger Bobby, holding a shotgun and smiling for the camera like an image of Bonnie and Clyde. He was stood in front of the open rear door of a cash van with two guards tied up inside it.

"Jesus."

"Cash van?" asked Debbie, who had leaned back to allow Penelope time to scan through the evidence.

Penelope nodded.

"Who takes photos of something like that?"

"Someone with an ego."

A few images later showed men dressed in eighties clothing, cigarettes hanging from their lips, and glasses of scotch or brandy on a table that was otherwise swamped with bundles of cash. The men were all smiling and laughing as the cash was being counted. A very young Bobby was on the far left of the photo with Billy. Some other unknown men filled the rest of the space. They were all young and fueled by greed and power.

But one man caught Penelope's eye. A man, slightly older than the rest, was sitting opposite Bobby. He had a shaved head and a few days' growth on his face. He was leaning across the table handing Bobby a wad of cash, but the photographer must have caught his eye, causing him to flick his eyes to his left.

Although the photo was black and white, there was no mistaking those piercing eyes.

She looked closer. The chin, the nose, even the shape of his shaved head.

"Who's this?" she asked Debbie.

Debbie glanced up from her phone to see the photo that Penelope held up.

"The guy on the right?"

Penelope nodded.

"The older guy."

"Isaac Black," she replied.

"Black?"

"You've heard of him?" asked Debbie.

"He's still alive?" said Penelope, ignoring the question.

"Prison," she replied. "Take a look at the last photo. That's where all of this began."

With tentative curiosity, Penelope slipped the last photograph from the stack and placed it on top.

Isaac Black stared back at the camera. He stood beside a much younger Bobby Carter, looking down at the young man with what Penelope could only describe as pride. Both men rested shotguns on their shoulders. Sat on the floor at their feet, in a pool of what looked to be back ink in the monochrome image, but what Penelope knew to be blood, were the corpses of two men.

CHAPTER NINETEEN

One of the attractions of where Frankie lived on the edge of London, with the luxuries and amenities of the city in one direction and the endless British countryside in the other, was the abundance of discreet locations where he could meet potential clients for ultimate privacy.

Along a winding lane, around thirty miles from his home and perched atop rolling hills of patchwork fields and shimmering streams that glistened in the summer sun, was a tiny patch of flattened grass just big enough for half a dozen cars to park side by side. Frankie's Range Rover was the only vehicle in the area. The lane itself was visible for miles, which allowed Frankie to see any approaching vehicles long before they became a threat. His Zeiss auto-focus binoculars scanned the tarmac below, found the pickup truck, and focused on the driver.

One steady hand held the wheel of the truck, and one elbow rested on the door frame, allowing the redundant hand to offer a one-fingered greeting at Frankie. Behind the gesture, hidden beneath the peak of a very recognisable peaked cap, was Nigel's face. His laughter lines clearly showed his amusement at his own joke.

Frankie scanned behind the truck as far as he could, then swept the entire area once more before Nigel skidded to a halt on the dry grass beside his Range-Rover. The window rolled down to reveal Nigel's smiling face.

"Nice spot," he said, as Frankie hit the down button on his own window. "Are we dogging or working?"

"And what if I said dogging?" asked Frankie.

"You'd be the first person to do it alone I guess," replied Nigel with a smile.

"Were you followed?"

Nigel shook his head as Frankie packed his binos away inside the little case and dropped them back into the door pocket where they lived.

"You're not your usual sparkly self, Frankie," said Nigel. "What's up?"

"Oh well, you know how it is, Nigel."

"No, mate, no I don't."

"Girl trouble," said Frankie.

"What do you need from me, instructions?" said Nigel. "Didn't your old man teach you all about the birds and the bees?"

The Range Rover began to chime as Frankie pulled the door handle and shoved open the heavy door. The chiming stopped once Frankie had shut the door and silence resumed. Striding around to Nigel's car, Frankie checked the hills for movement or a tell-tale glint of sunlight on a car windscreen, or worse, the scope of a rifle.

The paranoia never stops.

Nigel joined him at the front of the truck.

"I met someone, Nigel."

"Good for you, buddy." Nigel allowed his smile to spread across his round, freckly face. "That's great news."

A weak smile and a single nod were all Frankie could muster in reply.

"Oh god," said Nigel. "She's not pregnant already?"

This time Frankie shook his head, but couldn't face his old friend. Instead, he stared at the tyre print in the grass and let his mind wander with hypothetical scenarios in which the tyre track led people directly to his doorstep.

"So what then?" asked Nigel, pushing for more clues. "What's so terrible?"

"Do you remember Jacqui?" asked Frankie.

"Of course I do, mate. I was your best man, remember?"

"In all our time together, she never–" Frankie paused, hoping that Nigel would be able to full in the gaps. "You know?"

"Know what?" replied Nigel.

This time Frankie raised his head faced his friend and held his gaze.

"She didn't know about the unit, Nigel."

"They can't know, Frankie," said Nigel, his tone soft. "That's the whole idea. They wouldn't understand. Tracey didn't know either. Nobody can know. You know the rules."

"But that's just it, Nigel. The secret. What we did. Who we were. It's a lot for one man to carry."

"But we swore we would carry it, Frankie, and carry it we will." Nigel's tone had turned serious as if reminding Frankie of the oath the two of them had taken all those years before.

Frankie's head dizzied a little, then settled, leaving his mind clear to say the words.

"She knows, Nigel."

Nigel didn't reply. Instead, a silence grew, and a distance emerged from Frankie's foggy head. Had he actually verbalised the words?

"Did you hear me?"

"I heard you, Frankie."

"I need help, Nigel."

"Frankie, what have you done?"

"Nigel–"

"You know the rules."

"Don't, Nigel, please mate."

"It's a bit unfair, mate, don't you think?" said Nigel. He shoved off the front of the car and began to pace. "You get me to come all the way out here and then drop this on me."

"I didn't tell her."

"It doesn't matter, Frankie," said Nigel. "She knows. Are you sure she knows?"

"Ninety-nine per cent."

"Knows what?"

"Enough. She found photos."

Nigel's head flew back as if he'd been shot.

"Oh, Frankie."

"Nigel, listen to me. I've got an idea."

"Does your idea involve implicating me any further? Because quite frankly, I'm getting bored of that."

It was Frankie's turn for silence.

"Who is she?" asked Nigel.

"Do you remember Penelope Pike." Frankie said the words the way someone might introduce a new girlfriend to his circle of friends. Not like a friend might begin to describe the woman they both knew would be dead before the week was out. "She's the-"

"Journalist," said Nigel. "The Express, right? You're shagging the bird we pulled out of the desert? Bleeding-hell, Frankie. She knows you're special forces. We saved her bloody life. How? Why?"

"Not shagging," said Frankie. "Just-"

"Just nothing, Frankie. She's dangerous. You should have just cut all ties the minute you got back from the tour."

"Yeah, well. Things didn't really work out the way I intended did they?"

"Do you need me to take care of it?" asked Nigel.

"No," snapped Frankie. "Not entirely anyway."

"Frankie, we've got two options here. One, you do it. Two, I do it. If neither of us does it and she spills something in the paper, we'll both be taken care of. So either you do it, or I do it."

"Get her out of it," said Frankie. "Take her somewhere."

"You mean, *kidnap* her?"

"I mean get her out of it. Hole her up."

Sorrow spread across Nigel's face for the first time.

"Can't do that, mate. She's a journalist, Frankie. One slip and the whole team is blown. Why didn't you stop to think?"

"Think what?" said Frankie. "Think that she'd find out about who we really were? About my history? No Nigel, I didn't. I managed to keep it secret from Jacqui all those years."

"Jacqui wasn't a bloody journalist, Frankie. This Pike girl, she's different. How long have you been seeing her?"

"Remember the Crown murders?"

"Oh, of course," said Nigel. "That's where I know the name from. She was the lead journalist, right?"

"She contacted me, asked me to help find them. When the case was over, we just hit it off."

"And what's your idea?" asked Nigel. "How are you going to contain this?"

"I don't know, Nigel." Dejection seemed to suck the power from Frankie's voice.

"Good plan, boss," said Nigel. "Was you going to wait until she did a centre-spread on you?"

"What do you want me to do?"

"Take her out, Frankie. You know the rules."

"I can't do it."

"Then *I* will," said Nigel. "Nobody can know about us."

Nigel's last words stabbed at Frankie. He knew his friend was right. He knew the rules. But it all seemed so unfair.

The slamming of Nigel's car door shook Frankie from his daydream. He turned to face his oldest friend.

"I'll call when it's done," said Nigel through the open window of his truck.

He then pulled out of the small clearing and onto the narrow lane. There were no insulting farewell gestures as there usually was. There was no sign of humour at all as Frankie's best friend drove away. There was only the familiar feeling of loss again.

CHAPTER TWENTY

A LOUD BUZZER ACCOMPANIED BY A SPINNING ORANGE LIGHT announced the sliding steel gate was closing behind Isaac. For eight years he'd dreamed of the door closing, but in his mind, the scene had always been more ceremonial with far more grandeur. Instead, he stood staring at the world which should have been his new playground, a world in which he could go wherever he pleased and build a new life.

If it hadn't been for Shorty, Isaac knew that he'd already be dead. But his newfound freedom had come at a price, a price that could very well land him back inside, and if that happened, parole would be impossible. He'd be handed a life sentence from the judge with barely a pause for a breath.

Cars that Isaac had seen on the small TV that he and Smiler had rented for their cell passed by him as he strolled to the train station. He held an unmarked prison-issue bag, which was plain grey and contained the few items he owned. He wore the clothes he'd worn in prison, a pair of tracksuit bottoms, white trainers and a plain sweatshirt. The prison allowed prisoners to purchase a small amount of personal clothing, as long as the items followed the guidelines.

Eight years in prison had dulled Isaac's senses, but during the walk, they seemed to revive themselves with increasing sensitivity. He noticed the cool breeze on his skin. The summer was warm, the sun strong, and the gentle wind seemed to lick at his face. The train station was close by, a twenty-minute walk, but before stepping inside, and using the cash that the on-duty had made him sign for along with his belongings, Isaac stopped. He turned to face the world and one thing struck him hard.

The world hadn't stopped. If anything it moved faster.

Isaac's release should have impacted just one person; Isaac. In an ideal world, he'd have kept it like that. But Shorty's deal changed things. To take care of Carter, Isaac would need help.

The man behind the glass screen in the train station offered little help, other than directing him to the self-service machines that scared the hell out of Isaac.

"But, sir, can't you just print me one off, and I pay you? That's how it used to work."

"Sir?" replied the man. "I haven't been called that for a while."

"Old habits," said Isaac.

"Look, mate, it's not hard," said the man. "Just browse through the menu, find the station you want, and touch the screen."

"Touch the screen?" said Isaac, getting irritated by the lack of assistance.

It was then that Isaac witnessed, for the first time, the look on someone's face when they realised he was an ex-con who'd just been released. An awkward silence was broken by something that Isaac could only put down as an element of fear.

"Where you going, mate?" said the man with sudden helpfulness.

Isaac retrieved a small piece of prison-issue notepaper from his pocket and held it up to the glass.

"Oh, right," said the man. "You're better off with a daily travel card. You can use it all day on the buses or the trains."

Isaac slipped the twenty-pound note through the small gap

beneath the glass. It was the remains of his spend, what he'd earned mopping the floors every day, and within seconds, a pink card was returned.

"Thank you, sir," said Isaac.

"Pleasure, mate," came the reply. "Good luck."

During eight years of incarceration, cars had evolved into sleek futuristic works of art. Buildings of glass now framed the old factories that had once dominated the South London landscape. But the train that rattled to a squeaky stop beside Isaac on the platform seemed as if it had been dusted off especially for Isaac's release. Even the orange checkered velour seats were the same as he remembered them.

Taking a seat between the two carriage doors, Isaac sat and pocketed the little pink ticket. A few other people occupied the carriage but not many. Release time was timed to miss rush hour and the few strangers that shared the space were of no threat to Isaac.

The prison official who had offered guidance on re-integrating men into society had mentioned that old habits formed from a long prison sentence would be hard to break. Calling people sir or finding a place to sit while keeping everybody in view were just two examples. As the train entered Barking Station, Isaac pondered if killing someone should be added to the list.

Isaac checked the address on the piece of paper once more as the train drew into his stop. A part of him hoped that the ride would have been longer, another hour or two to give him time to prepare. He disembarked and made his way out of the station onto the busy high street. He had only a mental note of the map he'd seen on the Internet during association time a few days previously. It had been Shepherd that helped him use something called a search engine to find the address he'd been given, and he'd made it look so easy. Isaac turned right and began walking. The guilty feeling that everyone was staring at him as if they knew who he was, where he'd been, and why he'd been there, soon wore off. But still, the anxious twisting of his stomach remained as a constant reminder that, with each step that he took, the only thing that grew closer was uncertainty.

It was a full twenty-five minutes before Isaac stood outside the house. For the last time, he checked the piece of paper, then folded it and tucked it into his pocket. There were no cars on the drive, no lights on during the day, and no visible sign of life.

Twenty long strides took him to the side gate, where he took a deep breath, reached up for the sliding bolt, then pushed the gate open. He closed the gate behind him and entered the back garden. Isaac took a sweeping glance. The immaculate lawn, trimmed hedges, and beautiful simplicity assured him that he was in the right place. All he had to do was wait.

CHAPTER TWENTY-ONE

"Why don't we start at the beginning?" said Penelope. "Who is Isaac Black, and who is he in relation to your husband?"

Debbie sucked in an audible breath through gritted teeth, then puffed her cheeks and exhaled long and slow.

"He's the reason Bobby Carter is Bobby Carter. Why he is the man he is."

"Go on," said Penelope, encouraging Debbie to embellish on her answer. Interviews came naturally to her, and she found that when a victim began to get something off their chest, all sorts of information came flooding out.

"Bobby and Billy were abandoned as children. They never met their parents. As a result, they became problem children. They stayed together, took the usual jumps through various foster homes, were expelled from various schools. Life was hard for them, and I guess at such a young and impressionable age, all they really needed was some love and a firm hand. But society wasn't really able to provide them that back then. I don't know that it's any different now."

"Tough love?"

"Yeah, I guess," continued Debbie. "Bobby told me about it

once, but don't get me wrong, he doesn't talk about his past with pride. He doesn't really talk about any of it, not to me anyway. Whenever he spoke about his past, he'd speak matter of fact, like they did what they had to do to get by."

Debbie took a sip of her coffee, then placed the cup back down, but held it with both hands, as if warming them from the cold of the memories she was about to relive.

"As time went by, they began to steal. Just off other kids at first, lunch money and money for cigarettes. Then that turned into stealing for real money. They'd sell stolen tools in the local pubs for a quick buck, which progressed to cars and motorbikes that would see them through a little longer."

"Sounds like a natural progression for a criminal."

The word criminal seemed to strike a nerve. Debbie stopped, and for a moment, Penelope thought she'd blown it. She'd judged Debbie's husband, and as bad as the man was, she obviously still loved him to a certain degree. But then Debbie nodded.

"I guess if we're going to generalise," she replied.

"I'm sorry, Debbie," said Penelope. "That was out of line."

"No," said Debbie. "No, it wasn't out of line at all. He is what he is, and if he wasn't, we wouldn't be sitting here now."

The statement required no reply. Penelope simply acknowledged Debbie's words with a tight-lipped smile.

"By the time he was sixteen or seventeen, Billy would have been a couple of years younger, they'd sleep wherever they could. Couches mostly, or in a friend's parents' caravan in their garden. Sometimes even the railway arches out of the wind and rain."

"That's a tough start for any kid," said Penelope.

"It is," Debbie agreed. "Especially in East London. Sleeping with one eye open ready to defend himself and his brother. I just can't imagine what it must have been like for them."

"He worked his way out of it though," said Debbie. "Although I can't condone his methods, you can't take that away from him. They did everything they could to survive."

The shift in emotions from the scared woman who Penelope had joined at the table in the coffee shop to the woman who seated in front of her now, almost defending the man who repeatedly raped and humiliated her, was a sign that the interview was heading in the wrong direction. Penelope needed to steer the chat back onto Bobby's dark side. She needed to do it fast if the interview was going to provide any tangible results.

"I imagine there must have been a turning point in his criminal career," said Penelope. "A time when he transitioned from small time to the big time?"

"Yes," said Debbie. Her voice was thoughtful. A hint of empathy still remained in her tone. "He was stealing cars, sleeping in them sometimes, and then selling them for scrap. The usual tricks like filling the petrol tank with water to increase the weight and get more money for them."

"Very entrepreneurial."

"Yeah, you could say that. If there's a buck to be made, Bobby will make two. I'll give him that. We've never done without."

"And the transition?" Penelope prompted.

"Simple," Debbie replied. "One day, he stole the wrong person's car. Or tried to, I should say."

"Is there a right person?"

"I guess not. But of all the cars in the world that Bobby and Billy could have tried to steal, Isaac Black's was a sure-fire way to land himself dead in a ditch, the river, or the footings of Canning Town flyover."

"Canning Town flyover?"

"It was something Bobby used to say. A reference to the discarding of a body. I guess he learnt it from Isaac. When the Canning Town bridge was being built, they reckon a few bodies wound up in the footings."

"A concrete overcoat?"

"Something like that."

"But he didn't kill him. Isaac, I mean. He didn't kill Bobby. So what happened?"

"It was close, as I understand it," said Debbie. "Billy was supposed to keep watch but was distracted. Isaac caught Bobby at it, and Bobby gave him his usual mouthful of abuse."

A smirk crept onto Penelope's face. She knew the type of boy Debbie was describing.

"Isaac slapped him about a bit, but Bobby kept coming back for more. He'd knock Bobby down, and Bobby would be straight back at him. Little Billy jumped in for what it was worth, but they were no match for a full-grown man."

"Tenacious kids."

"He's a lunatic, Penelope. He's even worse now. You'd think he'd have calmed down as he got older, but no. I couldn't tell you the number of times I've just had to walk away from him while he told someone what he thought, and he doesn't care where he is."

"And Isaac?" asked Penelope, steering the conversation back on track.

"Isaac? He saw something in them. Maybe it was the tenacity. Maybe it was the hunger or the attitude. He ended up buying them both a burger. Can you believe that?"

"Somehow, yes, I think I can."

"Isaac had them running errands, small-time stuff, you know? He gave Bobby a little car and had them running all over the East End, dropping this off, collecting that, keeping an eye on someone."

"Isaac gave them a taste of the life?"

Debbie nodded.

"Yeah. It wasn't long though before Isaac had them working full time. Bobby was a driver at first. He'd learnt to drive by getting away from the police in stolen motors. Isaac saw the talent and had him as a wheel-man during robberies."

"And he worked his way through the ranks?" asked Penelope. "That's some achievement for a street kid."

"No. One of Isaac's men messed up, or grassed him up or something. I don't know the full story. But anyway, a fight broke out. A gun was pulled. Bobby stepped in and shot the bloke dead."

"Shot him dead?" whispered Penelope, aware that they were in a public place.

Debbie nodded.

"Just like that. He saved Isaac's life. Soon after that, Bobby found himself running jobs himself. Isaac soon came to count on him."

The image of a young Bobby and Billy Carter and a middle-aged Isaac Black stared back at Penelope from the old photograph.

"Handsome, wasn't he?" said Debbie. "I was young and foolish. He was young, confident and had money by the time I met him. I pretty much fell at his feet." She shook her head in dismay. "So stupid."

"Don't be hard on yourself," said Penelope. "As you said, he was a handsome guy."

"Yeah well-" Debbie began, letting the sentence trail off to an uneasy silence.

"So, what happened?" asked Penelope. "Between Isaac and Bobby? And where's Billy now?"

"Who said anything happened?"

"Well, I just figured. Seeing as Isaac is in prison and Bobby-" Penelope backtracked. She'd messed up.

"You think Bobby grassed on Isaac? Is that it?"

"No, I-"

"Well, he didn't. Bobby would never grass. I've seen what he does to grasses, and believe me, it's not pleasant."

"Debbie, I'm sorry. I didn't mean that at all."

"So what are you saying?"

"I don't know, I-"

"I thought you came here to talk about getting me away from my husband? All we've spoken about is Isaac Black."

"I'm just trying to get some background, Debbie. That's all. You know, build a picture of who Bobby really is."

Debbie's rigid back hunched over again. She leaned her elbows on the table, as she had done before Penelope had broken the flow of information.

"They did a bank job. It went wrong. Bobby got away and Isaac didn't."

"So Isaac isn't a grass either then?" said Penelope. "Is it fair to say Bobby grew to be like a son to him?"

"A son? No. There wasn't room for another son. But they were close."

If Penelope's earlier comment hadn't closed the shutter between the two women, her question about Bobby Carter being like a son to Isaac did. Debbie reached across, and with perfectly manicured fingernails, began to gather the photos.

"I'm sorry, Debbie," said Penelope. "Did I say something?"

"Who are you?" hissed Debbie. "And what do you really want?"

"I want to help you," Penelope said in earnest, Her hands held palms out in submission. "What did I say?"

The photos were stuffed into Debbie's bag in haste as she slid from the chair and strode towards the door.

"Debbie, wait."

Penelope followed suit and stood from the table. But by the time she had checked the table to collect her bag and make sure she hadn't forgotten anything, Debbie had left the coffee shop. Penelope composed herself, not wanting to draw attention. She stepped outside and chased after Debbie with a brisk walk through the mall. When Debbie walked to the right of people, Penelope followed in her steps. When Debbie cut between slow walkers or people walking while messaging on their phones, Penelope was just five steps behind.

"Debbie, wait," she said. "What's wrong?"

But Debbie had the large collars of her thick coat pulled up, and her hands stuffed deep into her pockets. Eventually, at the top of a set of escalators, Penelope reached the woman.

"Don't run, Debbie. Let me help you."

Debbie ignored the remark as if she wasn't known to her.

"Debbie?"

More from irritation than compliance, and with visible reluctance, Debbie turned around as the escalator was halfway down.

"All I want to do is help you, Debbie. But I need to know the truth. I need to know the history. I need to know what I'm getting into here."

Debbie gave a quick glance over both shoulders, then tugged at Penelope's sleeve, pulling her out of the way of the people stepping off the escalator.

"You honestly don't know?" asked Debbie.

"I swear," said Penelope, softening her eyes.

"Then you better listen close. The job they did-"

"The one that went wrong?"

Debbie nodded. "Isaac had arranged a driver, a last-minute job. By this time, Bobby and Billy were his numbers two and three. They did the job together. Isaac, Billy and Bobby, you know, plus a couple of others. They dropped Bobby off with the cash, which was something they always did, separate the guns and the cash. But when they got back to the garage, the driver started going crazy at Isaac, shouting at him and pushing him around, so the story goes."

"At Isaac?"

"Yeah. Two of Billy's men pulled their guns so the driver pulled a shotgun from the car and shot them both. He killed one and maimed the other."

"Maimed him?"

"Yeah, took his kneecap off. He lived. He still works for Bobby now. Harry. He's got a prosthetic leg. But that doesn't stop him doing what he does. If anything, it made him angrier. Anyway, Billy stepped in with another gun, but the bloke was too fast. He had the barrel in Billy's face before Billy could get a shot off. Harry reckons he was trained. He said the way he moved with the gun was just too natural."

"He shot him in the face?"

"No, they just stood there. It became a game of dare, I guess."

The scene played out like a slow-motion movie in Penelope's mind. The young Billy, the middle-aged Isaac, and the faceless driver, angry and bitter, who had come between the terrible duo.

"Isaac calmed them down," continued Debbie. "He convinced the driver to lower his gun, and Billy followed suit. Then, as Isaac made to leave, Billy pulled his gun back up."

"He shot Isaac?" asked Penelope.

"The driver shot him first. Just a flesh wound in the arm. But it was enough to push Isaac over the edge. He had a nasty temper, that man."

A moment of peace fell between the sentences. But Penelope knew what Debbie's next words would be before she spoke them.

"Isaac killed Billy?" asked Penelope.

"Killed him outright," said Debbie. Her voice croaked with exhaustion. "The police barged in seconds later and took them all away."

"And the driver? What happened to him?"

But Debbie gave a nervous look about her.

"I've said too much," she said. "You've got my number. Don't call it. Just leave a message, coded, if you can. Bobby checks my phone. Pretend to be a friend."

Debbie thrust her hands into her pockets again, held Penelope's stare, and then moved away.

"What about the driver?" repeated Penelope.

But Debbie didn't look back.

CHAPTER TWENTY-TWO

"Hello, Son."

The voice came from Frankie's right, from the lounge, below where Jacqui stood amid the stream of suited men in the rain. The gravelled and weary tones of the aged voice slammed into his chest. Frankie remained silent but felt his heart beating like a drum, so loud in his ears that he could barely hear his own heavy breathing.

"What? Aren't you going to say hello to your old man?"

"I don't have anything to say," replied Frankie. "Except you've got ten seconds to get out of my house."

"Can I at least finish my drink? It's the first one I've had for a few years."

With a shove of his hand, Frankie slammed the front door behind him, then turned and peered into the lounge to find his father sitting in the worn leather armchair with a crystal cut tumbler of brandy resting on the arm. The old man lifted the glass, swirled the ice cubes, then raised it high in a toast.

"To freedom," he said.

"How did you find me?"

"I had eight years of being locked inside with some of the most resourceful people I ever met, Frankie."

"And what do you want?"

"Oh, come now," said Isaac. "After all these years, I thought you might at least be civil."

"When did you-"

"A few hours ago."

"You came-"

"Straight here, yeah. Thought I'd go see my beloved son. I'm sorry about Jacqui, Son."

"I presume you have a plan? Somewhere to go?"

"I've got a plan, Son. I've got things that need doing. But somewhere to stay, no. Not yet."

"I'm sure you'll find somewhere."

"Frankie, come on."

"No, Dad," said Frankie, cutting him off before he had a chance to work his forked tongue. "No. I want you to leave."

"Can I meet him?"

"Who?"

"Little Jake," said Isaac. "I'd love to see him, just once."

"I suppose some little birdie told you his name as well?"

"Idle hands, Frankie."

The mention of Jake's name reminded Frankie that his son should already be home.

"You need to leave."

"You're going to deprive your son of having a grandfather?"

"No, Dad," snapped Frankie. "You deprived him of that a long time ago. Swallow the drink, savour the taste, and get out of my house."

"Why so hostile, Frankie?" said Isaac. "Why can't we just talk things out?"

"You cost me my life, Dad."

"Oh, come on. You did that yourself."

"I nearly went to prison, Dad. Because of you."

"Oh, that's a little unfair, Frankie. If you hadn't lost your temper, you'd have-"

"I was dishonourably discharged, Dad. From the army. My life. I lost my pension, my career, my friends-"

"It wasn't supposed to go like that."

"But it did, Dad. Because of you, I had to start again. And you know what? I lost my father. As bad as you were, at least I still had one back then."

"You've got one now, Frankie. If you want it."

"No, Dad. No. I don't want it."

"I took the rap for you, boy. You need to learn some respect."

Rage suddenly pulsed through Frankie's veins, a sensation he hadn't felt for a very long time.

"*You* took the rap for *me*?"

"I did eight bleeding years for it, didn't I?"

"You did an armed bank robbery, Dad."

"And you killed Billy Carter, Frankie," snapped Isaac. His own voice raised to compete with Frankie's. "You pulled the trigger on them, Son. Nobody asked you to."

"What's that supposed to mean? Was I supposed to let them go for you?"

"That was your call. All I'm saying is that if you hadn't kicked off, I wouldn't be in the mess I'm in now, Frankie. So no, I'm not bloody leaving. And you are going to help me get out of it."

"What mess?" asked Frankie.

Isaac rose from the chair. He was shorter than Frankie remembered but still stocky. Memories of his father throwing him into the sea with ease during a holiday in Cornwall flashed through Frankie's mind. He'd done the same to Jake and hadn't even thought of it then. He hadn't even thought about it since.

Isaac began to pour himself another brandy from the bottle Frankie kept unopened in the liquor cabinet since when Jacqui had been alive. Frankie offered no objection. Then Isaac stood with his back to Frankie, staring out of the window into the quiet street outside.

"It's a nice place you've got here, son," said Isaac. "You've done well for yourself."

"I've had to build a new life."

"As a photographer, I hear. Lucrative, is it?"

"It pays the bills," said Frankie. "It's a skill the army taught me. And it was about all I could salvage."

"That's not all you do, is it though?"

"What's that supposed to mean?"

"Remember that little birdie I told you about?"

Frankie remained silent.

Isaac turned to face Frankie, taking a sip of his drink. "That's not all you learnt from the army, is it?"

"Just spit it out, Dad."

"I'm not entirely sure of the name for it."

"For what?"

"You find people, don't you? That's your true talent."

"I've been known to help find-"

"Let's cut to the chase, Son," said Isaac. "You find missing people. You find criminals. And you charge a small fortune to do it. Unbeknown to Johnny Taxman, that is."

Frankie knew his silence was an admission of guilt, but no words sprang to his mind.

"And it's that gift you have, Son," said Isaac. "That is what will buy you your freedom."

"I'm already free."

"Your freedom from me."

"What's that supposed to mean?"

"You want me out of your life? You help me."

"Is that supposed to be some kind of blackmail?"

"No, it's black and white, Frankie. I need your help. You want rid of me. Help me, and you'll never see me again."

"And what is it you want help with?"

"I thought that much would be obvious."

"Maybe spell it out. I like to have clear terms and conditions with my clients."

"I'm a client now, am I?"

"Well, you haven't been a father and if you want a label-"

"Touché."

"What is it you want?"

"I need you to help me find someone."

"Who?"

Isaac smiled. It wasn't the smile Frankie remembered from Christmas or family events. It was the smile he remembered when his father had done a job and had taken them for a pub lunch. It was a greedy smile. One that simply said, '*I won, I beat them.*'

"Bobby Carter."

CHAPTER TWENTY-THREE

"No chance," said Frankie.

Isaac watched with sadness as his son turned to open the front door, a gesture clearly meant for Isaac to leave.

"Then I cannot promise I'll be out of your life, Son," said Isaac. "Or little Jakey's."

"It's Jake."

Isaac shrugged.

"It might be nice for him to meet his old grandpa anyway. Have you told him about me?"

Stubbornness ran in the family. Frankie didn't reply.

"Well?" continued Isaac. "Does he know who his grandfather is?"

"He knows who you *were*."

"Oh, he does, does he?"

"He's seen pictures."

"And does he know who I am now?"

"He knows what I want him to know."

"Which is?"

"You're dead. Buried in a cemetery in South London somewhere."

The news didn't shock Isaac. But the words still stung.

"Maybe he'd like me," said Isaac.

"Maybe. But we'll never know, will we?"

"Don't be hard on me, Frankie. I never meant for any of this to happen."

"But it did, and it was your fault."

Frankie remained at the door, with one hand ready to close it behind Isaac.

"I keep telling you, Son. It was you that shot him."

"You asked me to pick you and your mates up from the pub."

"Well, the bank was next door to the pub."

"You did a robbery, Dad, and implicated me as the getaway driver. What kind of father does that?"

"One that loves his son, and would do anything to make sure he had food in his belly and shoes on his feet."

"Don't give me that, Dad. I had a career. I was going places."

"You were in the army earning a pittance. How were you supposed to start a family?"

"Others did it. They still do."

"Not my son. I wanted the very best for my son."

"Well, you got it, Dad. The best thing that could have happened to me was to get you out of my life."

"And now I'm back. So what are you going to do about it?"

Just like his mum used to do, Frankie brought his hands up and covered his face.

"For God's sake, Dad," said Frankie, dropping his hands back down. "Don't you get it? I'm not interested. I'm not going to help you find some ghost from the past. I'm not going to ruin my life again, and I'm not going to help you ruin yours. Now get out. Or I'll call the police. I'm sure you're on parole, right? You're out nearly nine years early."

Isaac nodded.

"So if I call them and tell them you broke into my house, and now you won't leave, you'll be thrown back inside. You might even get your cell back, Dad. The bed's probably still warm."

Eight years in prison had taught Isaac many things about body language. Who's hiding something. Who's up to no good. Who's lying.

"You wouldn't do it," said Isaac, matter of fact. There was no need for a smart mouth. No need to be proved right. Frankie was a good boy. He always had been.

"Wouldn't I?"

Isaac shook his head.

"No, Son."

The pair met eye to eye. Neither spoke. Neither smiled, frowned, or displayed any emotion other than their own pig-headed stubbornness. At last, Isaac broke the silence.

"Tick-tock, Frankie."

"Do you have somewhere to be?" said Frankie. "Are you on a tight schedule?"

"No, Son. But the clock is ticking."

"What clock?"

"My clock."

Frankie let the door swing closed. The little brass knocker rapped of its own accord.

"You care to explain?" said Frankie.

Isaac turned and pulled the brandy bottle from the cabinet again, and began to pour himself another brandy.

"That's your last one of those," said Frankie.

"You very well may be right there, Son."

"Are you enjoying this?" asked Frankie. "Are you getting off on being cryptic. You break into my house, drink my brandy and give me an ultimatum. Tell me what's going on, Dad."

The brandy lined Isaac's throat as it passed through his gullet and into his stomach, where it warmed like a fire, then faded as his body absorbed the alcohol.

"You meet some nasty men inside, Frankie," he began. "You wouldn't know, of course, because I saved you from that pleasure."

"You were the one who..."

But Frankie's argument trailed to nothing as Isaac raised his hands to quell his son.

"Most of them are good men. The lifers and the long-timers. Yes, they did wrong to be in there, but at heart, they're good for the most part. But you never really make friends. You meet all sorts. Thieves, rapists-"

"Bank robbers..."

"And murderers, Son. Lots of murderers."

Frankie couldn't meet Isaac's stare. The guilt had got him, and Isaac knew it.

"And although you don't really make friends, you do sometimes meet people who can help you."

Frankie huffed at the statement and folded his arms as if to gesture that Isaac was wasting his time with the story.

"One such man helped me, you might be pleased to know. Saved my life, he did."

"Is that right?"

"It is," said Isaac. "About two days ago. I've got the wound to prove it." Isaac pulled the collar of his sweatshirt back to display the white patch across his shoulder.

"I doubt they'd help you for nothing, Dad. People rarely do that on the outside."

"You still have your intelligence, Son," said Isaac. "That-a-boy."

By confirming Frankie's statement was correct, his son's inquisition began to shine through his chiselled features. His eyes narrowed, and his down-turned mouth straightened to a horizontal slit.

"Is that what this is all about?" asked Frankie.

Isaac sank the remainder of what Frankie had labelled as his last brandy. He placed the fine glass on a coaster on the small side table. With nothing to hold, Isaac found his hands wandering to the pockets of his tracksuit pants. They slipped inside, clammy and hot.

"Dad?"

"If you don't help me kill Bobby Carter, Frankie, we'll all be killed. You, me and little Jake."

CHAPTER TWENTY-FOUR

"Hold me a front page," said Penelope, as she strode through the exit of the shopping centre. The scores of shoppers and commuters surrounding her passed by in a blur. The adrenaline and buzz of a solid case were alive inside her. Her phone was warm against her ear, her hands clammy with excitement. This was why she became a journalist. To make a difference. To reveal the world to the seemingly blind or ignorant.

"That's a bold statement," said Casey. She pictured him at his desk piled high with paperwork as other journalists submitted their articles for the weekend edition. Tammy would have made him a coffee and brought him biscuits. He'd be sitting in his big fat chair with his big fat gut hanging over the desk.

"One week from now," she said. "But until then, I need you off my back. I need room to breathe."

"Are you going to tell me what all this is about?"

"Remember the Crown case?"

"Of course."

"That's nothing compared to this."

"And you need a resource?"

It was the answer she was looking for. Despite his shortfalls,

Casey knew that Penelope would deliver the results. And to offer her the pick of the bunch meant two things. First of all, she had his confidence. Second, the deadline was now set in stone. He wouldn't offer the resource and then accept an extension. She'd need to nail the story, and she'd need to nail it this week.

"King," she said, without hesitation.

"How long do you need him?"

"All week, until I submit."

The pause in the conversation while Casey made his decision was barely discernible. But it was there. The longer the pause, the more chance of rejection, Penelope had come to learn.

"You've got him for two days," he said with finality. "Make them count."

Penelope didn't thank him. Casey didn't close off with a good-bye. The call simply ended, which she was expecting. She ran through the call history on her phone and found Jason's number.

"King, Casey's assigned you to me. I need you to look at something."

"Oh hey, Pikey," came the reply.

"Don't call me Pikey, Jason. Are you ready?"

"Well, I'm actually-"

"Drop it," she said. "Whatever it is, drop it. I need your attention."

King gave an audible sigh. But Penelope knew he'd rise to the challenge.

"Hit me," he said.

"Frankie Black."

"Your boyfriend? Penelope, we did him a few months ago, and we found nothing. I thought this was something work related."

"It is work-related, Jason. Frankie Black, Isaac Black, and Bobby Carter."

"*The* Bobby Carter?"

"Find me a link." Penelope disconnected the call and searched her call history for another number.

The unanswered dial tone played out, unconcerned and monotonous, in her ear until the standard thirty seconds had passed, and the automatic voice-mail message began to play. She hit redial, then pushed through the double doors into the car park where her little motorcycle was parked.

This time, the call was answered after just two rings.

"I need to talk to you," said Penelope. "Can I see you?"

"Now isn't the best time, Penelope," replied Frankie. "Can it wait?"

Penelope caught a sense of apprehension in his voice like she'd caught him off guard.

"I'm not sure it can, to be honest, Frankie."

"I'm in the middle of something. I'll call you as soon as I can."

"Tell me something, Frankie-"

"Can't it wait, Penelope? I've had some unexpected news."

"Who is Isaac Black?"

She knew the statement was too forthcoming. She'd played her cards early, but this wasn't about catching Frankie out. It wasn't about a story. It was about her life and the man she had begun to fall in love with. The rules of engagement were different.

"You've lost me, Penelope," said Frankie. He spoke the words cold and hard. Matter of fact. Had she lost him, or confused him?

"Isaac Black," she repeated. "Who is he to you?"

"Penelope, don't do this."

"I need to know."

"No, you don't. Nobody needs to know about-" Frankie stopped as if saying the name out loud would make it all real.

"He's your father, isn't he?"

"Penelope, don't-"

"You lied to me, Frankie."

"It's none of your business. It's nobody's business."

"It's my business when you lie to me. Just tell me I'm right, and I'll leave you alone. You won't see me again if that's what you want."

The tiny speaker in the phone hissed as Frankie exhaled. She pictured him, as she'd seen him do before, with his head rolled back as far as it would go.

"You don't need to do that, Penelope."

"So tell me I'm right. Say the words, Frankie. Isaac Black is your father."

"Penelope–"

"Say it, Frankie."

"I can't."

"Why not?"

No reply came, but she could still hear his breathing, controlled, but short and sharp.

"He's there, isn't he?"

Frankie's silence was replaced with the flat disconnected tone, signalling that the call had ended.

She unlocked the box on the back of her bike, pulled her helmet out, put her bag inside and closed the lid. The engine fired first time, and she slid onto the seat. A plan had begun to formulate in her mind, and as each step of the plan evolved, losing Frankie became more and more of a certainty.

She raised her visor to wipe at her eye with her index finger, hoping to stem the flow of the tears that she could feel welling up behind her eyes. She blinked a few times to try and clear her vision. As she rocked the bike off its stand and began to roll out of the parking space, an old truck pulled in front of her. It stopped, blocking her exit.

She blinked again, trying to clear her vision. The truck doors opened and the shape of a large man loomed above her.

"In the car," said the man. His voice was fast, confident and professional. "Don't make a scene, Miss Pike."

CHAPTER TWENTY-FIVE

"GIRL TROUBLE?" ASKED ISAAC WITH A SMILE.

Frankie disconnected the call, then checked for messages from Jake. There were none. He locked his phone and slipped it inside his pocket, before glancing at his wristwatch. Something wasn't adding up.

"Have you finished your drink?" he asked.

"I might have room for one more," replied Isaac.

"Later. Now, you're coming with me."

"Oh, are we going somewhere?"

"Just get in the car, Dad," said Frankie. He opened the front door.

"You always *were* the strong silent type," said Isaac. "I don't know where you get it from."

Isaac passed by Frankie in the hallway, stopping for just a moment, but it was enough time for Frankie to see the worry in his father's eyes, and catch the smell of brandy on his breath.

In a few moments, Frankie had the big SUV roaring away from the house. He checked for oncoming traffic as he approached the junction with the main road, and barely stopped to make the turn. The large engine raised the front of the car, as

Frankie accelerated towards town, then dipped as he broke hard and turned into the next side street. Isaac sat quietly with his arm on the leather-upholstered door. He rubbed his chin in thought.

"Where are we going?" he asked Frankie.

But Frankie's mind was elsewhere. To reply would break his chain of thought. The park where Frankie had found Jake the day before came up on his right, so he pulled the car to the side of the road, and scanned the area.

A group of kids played football. Some were still in their school clothes and likely hadn't been home. The thought hinted at some kind of normality, and for the briefest of moments, Frankie's mind was eased. But these kids were much older than Jake. Perhaps they were allowed to play out before going home, and besides, their situation was almost certainly different. Their parents would have normal lives. The children would be happy. Whereas Jake had lost his mum and his father had led a very abnormal life.

The reason for all of the abnormality sat beside Frankie in the car, staring out of the window in guilty silence. It was Jake's grandfather's life of crime that had wrenched Frankie from the army. It was the lies and the greed that had nearly put Frankie behind bars.

"Do you see him?" asked Isaac.

Turning in his seat, Frankie met his father's eyes.

He didn't reply. Instead, he pulled his phone from his pocket and dialled Sammy's mum. The call was answered almost immediately as if she was already holding the phone, and the noise of a busy, happy household accompanied her greeting.

"Hello? Frankie?" She covered the mouthpiece to tell someone to go away. "Sorry," she said when she returned to the call. "It's a madhouse here sometimes."

"That's okay," replied Frankie. "I'm sorry to have bothered you."

"There's no bother. Are you looking for Jake again?"

Again.

Doubt of his own capabilities began to cast a shadow over Frankie's thoughts. Was he being paranoid?

"He hasn't come home, Cheryl. He's having a hard time right now."

Cheryl's voice softened but failed to shake the hint of helplessness. She was moving around, probably clamping the phone between her ear and her shoulder, while cooking dinner for her own family.

"Listen, it's okay. I'm sure he'll turn up," said Frankie. "But if-"

"Hold on," she said, and then covered the mouthpiece again. Frankie could hear her call out to Sammy, and ask if they walked home together. "Sammy says they walked home together," said Cheryl, suddenly returning to the call once more. "He can't be far. It's only a few hundred yards."

"Oh, that's great. Thanks so much, Cheryl. Listen, when I find him, I'll let you know. I really appreciate your time."

"It's not a problem. I told you before, we love Jake. He's such a lovely boy."

Somehow, alongside the emotions of fear and anxiety, pride began to swell up in Frankie's throat.

"Thanks, Cheryl."

Frankie disconnected the call.

"Does he do this often?" asked Isaac.

Frankie ignored the question. He stared through the windscreen at the possibilities.

"Frankie, talk to me."

But Frankie ignored his father for the second time and slammed the car into reverse. The gearbox whined loudly then the tyre screeched a little as Frankie pulled the wheel around and bumped up into somebody's driveway. The car continued to roll back as Frankie selected *drive* and floored the accelerator, leaving a parallel trail of tyre rubber from the paved drive to the tarmac road.

Navigating the maze of back streets, Frankie slid the car

around corners, braved gaps between cars that he'd normally slow for, and pulled to a stop. The junction to the high street was ahead of him, along with the police station.

"Stay here," he told Isaac while shoving the door open.

"Frankie, you can't be serious," said Isaac.

But Frankie slammed the car door, quieting his father's voice.

Inside the reception of the station sat a youth trying his hardest to look tough. Cheap tattoos adorned his thin arms, and as much as Frankie tried not to judge, the shaved head screamed thug. He looked like he needed a good wash. He was sitting at the far end of a row of plastic seats that were fixed to the floor.

At the single glass counter, a woman holding a baby was arguing with a bored police officer who was trying his best to look empathetic.

"Why won't you do anything about it?" the woman asked, her voice full of frustration. "He comes around terrorising us. I'm scared to go out sometimes."

"Madam," began the officer. "If you've reported harassment, I'm sure the officer in charge of the case will be in touch."

"Yeah, but when?" the woman yelled. "What am I supposed to do while I wait for that to happen?"

Frankie stepped up to the counter beside the woman.

"I need to report a missing person. My son."

"You'll have to wait your turn, I'm afraid," replied the officer, gesturing to the woman.

"I want protection," said the woman, ignoring Frankie standing beside her. "I'm not going anywhere until-"

"He's only eleven," said Frankie. "Can I just talk to someone?"

"Sir-"

"Mate, wait your turn," the woman cut in. She started to shout something else, but Frankie snapped his head around to face her, and her voice trailed away. She pulled her baby close to her chest, stared back with wide eyes, then stepped away from the glass.

Frankie returned his attention to the officer.

"Sir," the officer began. "You really need to wait your turn."

Frankie stared at the man.

"Sir?" the officer continued.

His hand was raised palm out, indicating the chairs and the angry youth who was next in line. Frankie took a side step away, aware that the longer he tried to be seen first, the longer Jake would be out there alone.

The woman stepped forwards again with a cautious eye on Frankie. She talked, but the words muffled inside Frankie's head. His peripheral vision blurred and the tightness in his chest grew until he could feel his own heart beating wilder and wilder.

Unaware of how long he'd been staring, Frankie snapped from his daze, cleared his vision, and found the youth standing at the glass with his arms folded in a defensive manner that any police officer knew to be a subliminal admission of guilt.

A loud buzzer rang out in the foyer, followed immediately by a heavy thud. The youth was led into the station, leaving Frankie the only person in the foyer.

"Sir?"

Frankie watched the teenager disappear and the door close behind him. He couldn't help but think of his father.

"Sir?" said the officer again from behind the glass.

But as Frankie stepped back to the glass, he felt his phone vibrate in his pocket.

"It's my son," he said, reaching for his phone. "He's missing."

Frankie pulled the phone out. Aware that the officer may think his distraction impolite, he held the phone low.

The screen read, *Unknown Caller*.

"And how long has he been missing?" asked the officer.

Frankie typically ignored unknown callers, unless it was his other phone, his business phone.

"Sir?"

Returning his attention to the officer for a split second, Frankie apologised. The officer raised an eyebrow and placed his pen down on the small stack of forms in front of him to temple his fingers.

"This might be him," Frankie said. He stepped away from the counter, pushed through the double doors and into the car park of the police station, before sliding the button on the screen across to answer the call.

"Hello? Jake?" said Frankie, striving to hear above the noise of the passing traffic. "Jake? Is that you?"

"I wouldn't do that if I were you," said a voice.

CHAPTER TWENTY-SIX

"Frankie, you can't be serious?" said Isaac.

But Frankie had already slammed the car door closed and was crossing the road to the police station. Of all the places Isaac needed to be right there and then, sitting outside a police station was not one of them. He slunk down lower in his seat, thankful for Frankie's tinted windows.

The car was still running. Once Isaac watched Frankie disappear through the double doors of the police station, he flicked through the radio stations. Only the first preset channel was tuned to a station that played classical music. Numbers two through six played static and displayed the same first available frequency. The round centre button shut down the stereo, confirmed by a goodbye message that scrolled across the front of the unit in green letters.

Prison had given Isaac a deep sense of foreboding. The outside, the place he had longed to be for so long, seemed frightening. Not like the warmth and comfort of Frankie's house. Or even his cell back inside, where he knew the dangers and was as prepared as he could be. It had been just eight hours since he'd been released, and somehow, not a single moment of it had been enjoyable. The train journey had filled him with apprehension. Breaking into Frankie's house had been downright idiotic, although necessary. And now, he was waiting in what looked like a drug dealer's car on his first day of parole, in his prison skivvies, with a shaved head, and sitting outside a police station.

Paranoia kicked in.

His eyes scanned the road ahead, scrutinising everyone in sight, the clothes they wore, the way they walked. A row of shops with a cafe and an electrical store were on the main road opposite the police station. There was a pub at the end with four six-seater benches, where three teenagers were sitting with their hoods up smoking and glancing across at the police station. Members of the public whose journey took them near the youths redirected and walked behind the bench to avoid coming into contact with them.

A young woman stepped through the double doors of the police station carrying a small baby. She looked as if she'd been crying. She took a cautious look up and down the high street before making her way towards the bus stop a hundred yards away. The three teenagers' eyes all followed her. Then, when she clarified that she wasn't interested in them, by turning her head and pretending to look for the bus, they made their moves.

The first boy called out to her, but Isaac couldn't hear what he said. The other two boys laughed, and the first boy just stood across the street staring at her. The woman ignored his comments and continued to look away, holding her baby close to her chest.

The boy's boldness was almost admirable. Isaac wondered if his actions were considered normal now. He stood with one hand inside the crotch of his baggy jeans. The other adjusted his baseball cap as if trying different styles to see which one impressed the girl the most.

A white Mercedes van pulled up on the main road. It blocked the boys from Isaac's view and the girl from the boys' view. The scene came to a close, and Isaac imagined a sense of relief for the poor girl.

There was a movement to Isaac's right. It was Frankie, and his face bore a look of frustration. Frankie was Isaac's son through and through. And as much as Frankie wouldn't admit it, he'd inherited his father's temper but added with it his own flavour of control; an attribution no doubt garnered from his days in the army.

With a keen eye, Isaac watched as Frankie answered his phone and spoke. The way he carried himself with such strength made Isaac proud. Even if their relationship was rocky and possibly even irreparable, he was still Isaac's son.

Eight years inside had taught Isaac the basics of lip reading. Mouthed and silent warnings from Shorty or one of his boys. Guards discussing an imminent cell toss.

Frankie held the phone tight against his ear. *Hello? Jake? Is that you?*

The caller was clearly speaking now, and Frankie would be listening hard. A lull in the perpetual traffic brought with it a temporary peace on the main road; quiet enough to hear the side door of the white Mercedes van slide open. It was also enough to capture Frankie's attention, which, in turn, was enough to alter the expression on Frankie's face. His mouth hung open, his eyes widened and his mouth tightened from a worried father to boiling rage.

Glancing back across the street at the van, Isaac saw two things through the open door. A man in a black balaclava. And the feet of a small boy.

CHAPTER TWENTY-SIX

Although she was hooded, Penelope's hands had been cut free when the truck had stopped. She walked, unfettered, alongside the man. The journey had been against her will, but no violence had been used, no foul language and no threats of either had hung over her head.

The hood was a simple piece of cloth, which to Penelope's surprise, was also left loose, allowing her the occasional glimpse at her feet and the paved footpath below. The scent of flowers was rich in the air and Penelope tried to place the types, but the blends were varied, and the walk was too fast to single out an individual plant. In her mind though, tall sunflowers reached far above a bank of orchids, which in turn grew amid a plethora of wildflowers, violets with shades of pink to the sides of the footpath she was being led along.

The very fact her imagination found the freedom to picture the plants that scented the air brought with it the realisation that Penelope was not scared. There was little to suggest she was in any danger, save for the fact that the man had blocked her path, forced her into the car and made her wear a hood.

Forced? He hadn't forced her. She had climbed into the truck of her own volition.

Who the man was, was clear. Penelope recalled the meeting with Debbie. The idle time Debbie had spent tapping away on her phone had seemed harmless at the time. That she was giving evidence against her husband, Bobby Carter, suggested that Bobby Carter would be the last person she would message during the interview. But it was clear to Penelope now; she'd been set up.

"Where are you taking me?" she asked.

She was blind to the world, with just the occasional touch from the man who walked beside her for navigation.

No reply came.

The smell of flowers faded, replaced with freshly-cut grass and oil. It reminded her of her father's garage where he refuelled his lawnmower with a mix of petrol and two-stroke oil. The paved pathway gave way to rough concrete, obscured by the shade of what seemed to be a large roof. It was almost as if she'd been led into a big garage. The unmistakable smell of cut wood lingered with the scent of the two-stroke oil, casting visions of an old classic car with its bonnet up and wheels off. Perhaps there was a calendar with topless women and a steaming cup of tea on a bench beside a wrench, some screwdrivers and an old, oily rag.

Just like her father's garage.

"Sit," said the voice. A strong hand guided her to a worn plastic chair until she felt the seat on the back of her legs.

"Where am I?" she asked, and she felt her knees shake as she lowered herself into the seat.

"All in good time."

"Can I remove this?" she asked.

From somewhere to her left, a water dispenser gurgled as a cup was filled. Then, from beneath her hood, Penelope saw the cup being offered to her. To her surprise, it was clean with no oily finger marks or tea stains.

"Take it," said the voice. It was less harsh than it had been before, but more like that of a concerned parent urging a child to swallow medicine. Her request to remove the hood had gone unanswered.

Penelope grasped the cup in both hands and held it close to her chest, peering down at it beneath the hood. The man's hand lifted the lower part, which enabled her to raise the cup to her lips. She tilted her head back to drink, glancing around the room. There was no classic car with the wheels off and the bonnet up. There was no oily rag beside a bunch of tools. Nor was there a topless calendar. Instead, in front of where Penelope was sitting, a large plastic sheet hung from a wooden ceiling beam. It draped across the floor and then back up to the next beam to form a large U-shape.

The hood was pulled down as soon as the cup was removed from her lips. The man's hand removed it from her grip then coaxed her to stand. For the first time in the entire episode, Penelope felt fear. The plastic sheets. The chair. These were professionals.

Without warning, Penelope's knees buckled as she tried to stand. But his hands held her tight beneath her arms.

"Don't make it hard," he said; this wasn't his first time.

But Penelope's legs failed to hold her weight as if they too knew what lay in front and had begun their own struggle for survival. With reluctant ease, the man turned her around and dragged her to the chair sitting on the plastic sheet. Her feet scrambled for purchase. The rough concrete caused one of her flat shoes to be pulled off and her barefoot scratched on the abrasive floor.

The reality of what was about to happen kicked in. Her legs began to tremble.

Penelope was dropped onto the chair with as much dignity as the man could manage. Then her world became a sea of noise. It sounded as if more plastic sheets were being pulled across to close the gaps.

To stop the blood being spilt?

"Why?" she screamed between short, sharp breaths. "Why are you doing this?"

The man offered no response.

And then, despite the years of repressing her feelings, of forgetting her past, the tears came.

CHAPTER TWENTY-SEVEN

Acting on fatherly instinct, Frankie ran at the van.

The door slammed closed, and the driver pulled away into a fresh line of traffic to the tune of honking horns. The driver of the car behind displayed his anger by flashing his lights and driving close the rear of the van, which obscured the number plate from Frankie's view.

Frankie came to a stop in the centre of the road; the van was long gone.

Drivers from both directions sounded their horns at Frankie. He stood watching as the white van disappeared among the traffic, oblivious to the anger of the drivers around him who'd slowed and passed by with incredulous looks on their faces. A blue BMW screeched to a halt as Frankie suddenly bolted for his own car.

A single uniformed policeman emerged through the double doors of the police station and approached Frankie. But with his eyes set on his car, Frankie didn't stop. Nor did he offer a reply to the man's questions.

"Sir, is everything okay?"

He held his hands up for Frankie to stop, but Frankie ignored him.

"I understand your son is missing?" said the officer as Frankie approached. "Would you like to make a statement?"

Frankie kept on walking.

"Sir, can you stop? We'll just take a minute of your time."

The Range Rover rocked on its suspension as his father shifted inside the car.

"Sir, I'm going to have to ask you to come with me to the station."

"Am I under arrest?"

"No, sir, but you reported a crime."

"Did I make a statement?"

The Range Rover's reverse lights flicked on for a fraction of a second. Even in the daylight of the late summer evening, the reflection was clear to Frankie in the shiny bodywork of the car behind.

"I have reason to believe‑"

"Did I make a statement?" said Frankie. The policeman was now behind him and was staring.

"No, sir."

"Good day, officer. I'm sorry to have wasted your time."

Frankie crossed the side street where his car was parked without checking for traffic, but nothing was coming. His attention was on his car and his father, who had moved across to the driver's seat in Frankie's absence. Frankie wrenched the door open and found Isaac searching for the handbrake release.

"Going somewhere?" asked Frankie.

"Son, I was just‑" Isaac seemed surprised.

The police officer stared after Frankie.

"Move over."

The officer walked towards the car.

"Yeah, of course, Frankie," said Isaac. "Whatever you say."

The old man fought to raise his leg over the centre console. The bandage on his shoulder had slipped and his sweatshirt now brandished a patch of fresh blood.

"Move over, Dad. We've got company."

"I'm doing the best I can, boy," said Isaac. Then he noticed the young officer stepping into the side street.

"Well, do your best faster, Dad," said Frankie. But it was too late. The officer peered through the windscreen as he crossed the street. His inquisitive eyes fixed on Isaac who now straddled the centre of the car.

Frankie stood still, waiting for his father to finish moving across.

"Is there a problem, gents?" The officer walked around to the open car door and took a good look at Isaac.

"No problem, officer," said Frankie without turning. "I'm sorry to have wasted your time."

"You haven't wasted my time, sir," said the officer. "Do you mind if I take your names?" The young man retrieved a small notepad from his breast pocket and slid a pen from the top.

"That won't be necessary, officer."

"I'd still like to take your names if it's all the same to you." The officer moved into Frankie's line of sight and made eye contact. "Just to be on the safe side."

"We have done nothing wrong, officer, and you're holding me up from a very important engagement," said Frankie, folding his arms and straightening to his full six-foot-one height, a clear three-inches taller the officer.

The young man broke eye contact with Frankie, turned to Isaac, and directed his questions at him.

"And you, sir?"

But Isaac merely stared through the windscreen.

"Are you refusing to give your name as well?"

Tilting his head back and taking an audible inhale of air through his nostrils, Isaac stayed quiet.

"Officer, we are in a hurry. I promise you, we have nothing to say. Now if you don't mind?" said Frankie.

But the officer wasn't listening. He was fixed on the patch of blood on Isaac's sweatshirt. Frankie saw the flash of panic in his eyes, which triggered two further reactions. He watched the officer's instinct take control, as he reached for the radio on his shoulder. Frankie also watched as human nature's fight for survival kicked in; the officer stepped back to move away from the danger.

But it was too late.

With a swipe of his right hand, Frankie grabbed the man's wrist and pulled hard on his arm, extending the shoulder muscles and dislocating the arm. As the officer stepped back, Frankie stepped between the man's legs, shifting his balance.

In less than two seconds, Frankie had the officer laid flat on his front with a dislocated arm behind his back. A further three-seconds and Frankie had handcuffed the officer with his own cuffs. Another two seconds and Frankie had emitted a single one-second release of the officer's CS gas. Not too close to damage the man, but close enough for him not be able to read the number plate of the Range Rover.

The wide side street offered Frankie ample room to perform a U-turn. He gave a quick check of the mirror to confirm his actions had, for the time being, gone unnoticed. Then he floored the car.

"What the hell just happened?" said Isaac, checking his own side mirror once they were clear of the police station.

Frankie fixed on the road ahead.

"Frankie, gone is the time for being the strong silent type. What the bloody hell just happened? You do realise I've been out of prison for about eight hours? Any kind of infraction like that and that's it for me. It's game over."

Frankie remained silent.

"Frankie? Answer me."

Without slowing, Frankie wrenched the steering wheel to his right, sending the large SUV into a controlled slide around a corner into his street.

"Who was that in the van, Frankie?" said Isaac. "Was that Jake?"

Slowing to a sensible speed, so as not to alarm his neighbours, Frankie pulled into his driveway, hit the button to open the garage door, and pulled inside. He waited for it to close behind them, then turned the engine off. The two men sat in silence.

"Frankie?" said Isaac. His voice was now quiet and concerned.

Frankie let his father talk, airing his thoughts as he had always done. Preferring to let his own thoughts run amok in the chaos of his mind, Frankie ran the scenario over and over until Isaac eventually quietened, having answered most of his questions himself.

"Who was it, Frankie?"

He pulled the car into a space and checked the mirrors for signs of police.

Isaac lowered his voice. "Son?"

"He's got him," said Frankie.

"Jake? Who's got him?"

Frankie couldn't believe what he was about to say. He took a deep breath.

"Bobby Carter. He has Jake," said Frankie. It was Isaac's turn to remain silent. "And he wants you."

CHAPTER TWENTY-EIGHT

"And you're going to deliver me?" asked Isaac, when Frankie pulled the car into his garage and hit the button to close the door.

"This is you, Dad. It's all you. You want Carter. Carter wants you. But, now Carter has Jake."

"I'm sorry, son."

"We were doing pretty well without you in our lives, but in the past two hours you've managed to somehow destroy everything we have."

Frankie had laid the facts out plain and simple; it was unarguable.

"This is our chance, Frankie," said Isaac. "Don't you see it?"

"The only thing I see is a tired old man who has a debt to pay."

"But we can get close to Carter. We can take him down. And just maybe, Son, we can all get out of this alive."

In the confines of the car, emotions ran high. Frankie snapped around to face him. The dim light from the dashboard enhanced his son's features with deep, dark shadows to indicate the cleft in Frankie's broad chin and his high prominent cheekbones. Taut, lean skin ran from his face to the well-toned muscles of his shoulders.

"The last time I spoke to you, Dad, I very nearly went to prison."

"And it was *me* who paid the price, Frankie."

"You?" said Frankie. "You went to prison, but we all paid the price. Jake, Jacqui and me. I had to start a new life, Dad. And as I said, you've been out of prison less than a day and I've already assaulted a police officer. Do you honestly expect me to get involved in your gangland hits? Who the bloody hell do you think you are anyway? It's not nineteen eighty anymore. Isaac Carson is a nobody. Just a blast from the past. A man who had it all and lost it to greed. Whoever it is out there now, the gangs that took your place, do you think they aspire to be like you? No, Dad. You're a loser, and you always have been. The sooner you're out of my life, the better."

"Son-"

"No, Dad. Don't give me that, because I've had enough of you already. The one good thing you can do right now is come with me, give yourself up, and let me get my son back so we can get on with our lives."

Emotions coursed through Isaac's body. They tightened his chest. He felt tears of pride fill his eyes; his son had become a better man than he ever was. Fear gripped his clammy hands, causing them to shake as a reminder of his mortality and inevitable fate.

But love for a grandson he'd never met shone through the darkness.

"Okay, Son," he said.

For a moment, Isaac thought Frankie was going to talk. To thank him maybe or even apologise. To share the sense of guilt. But instead, Frankie opened his door, stepped onto the garage floor, and flicked on the lights.

Intrigued by the confidence with which his son moved, Isaac

stepped out of the car and watched as Frankie began to move a row of timbers that were laid across the floor.

"What's that?" asked Isaac.

Dropping the last timber to one side, Frankie reached into a dark hole that had been hidden on the garage floor. He fumbled inside and a lamp flicked on, lighting the dark space and disturbed dust that hung in the glow, as if basking in the new sun.

"It's a mechanics pit," said Frankie. "I had it installed when we moved in."

"What for?"

But the question seemed redundant. Frankie gestured with a nod to a heavy canvas that covered an old car on the far side of the huge garage. He ignored Isaac's question and lowered a wooden ladder to the bottom of the pit. Then, without a moment's hesitation, he turned and climbed into the hole.

"Is that what I think it is?" asked Isaac.

But once more, Frankie let him figure it out for himself. Ever inquisitive, Isaac raised the edge of the tarp.

"I don't believe it, Frankie. You've had it all these years?" Isaac ran his hand long the bodywork. He raised the tarp higher and saw the immaculate interior.

"She's perfect," he whispered, then called out. "Does she start?"

"First time every time. Now, take this," said Frankie from the ladder. Held a black case for Isaac to take.

Isaac took the case and laid it on the floor. Another case followed. Then Frankie climbed out. The first case was the size of a large briefcase. The second was slightly longer and deeper. Both had a series of catches that Frankie flicked open. He raised the lids to reveal a pair of handguns with magazines in the first, and a broken down rifle in the second.

"What the hell?"

"Don't run away with the idea that we're taking down Carter,

Dad. I'm not helping you. I'm going to find him and hand you over. An exchange."

"He'll kill me, Frankie," said Isaac, suddenly imagining all kinds of possibilities with the weaponry. But Frankie didn't respond. "Come on, you and me. We can take them down-"

His son looked up from the bottom of the pit. His face twisted into incredulity and Isaac's words faded away.

"Carter has Jake, Dad. Imagine how scared my son is right now. Imagine what's going through his mind. I'm not risking his well-being for you. You're not worth it." He slid the top of the handgun back and checked the action. "It's a straight swap. You for him."

They shared a moment. Isaac searched his son's eyes for a sign of humanity. Anything. But there was nothing and Frankie continued doing whatever it was he was doing.

"So why the firepower?"

"Security," said Frankie.

"Do you really need all that?"

"Better to have it and not need it, than to need it and not have it," Frankie replied.

"Did the army teach you that?"

"No," said Frankie. "I learnt it when I needed a father."

With a practised hand, Frankie loaded four magazines, then slotted two of them into the two handguns before setting to work assembling the rifle.

"When was the last time you did that?" asked Isaac. He was impressed at how fast the weapon came together.

"I clean them every now and then."

"Have you ever needed all this?"

"There's no harm in being prepared, Dad." Frankie began to load the much larger rifle magazine.

"What is that?"

"It's a Diemaco," said Frankie, dismissing any further conversation about the guns. He climbed down the ladder, pulling the larger case to the edge and then lowering it down to the pit floor. "Pass me the other case."

Isaac reached down with his good arm and grabbed the empty case, then slid it over to his son, who took it and disappeared back into the pit.

It was enough time for Isaac to grab one of the handguns and wrench the ladder from the hole.

There was no look of surprise on Frankie's face when he turned and noticed the gun aimed at him. He stood at the bottom of the pit with his usual casual confidence. Then he rested his hands on his hips and spoke with quiet control.

"What now, Dad?"

Isaac hadn't had time for a plan.

"Are you going to shoot me?" asked Frankie. "I suggest you get it right the first time."

Isaac fingered the safety catch as he'd seen Frankie do a few moments before.

"I'm sorry, Frankie."

CHAPTER TWENTY-NINE

THE CRUNCHING OF THE PLASTIC SHEET BEING PULLED ACROSS the gaps stopped. The area fell silent. Just a few quiet crinkles of the thin sheets settling. Already the little space began to warm, turning Penelope's already clammy hands to a full-on sweat. Moisture merged with her tears and dripped from her chin. It ran down her neck and her chest.

The urge to rip off the hood and run for her life was overwhelming. But the fact that she could no longer hear the man's footsteps was unnerving. His location was unknown; she wouldn't know which direction to run. Any possible chance of escape would be hindered by hysteria.

"What now?" asked Penelope, through a phlegm-filled throat. Her eyes streamed, but she fought hard not to break down. To show strength. And stay focused.

To her surprise, the reply came from over her shoulder. He was standing beside her. Maybe he was just watching her? Maybe that was his thing? How he got off?

"We wait for the instruction."

He sounded neither kind nor angry and made no attempt to scare her with his tone or demeanour.

"Instructions from who?" Penelope asked.

She found that, by talking, her mind was distracted from the incessant wondering. It was no longer a question of if it would happen. It wasn't even a question of when. She knew it would be soon. Instead, it became a question of *how* he would do it. Weighing up the options in her head, should the choice arise, she favoured a bullet to the head. A quick and painless death, if performed efficiently. Judging by the style and professionalism the man had displayed so far, it was likely. But the heavy screen of plastic suggested something much more painful and bloody.

She wondered if Bobby Carter would do it himself.

The man offered no reply to her question. So Penelope continued talking. Restraining her wandering mind was a continual process.

"Do you know who I am?"

"Penelope Pike."

"Do you know who I work for?"

"I do."

"They'd pay a reward. I'm sure of it."

"Not interested."

"How much is he paying you?"

Blind to her environment, the wild imagination that had sparked her career in journalism ran amok. The details of his face were coloured in by her mind with the imagery of a thriller novel or film cover. Heavy blacks and shadows outlined the shape of his athletic body. Bold, prominent colours lit his features.

He was a redhead. The thought hit her from memory. The visualisation of him adjusted.

"Come on," she said, finding distraction in conversation. "Everyone has a price. What's yours? How much are you getting for this?"

"There's no price, Miss Pike," he said. "Stop talking."

"So you're doing this for free? He must be a good boss."

"Some things are done out of duty. Not everyone needs paying to do what needs to be done."

Within the confines of the hood, Penelope raised an eyebrow. A hint of a smile cracked her dry lips.

He'd said too much.

"You have a duty to him?" she continued. Penelope knew that now he'd started talking, she could encourage more from him. Questioning, after all, what she was good at.

"To who?" the man replied.

"Oh, come on," she said. "No need to be coy. We both know who you work for."

"If you know who we work for, then you'd understand why you're here. I suggest you cease the questions, Miss Pike."

Twice now, he'd called her Miss Pike. It was polite. Formal. It seemed uncharacteristic of somebody who was part of an organised crime gang, and more like something a guard would say, a policeman, or-

A soldier.

"You know it was her that contacted me?" she said. Then she silenced to hear his reaction.

The visualisation of the man inside her now-spinning mind retained the athletic build, the red hair, beard and spattering of freckles. But now, the dark shape of his body stood at ease. His feet were shoulder-width apart. His hands locked tight behind his back. His arms bent at ninety-degree angles. His back was rigid and his head was up, looking dead ahead.

"I don't know what you're talking about."

"Debbie," said Penelope. "She contacted me, you know?"

No reply came. But in the noiseless space, she heard the faint sound of a day's growth rubbing across his cotton shirt. The image in her mind reflected the movement. He had looked down at her. He hadn't understood who Debbie was. That meant it wasn't Carter's man.

Her last call with Frankie-

Nausea came with the urgency of a wildfire, rising up from the very pit of her stomach, burning her throat and releasing bitter bile into her mouth. She lurched forward in spasm, lifted the edge of the hood and spat out the acid.

It couldn't be Frankie.

"Miss Pike?"

Torrid water formed at the back of her mouth. She gagged once. But before she could raise the hood, hot bile came flooding out. The foul smell that hung inside the material caused her to once more lurch forward. This time, she snatched the hood off. She leaned forward and let the congealed contents of her stomach spill out between her legs onto the plastic sheeting.

The nausea cleared, but strings of acidic bile hung from her lip. With one hand, she held her hair from her face. With the other, she leaned on her knee. Deep breaths helped to soothe her burning throat.

"You want some water?" the man asked. Again his tone was neither kind nor cruel. It just was. The guy was military through and through.

"Yes, please."

Penelope watched the man's boots pass her on the plastic. The gap he'd made in the side of the plastic tent allowed her a glimpse at the layout of the space. The room was bare. Not purpose-built, it served no obvious cause other than to host the abduction and murder of interfering journalists.

The low grumble of the man's voice disappeared through the doorway. His obscured silhouette vanished into the area of bright light to one side of the room, as if he'd taken a call and slipped outside to avoid being overheard.

It was now or never.

CHAPTER THIRTY

"I need help," said Frankie. There was no time for fluff or polite greetings.

"More help?" said Nigel. "Hold on. Let me step outside."

"Nigel, time is of the essence here, mate."

"Right, talk," said Nigel. "I'm babysitting your last cock up and haven't got time for much more."

"It's my dad."

"Your what?"

To repeat the sentence was unnecessary. Frankie knew how it sounded.

"Frankie, are you cocking me around? Because I'm just about to get to work and find out exactly what she knows. She's talking. She won't shut up."

"They've got Jake."

"Who has?"

"Bobby Carter. Remember him?"

"For God's sake, Frankie. Are we even having this conversation?"

"My old man was released this morning. I found him at my house."

"Frankie, sorry mate but this-"

"Just shut the hell up a minute, Nigel. Stop criticising and listen. My old man and Carter never shut the doors. Now he's out, it's all kicking off again. Dad wants him dead, and he-"

"Jesus, Frankie. Carter's got Jake and wants your old man in return?"

Thankful for Nigel being a fast thinker, Frankie didn't have to explain that Jake's life was in danger.

"It's not a pretty picture, Nigel."

"And where's your old man now?"

"Running away from it all, and leaving Jake to die."

"And where are you?"

"You remember where I keep my armoury?"

"In that little pit in your garage floor?"

"I *was* in there."

"Frankie, you couldn't make this up."

"He stole a gun then drove off. By the time I pulled myself out of the pit, he was gone."

"He drove off?" said Nigel. "In what? I'll get the boys onto it. They'll get the plate recognition and track him down."

With a sigh, Frankie's head dropped to his chest. He knew everything he was saying sounded weak. It all sounded like he'd failed in the biggest way possible.

"He's got the Aston, Nigel."

Only the sound of the digital connection filled the space, with a faint hiss of the wind from Nigel's microphone.

"Frankie, I want to help you, mate. But you have to help yourself. This is monumental."

"Nigel, right now, I need-"

"No, Frankie. In the last day, you've allowed some girl you hardly know to find photos of you and the team and who knows what else? And now she's fifteen minutes from having her head blown off. You've let your dad hold you at gunpoint and steal your car, leaving you to rescue your son from one of the nastiest and most notorious criminals this side of London. Which one do you want help with, Frankie? Honestly, I'm going to wind up in a bucket of crap myself for whichever one it is."

"I need Jake back."

"And to do that, we either need a ton of firepower or your old man, who, by the way, is missing in a nineteen-fifty-three Aston Martin worth enough money for him to retire on."

"Are you going to help or what?" asked Frankie.

He was growing tired of the insults. But he was reassured by the pause in Nigel's rant. If the answer was going to be no, he'd have said it outright with no hesitation. The pause indicated a willingness. A hint at a chance.

"What about the girl?" asked Nigel.

"Bring her with you. I'll take care of her as I said. I'll send her away. We don't even know how much she saw."

"It might be a bit late for that, Frankie. The scene is set."

The scene is set.

It was a phrase they had used in service. The preparations had been made. The suspect had been captured, the tools were in place and a clean up had been arranged.

"Have you told anyone else?" asked Frankie.

"Not directly. But I've got ear-holes out and about. Her apartment is being spun as we talk."

"Where did you find her?"

"In Stratford. She was having coffee with a friend. I've got a few of the boys tracking the friend down now to see if she's significant. To see if she needs containing."

"Nigel, just bring Penelope with you. I'll deal with it."

"Do you trust her, Frankie?" asked Nigel. "Do you trust her enough to put my life on the line as well?"

The brush of the gentle breeze on Nigel's phone eased away. His voice now bore a baritone echo as if he'd stepped inside out of the wind.

"Just bring her, Nigel. I'm running out of time here."

"We might have a problem there, Frankie."

"What? Don't tell me it's too late, Nigel. What have you done?"

"No, mate, it's worse than that," said Nigel. "She's bleeding gone."

CHAPTER THIRTY-ONE

THE AREA WASN'T ONE THAT ISAAC HAD BEEN FAMILIAR WITH, even back in the day. He'd passed through Upminster a few times and old friends had moved to towns close by in the eighties. A time when successful criminals sought larger properties on the outskirts of London. He took a gentle cruise to the main road, acutely aware that turning left would take him towards London where encounters with the police would be likely. The risk would be higher.

Turning right, he'd be facing the wild open countryside. Turning right, he'd face endless possibilities of freedom. To feel the wind on his face. To breath the open air. To see the patchwork quilted countryside rush by in a blur of greens and yellows, framed by the bright blue sky. The empty main road in front of him willed Isaac to turn right. Its avenue of trees reached across the dull grey tarmac and embrace the space overhead, allowing sprinkles of light through as if to entice a passerby.

Isaac lifted the clutch, powered down and felt the real bite of the Aston Martin. The torque from second gear pulled the car along with such ease that it almost felt a shame to double pump the clutch and find third gear.

Pride swelled inside him, as he thought of the meticulous attention his son had given to the old car.

To memories.

Large houses to one side of the road soon fell away to wide, empty spaces, leaving Isaac to enjoy the rolling hills and open fields. Towns and villages shot past in a blaze. Then nothing but open farmland welcomed the old convict to the world he'd left behind. There was no sign of the Internet, mobile phones, or electronic evolution of any sort. Farms remained farms. Streams remained streams. Rivers remained rivers. The air was fresh, and Isaac was alive and free.

For the first time in nearly a decade years, he laughed out loud to himself. Caught up in the excitement of freedom, he gasped at a stab of joy that moistened his eye.

There was so much he had missed. So much wasted time.

The road ahead wasn't paved with gold. It wasn't lined with opportunity. But it led to freedom. A future. Someplace where he could make amends.

A niggle of conscience twitched his cheek and cast a shadow over the future that spread out before him in his mind. The layer of cool sweat behind his ears, his neck and across his brow, brought with it light nausea. He found himself suddenly short of breath. Although the road before him was empty of cars and framed by the most glorious view he could imagine, the scene grew blurry. The vision of a peaceful existence faded away.

The sensation was familiar. The doctor in the infirmary just the day before had administered a shot of something to put him out. The sensation was similar. Isaac's head took on the weight of a cannonball and rolled from side to side with the contours of the journey.

Doubt squeezed at his heart. His chest grew tight with fear. His vision narrowed to a mere slit in the bright freedom. Through the cloudy haze of greens, yellows and blues, a patch of grey, wider than the road itself, grew closer. A lay-by.

Isaac lifted from the accelerator but his body lurched forward with the drop in power. His weakened arms guided the little sports car to the lay-by with a new tingling sensation as if electricity coursed through him searching for an outlet. He had no energy to lift his leg and hit the brakes, even if his mind could have commanded it.

Amid the haze of darkened greens and blues came a distinct shadow of colour. The shape moved with the fearful urgency of a deer, yet cautious, timid and afraid.

It stopped, frozen in its tracks.

It hung in the centre of Isaac's hallucination, wide eyes framed by the motionless trees and fields that seemed pinned to his periphery.

Until the car, too fast for Isaac to control in his weakened state, crashed into the form, sending the mass of colour and limbs across the front of the Aston, through the windshield, and onto the road behind him.

There was no time to look and no power in his body to do so.

As the car rolled to a stop, some two-hundred yards further, and teased itself into a drainage ditch at the side of the narrow country lane, Isaac's chest tightened once more as a vice-like grip squeezed his heart.

His feeble fingers clutched at his chest. Burning acid seared his throat. And the tingling sensation in his arms grew in strength until they no longer felt like his own.

A dance of dazzling lights spun behind his eyes like the heavens had opened their doors. Then darkness enveloped him as heaven's doors slammed closed.

Isaac rolled to his side. He gasped a burning lungful of air.

And closed his eyes.

CHAPTER THIRTY-TWO

AT FIRST, THE SMALL TRACK INTO THE FARM SEEMED LIKE THE only way out. But with a small paddock to her left, which was closed in with a neat simple wooden fence, and wild, open grassland to her right, Penelope felt exposed and vulnerable.

She stopped running and listened. No cars could be heard. There was no pounding of heavy boots on the track behind her. She dared to glance back at the collection of small farm buildings. Nothing moved. Behind the where she had been prepared to die, she saw a large farmhouse. It was old but well-maintained, and on any other occasion, Penelope would have called it pretty. An open barn was opposite the house and there were stables. The docile bobbing of a feeding horse's head was the only sign of life.

The track ahead of her ran on for another five or six hundred yards. It was too far. It was too open. She gauged the open field to be perhaps one-hundred yards, beyond which a woodland ran on for as far as she could see.

An engine fired somewhere behind her.

Grateful for her love of flat shoes, Penelope ran. She bounded off the track, which was wild and unkempt with divots and large clumps of wild grass to trip over. Moving as fast as she could, with her eyes on the ground directly in front of her, she waded through the long grass seeking safe placements for her feet. The trees ahead grew closer, but with an almost tantalising lethargy.

Somehow, above the train-like thudding of Penelope's heart in her ears and the noise of her own breathing, which was loud like the rushing of breaking waves over and over, she heard wheels crunching the gravel track. The sound was coarse and harsh against the pulsing beat of her heart.

Thirty-yards.

The truck emerged from behind the buildings, its noise no longer walled in by the small buildings, the difference in tone was all Penelope needed to hear just how close he was and how little time she had.

Twenty-yards to the fence.

Fearful of stopping to look back, Penelope continued to run, searching for footholds. A wooden fence bordered the field. A final obstacle for Penelope before freedom and life.

Tyres skidded on the gravel.

She dove to the ground, praying that the long, wild grasses would cover her. Turning to scamper backwards on her hands and feet, she saw the roof of the truck on the dirt track. It had stopped exactly where Penelope had left the road.

And then she saw his red hair.

He was out of the truck peering into the field. His red beard against his pale skin was clear against the pastel surrounding colours.

Slowly she crept until she reached the fence. Penelope rolled onto her front and dragged herself beneath the wooden fence. Sh Head to turn her head and wiggle through. For a moment it felt as if her chest would get stuck and she would be trapped. But she gave everything she had. Tears streamed down her face and for the first time in her life, she was thankful for her small bust.

Then she was through. She turned to check on the man,

raising her head above the fence cautiously. She searched for the crop of red hair. The glimpse of pale skin.

But she saw nothing.

He was gone.

A frantic scan of her limited view bore no sign of him. No movement at all.

With a sudden awareness of how loud her own breathing was, Penelope tried to quieten herself. Instead, her short, sharp exhales burst from her and her heart pounded like a train.

With cautious, sudden movements, Penelope crouched. She dragged herself to the trees with slow, methodical movements. Adrenaline surged through her, her eyes were alive to the acutest movement.

Then, it felt like time itself had stopped.

As if somebody had called, *'Game over.'*

Peace fell. A silence seemed to lie across the field like a blanket. But that moment of tranquillity, as Penelope sat between the field and the forest, was shattered by a bullet ricocheting off the fence and sang through the air as it passed her face. The roar of a high-powered rifle followed.

She turned. And in that split-second, she made a decision. And she ran.

Blinded by fear and tears that now streamed from her eyes and with legs that seemed feeble and unsure of their own strength, she tore through the thick brush that clawed at her dress like evil, twisted fingers. It was as if they were an extension of the man; the land, the wildlife and he were one. All seeking to bring her down. But the will of Penelope's spirit powered through. The skin on her legs tore and bled. Some wild and thorny plant reached up and stung her arms. Low hanging branches of the trees drooped low and jabbed for her eyes with sharp, pointed twigs.

And then she was through.

Daring herself once more to look behind her. She saw no truck. No man. She heard no chase.

But she felt his eyes.

She ran on.

The trees opened up inside the woodland, and though there was no clear path, Penelope ran on downhill. A few fallen trees gave her the chance of a reprieve, to regain her breath, check behind her, and then seek an opening beyond. Another house. A road. Anything.

Dried tears stiffened her skin. Frantic fearful breaths had dried her throat so that it itched and scratched with every breath.

She was on a rise in a forest with a view of the trees all around. A layer of grey lit by the sun was just visible through the bushes below.

A road?

Without slowing to ease herself through, Penelope tumbled down the hill. She tore through the branches. Her momentum ripped the wild, thorny weeds from the web they'd formed across the outer perimeter of the woodland and she stumbled through. She stumbled free.

The open sky and beaming sun welcomed her and tears of joy overcame the fear. There was hope.

But there was a noise. An engine. She spun to face the sound. But it wasn't the truck. It was a sports car, low and sleek. The driver had seen her. He was stopping. Relief washed over Penelope, cleansing her of the adrenaline that lined her veins in a wave, trickling from the tip of her head through her shoulders and organs, then through her weakened legs. She could barely walk any further. She could barely stand.

She was pinned to the spot.

The car approached. It was moving fast. Too fast. There was no time to move even if she could have. Only that wild, carnal instinct had warned her of the truck. The survival instinct released a surge of energy. It was barely enough to lift her feet from the ground. The low, front end of the car swept her feet from beneath her. She hit the bonnet hard, and the world turned dark. She felt her body roll across the car, then bounce off the windshield, high into the air.

She hit the tarmac in a heap of blood and tears.

CHAPTER THIRTY-THREE

"WHERE ARE YOU?" ASKED FRANKIE.

He could hear Nigel running across gravel. The truck door squeaked then slammed.

"Nigel? Where are you?"

"If I said it was classified-"

"You're at the farm?"

"I didn't tell you that."

"I'm on my way. So you better find her and find her fast."

Leaving Nigel's argument to deal with the disconnected dial tone, Frankie collected his weapons from where he'd left them. One Diemaco and a Sig handgun. The rear seat of the Range Rover folded down with ease, providing a space to stash the rifle. It would be out of sight but easy to reach. He dropped the Sig into the pocket of the driver's door, climbed in and fired up the engine.

But before putting the car into reverse and clicking open the garage door, he closed his eyes, took a deep breath and let his head fall back onto the headrest. A few seconds of contemplation, during which he considered everything he was about to do.

Remnants of a plan skirted the core of his mind. Potential events showed themselves in tantalising flashes of hope before slinking back to the whirlwind of thoughts, possibilities and outcomes.

An unshakable image of Jake, tied up, hurt, lonely and afraid, remained fixed at the epicentre of his imagination. He glanced at the empty space where his Aston had been. He might never see it again. He might never see his garage again. The possibility of spending the rest of this life in a cell with just four walls was strong. But one thing was for sure, Jake would be alive.

He clicked the fob to open the garage door and let the whining begin. Half-expecting to find a line of police cars with the flashing blues blocking his driveway, he was surprised to see an empty road in his rear-view mirror.

The five-litre V8 engine responded to his touch of the accelerator and the car eased out of the garage. Without wishing to draw attention to himself, Frankie refrained from pulling a J-turn out onto the road. Instead, he closed the garage door and casually reversed onto the street. But when the main road welcomed him with those open arms of oaks and elms, he took the right turn towards the countryside and opened the engine up.

Once he'd settled in, and had joined the winding network of country lanes, he hit redial on his phone. The car's hands-free system took over, playing the call through the speaker system. It was answered after just two rings.

"Frankie," said Nigel. The background noise was filled with a loud diesel engine and rushing wind.

"Did you find her?" Frankie asked, having to raise his voice to be heard.

"Negative. She ran into the woods. I'm in the truck now, trying to head her off on the road."

"Nigel, I need to find my dad," said Frankie, his tone harsher than necessary. Then, realising that Nigel was the only man who could empathise with what he was going through, he softly added, "I need Jake back."

"And I need to find this girl of yours. You know she mentioned Carter?"

"Who? Penelope?"

"She thought I worked for him. Don't ask me how."

Too much had happened in the last few hours for Frankie to take it all in and assemble the news in any kind of cohesive form.

"Do you think she's part of it?" he asked.

"No. Well, not directly. I think she knows who the players are, but her motive wasn't to help Carter take Jake of that's what you're thinking."

"She wants a story. That's all she's ever wanted."

"But is the story about you, me and the team or is it Carter?"

"What else did she say?"

"She mentioned Debbie-"

"Who is Debbie?"

"You tell me, Frankie. You're the one who seems to be mixed up with convicts, criminals and tabloids. I'm just a guy who runs a farm."

"Well give me context, Nigel. What exactly did she say?"

"Context, Frankie. She was hooded, and I had a gun aimed at the back of her head. She said anything she could say to stay alive."

"You were that close to it? What stopped you?"

"I don't know. We don't even know what she saw on your computer."

"She clearly knows something, Nigel," said Frankie as he manoeuvred a bend in the country lane. "So we've got three missing people; my son, my dad and Penelope."

"Roger," said Frankie.

"We need to find my dad to get Jake back and we need to find Penelope to find out what she knows. We can work alone, or we can partner up. You choose."

"You should have been a salesman," said Nigel. The loud horn of a car and the screeching of tyres sounded through the Range

Rover's speakers. "I don't know how you got me into this?" he said, ignoring the near-miss.

"Are you in?"

"I spend my life staying below the radar-"

"Are you in, Nigel?"

"I'm in. Of course, I'm in."

"Good. Get Penelope back, then we need to find my dad. He's the key."

"And how the bloody hell do we do that?"

"He's driving the Aston. Do you have any favours to call in?"

"Already done. But the number plate recognition is only good when your old man drives past a camera. And there aren't too many cameras out here in carrot-crunching land, boyo."

"How hard can it be to find a bright green seventy-year-old Aston Martin? He'll have to pass by a town or a village at some point," said Frankie. But then it hit him. "No, wait. He's just been released. He'll be wearing a parole tag."

"GPS?"

"I'm sure of it. Do you have anyone with access?"

"Not officially," said Nigel.

"Unofficially?"

"Unofficially, we have the entire British Intelligence at our disposal. Or at least their tools."

"I'll meet you at the farm," said Frankie. "I'm ten minutes out."

"Whoa, hold on," said Nigel. The rushing of wind faltered, and the engine quietened.

"What's going on?"

"You're not going to believe this," said Nigel. "I just found an old, green Aston Martin ditched on the side of the road."

"Location?"

The sound of the wind and engine died down and Nigel spoke with caution as he read the scene.

"I'm a five-minute walk south of my farm. Acre Dyke Lane."

"Tell me what you see, Nigel."

"I see nobody. It's empty."

CHAPTER THIRTY-FOUR

THE FRAGRANT SMELL OF FRESH WILDFLOWERS CAST IMAGES OF a field of green with pollen hanging in the soft breeze that tickled the tops of long grass. But an overwhelming taste of iron cast dark suffocating clouds on the horizon of Isaac's dream. Repressive and restrictive, the weight of the foreboding darkness squeezed the air from his lungs and clamped their steely grip into his chest.

Light and darkness battled overhead as if they fought for Isaac's soul. The breeze ran across his face, gentle as the touch of a child, while invisible forces sucked the life from his body. Instinct clutched his hands to his chest, pawing at the foreign claws that held his heart in its grasp.

An angel spoke. Soft and with the chorus tone of the heavens. The voice came from afar, from all around, carried by the wind across the grasstops and through the trees. But the evil was already within. Sharp talons wrestled with Isaac's heart, wrenching his soul from his body with the tenacity of death as if his heart was the one part of him that clung to life. Pain no longer shot from his arms. The electricity no longer coursed through his torso to his legs. His limbs were already dead, just heavy lifeless weights that pinned him to where he lay.

"Isaac," the voice said, closer now. The smell of flowers was strong. The warmth of the voice eased the pain. A damp cool sweat formed on his brow; the touch of the demons there to carry him away. "Isaac. You're alive."

His desire to reply was fierce. But the effort rewarded him only with tiny, sharp stabs to his dry throat. He coughed and felt a run of warm saliva run from his mouth onto his arm where his head lay and the stab of a talon in his heart.

"Relax, Isaac," said the voice. His eyes opened. Bright sunlight flooded in. He gasped a lungful of fresh air, and then coughed once more. Though the angel spoke to him and reminded him of life, the demon remained inside his body. It still clung to his heart like a shadow.

A warm hand rested on Isaac's brow. The skin was soft and smooth.

"Who are you?" he asked, his voice quiet, and barely perceptible to himself.

"Shh," the angel replied. "Relax. You need to rest."

"My son-" Isaac replied. He tried to straighten, but the demon denied him movement and Isaac laid back down, succumbing to the whim that still played out inside his body.

"Don't move," she said, quiet but clear. "I'll get help."

The shadow of her face on Isaac's eyelids faded, and brightness began to warm the cool layers of sweat on his brow.

"No," he whispered. "Don't leave."

The shadow returned.

"I have to get help. You'll be okay. Just don't move."

Bright sunlight once more filled her void, leaving Isaac to witness the battle for his soul alone. But a calm had fallen over him. Conscious thought returned in waves of guilt with images of Frankie and his faceless grandson.

A single tear formed in the corner of Isaac's eye and rolled across his face, refusing to let go. The light that now flooded his stinging eyes showed a picture so clear and vivid of who Isaac really was and who he could be. It was as if the two sides of his soul, in the midst of being torn apart, had somehow separated his identities.

What have I done?

The old Isaac Black had run away like a coward and left his grandson to die. But the Isaac they'll remember was right there, awakened from a long sleep, quenched by the misgivings of his alter ego. The battle for Isaac's life was lost. But the life of his family would go on.

As if hearing his thoughts and sensing his growing strength, the demon struck out with his sharp claws as Isaac reached for the steering wheel. The demon squeezed. But Isaac pulled away, his face contorted with pain until he sat upright; the demon eased his attack. Isaac coughed a dry cough and felt stabs at his heart like hundreds of tiny pins.

A trickle of pinkish blood ran from his mouth, which he wiped away with the cuff of his sweatshirt, leaving a smear across the fabric, lighter than the dark patch of blood that spread across his shoulder, but a reminder of his imminent death all the same.

Being upright in the car exposed his cold sweats to the breeze. His chest tightened as shivers ran across his skin the way fine sand dances across the arid desert.

Memories of the angel returned, but there was no sign of her. Perhaps she'd brought him back from the cusp of death, and had moved on to spread the joy of life to others, content that her work was either complete or futile.

As if answering his thoughts, the sound of an approaching car grew louder somewhere behind him. It slowed and brakes squealed. Men's excited voices, rough and loud, like those of the men he had shared eight-years of his life with.

He was saved.

"Get him out," the first voice said.

"Wait," said Isaac, and the demon stabbed as he raised his hand to protest.

"Boss, he doesn't look too clever," said another voice, younger and subservient. The young man stood beside Isaac, peering down, but all Isaac saw was his silhouette. "He looks like he's just about hanging on."

The silhouette was joined by a second man, a larger man who didn't peer down for a closer look. He seemed to appraise Isaac from a lofty height.

"Pull the van up here," he called to the driver behind.

The diesel engine grumbled closer. A door slid open. It was metallic, like the iron taste in Isaac's throat. Strong hands pulled Isaac from the car, waking the demon inside him who fought the attack like a caged beast. Isaac screamed out, but another man lifted his lifeless legs, and between them, they lowered him to a rough carpet in the back of a van.

"The angel-" But Isaac's words induced another spell of dry coughs that invigorated the efforts of the demon and its claws.

"What angel?" said the man, the youngest.

"He's delirious," said the man in charge. His voice was familiar.

Isaac let his head fall to one side and his eyes rested on the wall of trees and brush through which she had vanished.

"Let's go," said the leader, banging his hand on the side of the van. But as the door slid to a close, faintly in the shadows of the trees, a face peered out. Pale skin against dark, rich hues. Long, auburn hair as wild as the trees around her.

"The girl-" said Isaac. But his arm was too dead to raise and point and his throat was too dry and cracked to speak.

"The what?"

"There," he grumbled.

The action paused. The lead man studied the trees and bushes.

"Jammo," he said. "Earn your keep. Wait here until we get back."

The young man he'd called Jammo stepped past Issac and dropped to the ground. The man in charge leaned out and spoke to him.

"The old man said he saw a girl. Find her and shut her up."

"On my own?"

"You can handle a girl, right?" The door slammed shut, leaving the youngest outside.

With his back resting on the seat behind him, Isaac clutched his chest, holding the demon in place. In front of him was a man in pressed jeans and smart brown shoes. As Isaac's eyes traced the man's body, he noted the expensive-looking shirt and the silver wristwatch that hung loosely from his wrist.

And Bobby Carter's smiling face.

"Hello, Isaac," he said. "Long time no see."

CHAPTER THIRTY-FIVE

IN THE SHADOWS OF THE TREES, PENELOPE WATCHED AS THE man she'd heard being called Jammo stepped down to the ground. The van door slammed closed behind him and then drove off.

Hope had enthused her. She'd come close to stepping from the bushes to make sure the old man was okay. It had only been as the van door closed that she had seen the man's face.

It was a face she would never forget.

The coffee shop.

Debbie with her black eyes and over-sized sunglasses.

A pack of photographs.

Bobby Carter.

So, Penelope had dropped to the ground and hidden in the thicket of wild, thorny weeds that brimmed the edge of the forest.

Jammo watched the van drive off. His shoulders dropped and his face was an open book of disappointment.

Then there was silence.

At first, Jammo admired the old car. He walked around it, studying it from all angles. But it was as he opened the door and climbed into the driver's seat that he just seemed a little bit odd.

She imagined the car to be the old man's pride and joy. Someone had loved it. Someone had kept it shiny as if it had just rolled from the factory. Jammo seemed impressed too.

He spent a few minutes searching the car for what seemed like anything he could steal. He checked the small give compartment, the door liners and even under the seats.

That was when he found the handgun.

He pushed the car from the brink of the ditch, back into the lay-by. He pulled the brake and closed the door. Then, without warning, he took a few steps to the tree line and stopped just a few feet from Penelope. For a moment she thought he had seen her and that she would be dragged from her little spot in the weeds.

But it was far worse than she could have imagined.

Jammo opened his fly and began to urinate.

There was no time to move. He would have heard her scramble on the forest floor. Instead, she was forced to remain still and let the warm urine splash through the trees onto her legs and dress. She dry-heaved, sickened by the thought of what was happening, telling herself over and over to keep quiet and not to move. But the rain came heavier, finding a direct path through the leaves that shielded her. With her eyes set on Jammo watching his eyes as they scanned the forest, Penelope pulled her bruised leg out of the stream.

"Oy," said Jammo, hearing her shoe scrape in the dirt. "Who's there?" His young voice was clear in the calm fresh air.

He zipped up his pants and moved the leafy branch of the bush that she lay beneath. His ugly face peered down at her in bewilderment.

"You." He smiled a cruel smile.

Penelope rolled.

Through what, she didn't care. She knew there was something not quite right in those eyes of his the second she had seen him.

Thorns, sticks and stones pricked, stabbed and bruised her

skin. The bushes came alive with noise like some giant predator was tearing a path behind her. Scrambling to her feet on the forest floor, she stood and felt her bruised legs company at the weight. She had no direction to escape except towards the hill that she had run down from the farm.

The ripping of bushes and branches stopped. Jammo was free of the entangled foliage at the forest edge.

She limped toward the hill, cradling a damaged elbow.

Heavy footsteps gained speed behind her as she gave everything she had to climb. Her flat shoes slipped on the loose forest floor, and she fell to her hands. She scrambled to the top, pulling on the roots of trees, on nettles that stung her hands, and on the thorny stems of bushes that blocked her path. Until finally, she reached the crest of the small rise, where the forest was in full view below her.

Her heart pounded in her ears. Her breathing was the only sound she could hear. Penelope turned back, expecting to find the young man on her path. But there was nobody there.

No footsteps. No sounds of someone tearing through the brush behind her. Just the quiet of the forest below and the silent world of the birds above.

Aware of how exposed she was once again, Penelope rose to her feet using a small tree for balance. She scanned the ground below her and to the sides. The feeling of being trapped was overwhelming. She knew the farm was behind her, along with the wall of plastic sheeting and the red-headed man with the truck. To her left was unknown, and to her right, deep forest as far as she could see.

She turned around towards the farm, but in the same instant, she saw Jammo's boots on the ground above her. She felt the blow to her head, and she stumbled to the ground. Dizzying lights danced across her eyes and a high-pitched monotone ringing swelled in her ears with the beat of her pounding heart, repeatedly fading then returning to taunt her a second later.

"Where do you think you're going?" said Jammo.

He stepped onto her ankle with all his weight.

"No, please," she cried, surprised at how controlled her voice sounded. She tried to pull away, but his weight pinned her to the spot. "What do you want?" she spat, turning to face him.

"It's not what *I* want. It's what the boss wants," he replied.

The sudden reality that death might not be the only outcome hit Penelope when she realised how vulnerable she was and how alone they were.

"Carter?" she said. "What does he want with me?"

"Oh, he's a very nasty man with very nasty habits."

"And I've upset him?" asked Penelope, buying time. She searched left and right for a weapon, a stick or a rock. But there was nothing close.

"Not directly. But he likes to keep things under control."

"Is that right? All I've done is help an old man who crashed his car. I don't see-" But Penelope's words trailed off as Jammo whipped his belt from the loops of his jeans.

He stared down at her, smiling with the confidence of a child and eyes that were adulterous and lustful. It was that look in his eyes that awoke newfound energy in Penelope's body. She twisted and turned beneath his foot, trying to drag herself away. But the weight of Jammo on her legs surpassed her strength, and when he dropped to his knees, pinning her legs apart and lifting her dress, she fought back with her mud-stained hands, scratching and clawing at his face. An inner fight took over inside, protecting all that was sacred. All that was hers.

But Jammo was strong. He caught her arms and pinned them to the ground above her head, bringing his face close to hers. Even when Penelope dredged up the dry, foulness from her throat and spat it into his face, Jammo just smiled. It took just a few deft movements to bind her hands with the belt, and one more to release the buckle on his jeans before he leaned in and kissed along her neck.

Her worst fear was coming true. It was alive, and all she could do was scream a soundless scream. To cry a silent tear. And feel him working himself against her.

His dirty hand moved down to remove Penelope's panties. The sharp tugs that broke the thin elastic rocked her body, but her fight had gone. She closed her eyes, rolled her head away, and suddenly, she felt his weight from her body released.

Jammo grunted.

Penelope's legs were free. She didn't dare to see what he was doing. But there was no feeling of intrusion. She no longer felt him on her legs.

A scream, wild and carnal, pierced the forest. Birds scattered from the trees. The thud that followed like the beat of a dead drum preceded a sickening crack of bones.

Penelope snapped to and scrambled to her feet. Beside the tree in front of her, Jammo lay on the ground curled in the foetal position. His blood-soaked hands covered his groin, and an anguished expression of unthinkable pain spread across his spotty face as he issued his own silent scream to the empty forest.

A man stood over him with his back to Penelope.

Another stood beside her with a rifle aimed at her head. It was the red-head. It was the redhead but she didn't care.

"Cover yourself," he said, then turned away. Penelope pulled her dress down and made to stand, but the man held his hand up. "That's far enough. Just take it easy."

He turned his head to the other man who, with peered down at Jammo.

He raised a handgun and aimed at his head. It took a few moments for Penelope to register what was happening, but before she could say anything, it was too late.

He pulled the trigger.

It was all Penelope could to scramble away on her hands and feet. It was all she could do to suck in the hot air but exhale nothing. And it was all she could do to issue a silent scream through her dry and cracked throat.

"No," she breathed to herself, shaking her head at what she had just witnessed.

The redhead followed her with his rifle.

"Do we kill her?" he called to his friend.

"No," he replied. He gave Jammo one last look, then turned and Penelope's world crumbled. "No, she knows more than she's letting on."

Frankie stared at Penelope, his face a picture of disappointment. "Bring her with us."

CHAPTER THIRTY-SIX

"Leave her to me, Nigel," said Frankie, his voice cool and calm. "There's no need for that." Frankie gestured at the rifle.

Nigel lowered the rifle, not questioning Frankie's word, then helped Penelope to stand. There was a brief awkward moment as he reached for her ripped underwear from the ground, then stopped. Penelope snatched them up and screwed them into a ball in her hand.

"You okay?" he asked.

She nodded once, unsure if it was shame, gratitude or fear she felt towards the man.

"You want a few minutes?" he asked Frankie.

A single nod of Frankie's head was enough of a reply, and Nigel turned away towards the field.

"Are you hurt?" asked Frankie.

"Physically?" Penelope asked. "No. Bruised."

"Do you know who he was?"

"You mean the man you just killed, Frankie?" Penelope fought hard to control her wavering voice, but the tremors of the emotion signalled a rising breakdown. "I'd rather know who you are. I'd rather know about the man who's been lying to me for the past six months."

"There are no lies."

"No lies? Frankie, look at him lying there. You just shot a man in the head. You're standing there as if you just helped me cross the street."

"He was raping you, Penelope," said Frankie, keeping his voice low. "What should I have done?"

But Penelope wasn't convinced. She shook her head and stepped backwards away from Frankie. He watched her move, making no attempt to follow. She couldn't escape.

"Tell me who he was," said Frankie.

"I don't know who he was. He was left here by some guy in a van."

"A white Mercedes van?"

"I don't know what make it was. I was busy hiding."

"Hiding from who?"

"I don't know, Frankie. Look, today has been a complete mess. I had coffee with someone and you're friend here kidnapped me. I escaped and got hit by a car-"

"Did you see the driver?"

She had been right.

"Your father."

"Where is he, Penelope?"

The words wouldn't form in her mouth. It all seemed too incredible.

"Bobby Carter?" said Frankie. "It was him in the van wasn't it?"

"What are you mixed up in, Frankie?"

"I'm not mixed up in anything. Not anymore. Where's my dad?"

"The van came," she replied. "The van came. Men got out and carted him away."

"Did you see Jake?"

"Jake?"

"Did you see him? Was he in the van, Penelope?"

"No. I don't know. I didn't see. They dropped this guy here, took your dad and left."

"Why?"

"Your father saw me. He said something."

"Did they hurt him?"

"No," she said. "No, they didn't need to. Frankie, he's hurt."

He stared at her. The trust had gone, but she retained a sliver of credibility.

"The car crash? How bad? The car looks fine."

"No, it wasn't the crash. I think he had a heart attack. I think that was *why* he crashed."

The urge to reach out and give her a hug was overwhelming, but one glance from Nigel reminded Frankie of the next part of the conversation. He took a breath, waiting for her to calm, and watched as she stood before him, hugging herself with dirty arms. Her torn dress, straggly hair, and bright red eyes gave the impression of a homeless woman or a junkie.

"Please hold me, Frankie," she said at last and peered up through her hair at him.

"Just a few more questions."

"But-" she began, then stopped to retain her emotions. She sniffed hard. Frankie tore the arm from his t-shirt and held it for her to take.

"Tell me what you know about me, Penelope."

There was a shift in her demeanour, from the vulnerable girl who'd been attacked to the guilty stare of someone whose mind was fabricating a story before his eyes. He'd seen it in the military. It was the type of communication that no language barrier could withhold. No translation was needed.

"What do you mean?" she asked. Another sign. She was buying time.

"I saw you on my computer, Penelope. Tell me what you saw."

"I didn't see–"

"Lets cut to straight to it. I know what folders you opened."

"So, why ask?"

"Tell me what you saw, Penelope."

"Or what? Or your friend will kill me? You know what happened to me earlier?" She glanced across at Nigel.

"I can imagine."

"And you *let* it happen?"

"I had bigger things on my mind."

"Bigger than me being executed?"

"Don't be dramatic."

"Dramatic, Frankie?" snapped Penelope. "Dramatic would be crying my heart out pleading with you to help me. Dramatic would be screaming at the top of my lungs that I was nearly raped, but I'm not Frankie. I'm not." She seemed to calm, the outburst relieving some tension. "Today, I have been abducted and nearly killed, run over by a man having a heart attack, and I came this close–" She held her index finger and thumb up an inch apart. "This close, Frankie, to being raped. And to top it off, the man I've been falling in love with for the past six-months has just committed cold-blooded murder before my eyes."

Penelope stepped closer to Frankie for the first time.

"So why don't you tell me what you *think* I saw and be done with it?"

The statement had finality.

"You're falling in love with me?" It was the only thing he could say.

"No," she replied. Frankie's heart jumped. "I *was* falling in love with Frankie Black. I don't know who this man is in front of me."

The words tore at Frankie in a way he hadn't felt for a long time. Suddenly, Penelope mattered. It mattered what she thought of him. It mattered that she cared. It changed everything.

"The man that stands before you now, Penelope, might not be the Frankie Black you thought you knew. But let me tell you this.

This is the real me. And there's a reason the real me doesn't show his face too often."

The hostility faded from her eyes. They narrowed with intrigue.

"There's a man who wants my father dead. It's an argument from long ago-"

"Bobby Carter?" she said as if she'd known all along. As if it was common knowledge and Frankie's entire life had been aired to the public from day one.

"You know him?"

"I know of him," she replied.

"Penelope-" said Frankie.

He reached for her shoulder, but at the very touch of her body, he pulled in her in close, wrapping his arms around her, unsure for whose benefit the hug was. He felt her body ease against his own. The weight of her head against his chest conveyed her emotions. Then, reaching for her shoulders, he pushed her away to arm's length and looked her in the eyes.

"He's got Jake."

CHAPTER THIRTY-SEVEN

"Do you know how long I've waited for this day, Isaac?" said Carter.

A length of gaffer tape had been wrapped around Isaac's head to cover his mouth, but he hissed a response anyway, then regretted the effort as needles stabbed at his heart, turning his curse into a low guttural growl.

Directly in front of him stood Carter, his feet shoulder-width apart, his arms folded, and his back ramrod straight. To one side, Isaac could see the rooftops of London below and a small slice of the River Thames. The room itself was large, the size of an apartment, and the smell of concrete and dust was heavy in the air. There were no windows or doors, just gaps where there would be one day. The floor was unfinished concrete, as was the ceiling, but with a few sparse copper pipes and thick armoured cabling leading to nowhere.

Given the chance, Isaac would estimate they were thirty or more stories high.

Given the circumstance and Carter's tone, he knew he was about to find out the hard way.

"No?" said Carter with a smile. "Eight years, Isaac," he continued. "That's how long I've waited. That's eight years of borrowed time you've been living on, Isaac. I don't know how you got parole so early and I honestly don't know how Bruno didn't get you. But, that's all okay. I'm not letting you go anywhere. What do you say about that then?"

Isaac sat, resolute, and swallowed the blood that was seeping into his mouth.

"You honestly thought you could get away from me? You? You betrayed me, Isaac," said Carter. He stood and paced the bare concrete floor with the leather soles of his smart brown shoes tapping the slow rhythm of his casual stride. It was as if he had all the time in the world.

It was as if he was waiting for something.

He stopped beside the gap where a set of double doors might one day lead to a balcony peering out over East London. A single scaffold tube fixed to the wall either side prevented him from walking out. But to lift a man over and drop him to the ground far below would require little effort.

"You were like a father to me, Isaac. You showed me the way, you know? And I'm grateful, truly, I'm grateful for it. For everything you taught me. But times change. People change. And if you don't move with it, if you don't absorb the changes and roll with the punches, Isaac, you get left behind."

Carter twisted and stared at Isaac.

"You got left behind, Isaac," he finished, then nodded to someone behind Isaac. Within moments, the gaffer tape was ripped from his face, taking it with the growth of the day and a few stray hairs from the back of his mostly bald head.

It felt good to suck in the cool air and spit the pinkish phlegm from his throat.

"You never did have much style, did you, Isaac?" said Carter. His face sneered at the atrocity that Isaac had coughed up. "You're just scum. That's all you ever were."

"Just do it, Bobby," said Isaac. "If you're going to do it, just do it. I don't have time for games."

"All in good time, Isaac. All in good time. We're waiting for the cavalry, aren't we? Speaking of which, how is Frankie?"

Isaac froze at the mention of his son's name.

"Now Frankie, on the other hand, *he's* got style. He could have done well for himself."

"Leave them out of this, Bobby. Where's Jake? I know you've got him."

As if a moment of fatherly understanding passed between them, Carter stopped his jeering.

"He's okay. He's safe."

"Just let him go, Bobby. He's just a kid," Isaac wheezed. Each word was a strain on his heart, and each breath felt like the last his lungs would issue.

"Do you know what you took from me?"

"It was a mistake, Bobby. Leave it. Life is short."

But the words angered Carter. He pushed off the scaffold tube, gave four long strides and slammed his fist into Isaac's face, sending him and the chair over backwards. Isaac's head hit the concrete floor. A thousand tiny claws gripped his heart and his lungs issued a stream of blood into his mouth. Isaac coughed and growled to absorb the pain in his chest. The urge to hold his heart, to ease the pain, was irresistible, but his bound hands were useless.

"You're damn right life is short, Isaac. For some anyway. Billy deserved to live. He deserved a longer go. While you, you bloody coward, hid away inside. And the rest of us out here picked up the pieces."

"So why didn't you get me inside? You had eight years to get me and you sent Bruno on my last day."

"Get you inside?" said Carter. "What? And allow you to miss all the fun? No, Isaac. I wanted to make sure you suffered. You see, while you stared at your four walls, while you endured the mindless rigmarole of prison life, the beatings, the humiliation, and the wondering if the next day was going to be your last, I was out here *planning* your last days."

"So, why send Bruno?"

"Think about it."

"You knew I was being released?" said Isaac. "Nobody knew."

"Nobody on the outside knew. But I just happen to know a little birdie on the inside."

The chair was suddenly snatched up by two strong arms either side of Isaac. The movement shook his insides. But at least he could spit his blood to the floor.

"Can you stop doing that?" said Carter. "That's disgusting, that is."

"I'm dying, Bobby."

"Not yet you're not."

"There's not much I can do about it. This birdie. He wouldn't happen to be a screw, would he?"

Carter laughed once, short and sharp.

"I can see where Frankie got his brains."

"So you've got me, Bobby. What now? You've won. Well done. Why don't you pat yourself on the back? I'd do it myself but-"

"What was the worst thing about being inside, Isaac?" said Carter. He turned and looked out across London once more with his arms behind his back, and rocked from his toes to his heels. "I want to know."

The question was simple. The answer was even simpler. But it led somewhere Isaac dare not go. So he said nothing.

"Come on, Isaac. Spit it out. You've had eight years to think about it, after all."

"Missed opportunities," said Isaac, leaving the response vague.

The reply incited a look of contemplation from Carter, who for a second, seemed impressed, but continued to study the horizon outside.

"Missed opportunities," he repeated as if he were deciphering a puzzle. "Family?" He twisted once more to face Isaac. "I'm right, aren't I?"

The hands that squeezed Isaac's insides tightened with the timing of his pulse, which felt at least double its usual speed.

He said nothing.

"You haven't seen your grandson yet, have you? You've never met him."

Preferring to let the silence speak for itself, Isaac remained quiet.

"The question is, Isaac. Who do you think Frankie loves the most?"

Only the sound of the city below them murmured a response.

"Let's find out, shall we?"

CHAPTER THIRTY-EIGHT

IT WAS ONLY WHEN BOTH FRANKIE AND NIGEL HAD WALKED away, and Penelope had sat on her haunches against a tree to call Debbie Carter, that the first true tears fell. She had suppressed them well by keeping her mind busy and diverting the conversation with Frankie, but they were a ticking time bomb. Nobody ever saw Penelope Pike crying. They hadn't since before she could remember.

The two men were at the foot of the hill heading towards the old car. Debbie's number was displayed on the screen of her phone and the green dial button was ready to be hit. But three breaths in quick succession came from nowhere. Her eyes flooded and her mind tensed. Only when she was sure she was unobserved, did she let the tears flow.

It was as if she'd both pulled her thumb from a dam and released the air from a balloon simultaneously. The emotions came pouring out. Though she maintained the low volume, and although the two men were too far away to see her crying, she rolled to her side, curled up in a ball, and let her vulnerability, her wounds and her fragile state drain from her body, heart and mind in a flood of tears and sobs.

It was Frankie's torn sleeve that she used to wipe her face, but it was her own dress that she held together at her neck and around her legs to cover herself. To cover her weakness. Her hair fell across her face, lank, lifeless and festooned with the scatterings of the forest floor. Mud, small twigs, leaves and bark from the trees shielded her anguish from the sorry eyes of Frankie and Nigel.

A few minutes had passed when the forest peace was broken by Frankie calling her name. No matter what she tried, she knew her tears would have left tracks through the grime, and her eyes would be lined with the red rings of her fragility.

"Penelope," Frankie called again. "We're leaving."

The men stood at the bottom of the hill peering up. So, Penelope leaned around the side of the tree, waved her hand, and cleared her throat.

"I'll just be two minutes," she called back. "I'm calling Debbie."

Thankful for the extra time alone, time that might allow her bright red eyes to settle a little, she hit the dial button on her phone. The dial tone played on loop for a suspense-filled thirty seconds. Then it rang off, leaving Penelope listening to the sound of her own laboured breathing and beating heart.

"Let's go," called Frankie from the bottom of the hill. He waved her down to him when she caught his eye.

It was during the scramble down the steep hill that Penelope realised just how unsteady she was. Her shaky her legs had become a sign of weakness, which she would need to hide from Frankie and Nigel.

They were standing a few feet from the spot where Penelope had been urinated on, but she said nothing of the incident and let Frankie, who had gone from a quiet, thoughtful man, to a man used to being in control, to issue his instructions. While he spoke, Penelope compared the two variations of Frankie as if they were two separate people. Right there and then as she admired him, she realised just how much she needed him.

"Penelope?" said Frankie. "Are you with us?"

Her daze was snapped away when she realised Frankie was asking her something.

"Did you get hold of Debbie Carter?"

"No. She didn't answer."

"Try again. Do you know where she lives?"

With her phone beside her ear, Penelope waited for the call to be answered and shook her head.

"Can you find out? Your research man?" asked Frankie. Waiting for a call to be answered would not pause his plans.

She nodded.

"Good. Get your man onto it. We need an address."

The phone slid from Penelope's shoulder to her hand when the call rang out again. She found Jason King's number and hit the green dial button.

He answered with what sounded like a mouthful of crisps.

"King, what's the news?" she asked, her voice cracked and weak.

"No news yet. Your man Frankie Black is elusive. There's barely a record anywhere but I have some ideas-"

"Forget about him. What have you got on Carter?"

"Ah well, Bobby Carter is very different. Nothing that directly ties him to any criminal activity, as you can imagine. But he's got his fingers in several pies. Mostly cash businesses. He recently acquired a construction firm and is now the proud owner of what will be a very swanky-looking apartment building, if the 3-D visualisations on the Internet are anything to go by."

"What about Debbie Carter?"

"Debbie Carter?" said King. Penelope listened to the noise of him flicking through a pile of papers on his messy desk. It would be cluttered with takeaway containers, drinks bottles and general filth.

"Come on, Jason. I need her address. Where does she live?"

"Just a minute," he replied.

With a flick of her head, Penelope nodded to the road, indicating that they should go. The address was coming. She also knew something else was coming.

"How about-"

"If you mention drinks, King, it's off. I have had the worst day in history. The last thing you want to Dosi push me right now."

There was a silence as King contemplated a retort.

"Debbie Carter's address is on its way," he said.

"Thank you, King," she said. "We'll take it from here."

She hit the disconnect button before King could ask who *we* Incorporated. She looked up at Frankie and, for the first time, felt equal to him.

"Carter's building a block of apartments somewhere. But to find that, we'll need Debbie Carter."

CHAPTER THIRTY-NINE

"Nigel, let's do this," called Frankie, as he took Penelope's hand. "We've got two objectives. Save Jake, and take Carter down."

"What about Debbie?" protested Penelope.

"She's not important. We can trace my dad the same way Carter did, with his parole tag. We find my dad and take Carter down. End of story."

"You're going to take him down?" asked Penelope. "You mean you're going to kill him?"

"Nigel, can you get Penelope somewhere safe? We'll rendezvous in an hour," said Frankie, ignoring Penelope's outburst.

"Oh, no," began Penelope. "You're not leaving me out of *this*."

"She can hide on the farm until we're done," said Nigel.

"Can you guys even hear me?" said Penelope. "I'm coming with you. After everything I've been through today–"

"Wait, Penelope? After everything you've been through today, you want more? We don't know what Carter is capable of, and if I'm honest, I don't even know what he looks like anymore."

"*I* do," said Penelope. "I saw him, remember?"

"Hold on. We've got a problem here," said Nigel, studying his phone. "I had the boys track your dad's parole tag. GPS says your dad is right here with us."

The two men both glanced up at Jammo's bloodied body. Nigel began the search. A few minutes later, he waved the broken tag at Frankie.

"We need a new plan," he said when he returned. "Without this, we have no way of finding your old man."

"You *need* me," said Penelope. "Take me with you to get Debbie. She's our only chance of finding him."

"Just give me the address, Penelope."

"I spoke to Debbie. She told me things."

"What things?" said Nigel. He stepped up to her, closing the gap.

"Carter leaves men there to stop her from running away. But he says it's to protect her."

"How many?" asked Frankie.

"I'll tell you on the way," she replied.

"You don't have to do this, Penelope. It could be very dangerous."

"I know. I know all about him. I know what he looks like. I know about the robbery and your dad and what happened after. I know everything, Frankie."

"Have you been researching me? Am I a story? Is that what all this is about?" asked Frankie.

"Why would you be a story? You're just a photographer with a particular set of skills, right? You're good at finding people."

"Right," Frankie agreed.

"I met with Debbie Carter. *She's* the story."

"*Debbie* is the story?"

"She came to me. She's looking for a way out and she's afraid Carter will kill her if he finds out."

"So you were going to expose him? Do you have any idea who you're up against here?"

"I know the risks involved."

"And the story is worth the risk?"

"It was at first, the story, I mean. But now it's about getting Debbie Carter her freedom. He's a monster."

The final statement needed no confirmation. Frankie knew all too well what the man was capable of.

"So how do you know about my dad?"

"Debbie showed me photos. I recognised the name."

"Black is a common name."

"You look like him," she said, and the words stung.

"Well, the eyes anyway. And the shape of your face."

He raised his eyebrows at her, asking if she had finished.

"And you have the same mouth. It could have only been your dad."

"Anything else you want to confess?" asked Frankie.

Penelope looked away.

"Tell me what you saw, Penelope."

She shook her head.

"I saw photos of a man I knew once when I was stationed in the Middle East."

"Anybody else?"

"Just some guys that pulled me out of a little fix I got myself into."

She stared at him.

"That's all, Frankie. I know you were special forces and I know you were something beyond that. You and your redhead friend. I know its something you'll never share with me and that's okay. Honestly, all I care about is who you are now. I'm not going to write about you."

Frankie studied her face. There were none of the tells that he'd been trained to spot liars. No muscles twitching, no averting of eyes and no shuffling of fingers and feet. She was sincere. Probably the most sincere he'd ever know her to be.

"Frankie?"

"It's okay. I believe you."

"So how do we do this?" asked Penelope.

"That depends," said Frankie. "How do I know you won't write a story about the team?"

"What team?"

She smiled.

"They don't mess about, Penelope. What Nigel was going to do earlier was standard protocol. All you need to know is that you need to forget what you saw. If any of it made print, you'd vanish off the face of the earth and there would be nothing I could do to stop it."

"Are you worth a story?"

"Not really."

"So I think I'd rather keep you to myself."

Somewhere in the flick of Penelope's eyes was a hint of disdain at Nigel.

"He's a good guy," said Frankie. "He didn't hurt you. Like I said, he was following protocol."

"He was going to kill me."

"Where do I find, Debbie Carter?" said Frankie, ignoring her question, as true as it was.

"*You* don't find her, Frankie. *We* do."

____

CHAPTER FORTY

"Do you know who this is?" asked Carter, with his hand resting on the boy's head.

The touch was threatening to Isaac, but Jake's innocent naivety perceived it as little more tan affection; much like the beautiful view across London that Carter showed him. It was clear that the threat of being pushed hadn't occurred to Jake.

Jake studied Isaac's face for a moment from where he stood beside the single scaffold tube. Then he looked up at Carter and shook his head. A stab of pain shot through Isaac's body.

"Why don't you tell the boy who you are, Isaac?" said Carter.

It was a conversation that Isaac hadn't prepared for. He'd imagined a similar grandfather to grandson discussion so many times before but never had he envisaged a scene with so much volatility, with the constant threat of death and pain hanging in the air. A walk in the park maybe, the three of them, Frankie, Jake and Isaac. Or even a day out somewhere, the beach or a museum. But the forty-something floor of a partially built tower block had never been the scene.

"Go on," said Carter. "We're waiting."

A rough and ragged tongue coated in blood flicked from Isaac's mouth to wet his lips but served little purpose.

"How about a minute alone, Bobby, eh?"

The question hung in the air. No expression appeared on Carter's face. There was no sign of a reaction at all until, after a few long seconds, he laughed out loud. A short, sharp, stab of laughter.

"Alone?" said Carter. "Me? Leave you alone with young Jake here?" He moved his hand from the boy's head, and let it fall to his shoulder, then gave him an affectionate squeeze, like a friend might, or an uncle. "Oh, I don't think that's wise, Isaac. Do you? After all, I have been charged with the care of the boy. What would I tell Frankie if anything should happen?"

He spoke the words consistently with the split adult and child agenda he'd been portraying since Jake had been brought into the room. To Jake, Carter would appear caring and responsible, someone to look up to, perhaps. But to Isaac, sarcasm ran through Carter's tone, twinned with that endless quest for power Carter had always had.

"Come on, Bobby. Just two minutes," said Isaac, then fell into an agonising coughing fit. He spat blood to the floor and watched the boy's eyes widen as he recognised the glistening red hues on the floor.

"It's okay, Jake," Isaac reassured him. Then, without removing his eyes from the boy, he added, "Bobby, come on. Two-minutes. That's all I need."

With a scrutinising glare coupled with an unsmiling face, Carter nodded slowly.

"Two-minutes. That's all." Then he turned to the boy. "You'll be okay in here, Jake. He won't hurt you, okay?"

Jake nodded. Isaac's heart folded in two as his grandson watched Carter leave with a look of abandonment. The sound of Carter and his two goons faded to nothing, leaving Isaac alone with his grandson for the first time.

A thousand introductory lines came to Isaac's mind in a tangle of emotions, but Isaac could speak none. All words were ill-fitting and inadequate. What Jake needed to hear was one thing, but if Isaac was to make an impact on the boy, if he was to gain his love and maybe even respect, his first words would need to be memorable. It was likely to be the first and last time Jake would see his grandfather. It needed to count.

But still, the right words failed to fall into line.

Jake looked at him expectantly, his head cocked to one side. Perhaps wondering who he was. Perhaps wondering why he was tied to a chair forty-something floors above London and coughing up blood.

But then the boy did something unexpected. He took three steps forward until he was within reach of Isaac. The patch of blood on Isaac's shoulder had caught the boy's eye and with a tenderness that could only come with innocence, Jake reached out and placed his hand on the wound. Big eyes looked up at Isaac. They were white with purity and had dark centres that were large, to take in the new surroundings, new information and new people.

"Your mother was the most beautiful woman I ever saw," said Isaac.

The boy gave no response but blinked away a glaze that formed at the mention of her name.

"Do you remember her?" said Isaac.

The boy nodded.

"So do I, Jake. And you know what?"

Somehow talking with his eyes, Jake merely altered his expression as if to say, "*What?*"

"You look just like her."

The boy's expression changed to that of intrigue.

"Your eyes, your cheeks, your chin, and your hair."

The boy's hands followed Isaac's words, touching his own face and hair in confirmation.

"But do you recognise anything about me?"

The question was lost on Jake, so Isaac crossed his eyes and looked down, inciting a smile form the boy. The first smile Isaac had seen.

"Do you see my nose? I'd show you, but-" Isaac glanced over his shoulder as if telling the boy something he shouldn't be. "My hands are tied."

Another smile.

"You see my nose?"

Jake nodded and stared at Isaac's face.

"It's the same as yours."

Small hands felt the shape of Jake's nose.

"Do you know who else has that nose?" asked Isaac.

Still, without uttering a word, Jake's expression answered for him. This time, it was as if an intruder shared their nose, somebody who had no right to it.

"My son," said Isaac, unsure if he should continue. But something in Jake's expression coaxed the rest of the sentence from his parched lips.

"Do you know who my son is?" said Isaac. "Do you know why you and I share the same nose?"

After a brief pause to consider the question, Jake shook his head. His mouth hung open in the way a child's mouth does. But his eyes searched deep into Isaac's like he was building his own picture inside. His own memories.

"Your dad, Jake. Your dad is my son."

He said it. He put it out there.

But still no reaction.

"Do you love your daddy, Jake?"

"Yes," he replied, his first words to Isaac.

"He's special to you, yes?" continued Isaac, keen to maintain the momentum.

The boy nodded. "Of course he is. He's my daddy."

"Well, I'm your *daddy's* daddy," said Isaac. "Do you know what that makes me to you? Do you know what to call me?"

It was as if the last statement had offended Jake, or confused him. Isaac couldn't tell. But Jake's lower lip stuck out, and his brow dropped to form a horizontal line across the top of his eyes, just how Frankie's did.

"You call me Granddad," said Isaac. "Can you do that for me?"

"You're not Granddad. I already have a granddad."

"That's right, I remember him. But he's your mummy's father. I'm your daddy's father."

Jake stepped back once, shaking his head in disbelief.

"Jake, don't go."

But he stepped back further.

"You're not my Granddad," said Jake. "My daddy doesn't have a dad."

But before Isaac could reassure the boy, before he could coax him close once more, Carter burst into the room, strode across the concrete floor and stood behind Jake with his hands on the boy's shoulders.

"Did you two have a nice chat? asked Carter.

But Issac was transfixed on Jake's down-turned face. It would be his only chance, and he'd blown it.

"Good," said Carter, breaking the silence. "Because we need to get ourselves ready."

"Ready for what?" asked Isaac, blinking his eyes clear.

But Carter simply laughed in reply, scooped the boy up to sit on his arm, and stared down at Isaac.

"In a few hours, Isaac, all of our lives will be very different."

He stepped closer to Isaac and leaned down, keeping Jake at a distance. Then, with the callous snarl of a man who had it all, he whispered into Isaac's ear.

"It's showtime."

CHAPTER FORTY-ONE

"This is it here. The big house on the right," said Penelope.

She was sitting in the rear seat of Frankie's Range Rover, leaning forward between the two front seats. Nigel drove in silence while Frankie peered through the window, firing questions at Penelope; he was trying to build up a picture of everything Debbie had told her.

"Drive past, Nigel," said Frankie. "Let's have a nosey and see who's who."

They rolled past the large house, which was set far back from the road behind a long curved driveway and partially hidden by tall conifer trees. The house was tucked away in a very well-to-do street on the border of East London and Essex, in a small town called Chigwell. It was an area Frankie knew to be a haven for the East End criminals who wanted out of the rat race, but not too far away.

"Sounds like the bloke needs a good seeing to anyway," said Nigel, as he did a three-point turn, checked his mirrors and pulled to a stop. "Who the bloody hell does that to his wife? Especially in front of others."

"She tried to leave him a few times already. But he uses emotional blackmail to make her stay. Says he can't live without her. Then a few days later, the whole thing starts over."

"And you're sure she can lead us to him?" asked Frankie.

It was the first time Penelope had stopped to watch him under stress. On the surface, he gave the image of a man in control. But the way he fidgeted in his seat, the way he adjusted the temperature every thirty seconds, and the way he drummed his fingers lightly on the door, all revealed his agitation.

A plan was forming in his mind. What arm of the elite services Frankie was in would likely never be shared with her. Any chances of him divulging even a hint of his military career after what happened that day were slim to none.

"Penelope?" said Frankie. His abrupt tone snapped her from her daydream

"Yeah," she replied.

"Come on, I need you switched on. Are you sure she can lead us to him? Because after what I'm about to do, there'll be no turning back."

The seriousness of his voice weighted heavily in the confines of the car.

She nodded once to confirm.

"She's our best chance."

Twisting his body to one side and lifting himself from the seat, Frankie pulled a handgun from his waistband and dropped it into the centre console. Then he reached into the back and slid his hand beneath the folded-down seat beside Penelope.

"You need help?" she asked.

But Frankie didn't reply. He pulled on a strap until the butt of a semi-automatic rifle slid into view. He took the weight of the weapon and set it, muzzle down, in the foot well beside his leg.

"Tell me what you saw, Nigel," he said, as he ejected the magazine, felt the weight and re-inserted it.

"Double gates. Probably electric. Two cars. One Porsche and a large SUV."

"Agreed," confirmed Frankie.

It was as if they were back in the army. The whole thing was an operation to them, which should have instilled an element of confidence in Penelope. But fear gripped her as she realised that they weren't going in just to get Debbie. They were going to start a war.

"Entrance?" asked Frankie.

"Double doors. Glass porch. Living space to the left of the doors. Double garage to the right."

Between the panic attacks that Penelope was striving to contain, she marvelled at the discussion the two men were having. It was like they were stood at a bar, sharing a beer.

"And where would you place the guards?"

"I'd have a man outside, although I didn't see anyone. I'd have one by the front door and one at the back of the house. There are possibly more if they're working shifts and Carter wants to keep tabs on his wife."

"I'd agree with that."

"There'll be armed too."

"Do you remember Sarajevo?" said Frankie.

"The embassy?" replied Nigel.

Frankie nodded. He remained focused on the house two-hundred yards away. Nigel didn't respond. Whatever they had done in Sarajevo formed the basis of the plan they were making now, while parked outside a one-million-pound house in the heart of Essex suburbia.

"Right. We're on in thirty-seconds," said Frankie. Then he turned to face Penelope. "You need to get out. Walk the other way. We'll pick you up in less than five minutes."

"No way," said Penelope. "You're not leaving me here. No. After all-"

"Penelope," said Frankie. He hadn't raised his voice, but there was something in the way he spoke, a confidence, with which

Penelope couldn't help but stop and listen. "Inside that house is the key to getting my son back. Now get out of the car." His harsh eyes softened when they saw Penelope's widen with fear. "Please. It's too dangerous."

Penelope was frozen to the spot. She was unsure if she should try to talk him out of it and call the police, or if she should just run. In the end, it was Nigel who made the decision for her. He got out the car, opening her door and pulling her out, with firm but gentle hands.

"Always the gentleman, Nigel," she said, resisting him only slightly.

The door slammed closed, leaving Frankie to slide across to the driver's seat.

"Go," Nigel said to her. "He'll be okay. I promise I'll keep an eye on him."

The red-headed man winked, then made off on foot in the direction of the house on the far side of the street.

Penelope began walking but turned every few steps only to find the Range Rover in the same spot, and see Nigel growing closer to the house with his rifle held inside his long jacket. He walked as if he were fetching a newspaper. Prying eyes wouldn't look twice.

The street ahead curved away, but before Penelope had made the turn, she took a final glance back. Just as Frankie gunned the engine. The sudden noise shattered the tranquil neighbourhood. From her spot in the road, Penelope could only see the gates and a side view of the house.

As the Range Rover passed Nigel, the red-head sprinted behind it. Expert hands guided the large SUV into a tight curve and smashed through the two iron gates. For a moment, Penelope thought Frankie would jump from the car and kick the door in. But instead, he cut across the lawn between two of the evergreen trees without releasing the throttle once and drove the Range Rover into the front of the house.

CHAPTER FORTY-TWO

JUST SECONDS BEFORE THE RANGE ROVER TORE THROUGH THE wall of the large house, Frankie pulled the door release to prevent the door being jammed shut. A shower of bricks and glass rained down on the front of the car. A cloud of hissing steam sprayed up from the grill as the vehicle came to stop.

Shapes in the fog of dust and steam ahead darted towards two double doors before Frankie jumped out and crouched low. Above the noise of the settling bricks, a groan came from beneath the car where it rested on a flattened and ruined couch. To Frankie's right, Nigel ran into view across the lawn. He caught Frankie's eye and followed his silent command to take the front door.

The large living space was cut in two by a wall of glass doors. The exit to the hallway was on the right. A three-round burst into the dying man beneath the car stopped the groaning, allowing Frankie to concentrate on the scuffling of boots on the hallway's wooden floor outside. A shadow passed the frosted glass to what Frankie presumed to be a dining area. Another three-round burst shattered the glass, and something heavy dropped to the floor.

Taking a wide arc towards the hallway, Frankie's senses were on high alert. More heavy boots. The faint click of a weapon being armed somewhere in the hallway. Then Nigel forced the front doors open. The man with the gun stepped into action but showed just a little too much of his boot. Frankie took him down. Nigel stepped into the living room to join him.

Both men listened to the noises of the house. From the kitchen at the back of the house, a hushed whisper cut through the temporary peace. With his Diemaco tucked into his shoulder, Frankie pointed for Nigel to take upstairs and then slipped through into the L-shaped kitchen. In his mind's eye, Frankie saw two men, nervous, adrenaline-fueled and untrained. They would be waiting for him to step around the corner. If they had weapons, they'd be handguns. At twenty-feet, the chances of one of them actually hitting Frankie were slim. But the army had taught him caution and preparedness.

He coughed once and tapped his boot on the flagstone kitchen floor to tell them he was there.

As if it was all a rehearsed play, the first of the men peered around the corner with a Glock poised to shoot. A single shot from Frankie's Diemaco took him down. He dropped to the floor, twitched and moaned, then silenced.

Loud, nervous and uncontrolled breathing came from around the corner, as the second man waited for his turn. He would have his back to the wall, possibly slid down to his haunches and his gun would be in both hands, which would be sweaty and shaky. But a person's fight for life was tenacious. A cornered criminal was dangerous.

Upstairs, two single shots from Nigel's rifle sounded off. A loud and piercing scream cut through the space, and doors slammed as Frankie imagined Debbie running through the house to get away. Speed was of the essence.

"Why don't you show yourself?" said Frankie to the last man in the kitchen.

The jittery exhales of the man were loud, as if they'd been suppressed and he was now free to breathe.

"The way I see it," Frankie continued. "You're going to die anyway. Why make it hard on yourself?"

The man whimpered, then sniffed, wet and thick.

Beside Frankie on the side of a large American style fridge, photos were pinned up with tiny magnets, much like in his own home. Nearly every photo was of Bobby Carter with one or two of his friends. He couldn't be sure, but the man who'd died on the couch beneath his wheels looked like one of the men with Carter. They were somewhere hot. They wore shorts, sunglasses and both held large European-sized glasses of bright, amber beer. In another photo, Carter wore a tuxedo and was sitting beside two men at what appeared to be a charity gig or a fancy dinner. The confidence of a man who had it all shone from Carter's eyes, almost daring Frankie to get him.

"Just leave," said the voice. It was younger than Frankie had imagined, mid-twenties maybe. "I won't come after you. I haven't seen your face."

"You won't come after me?" said Frankie, still admiring the photos. "That's good of you, and I have to say the offer is tempting." He left a pause, enough to build hope in the poor guy's ill-fated heart. "But I don't like loose ends."

The boy sobbed. Just once. It was almost as if he'd lost control. His face would be streaming with tears of fear. His vision would be channelled, his peripheral darkened.

"I know you're scared, boy," said Frankie. "I was like you once."

There was traces of white powder on the granite kitchen surface along with a set of digital scales. The room bore the unmistakable smell of marijuana, sweet and pungent.

"I'm not scared of you."

Defiance. Weak but admirable.

"Is that right?" said Frankie.

"If you come around that corner, I'm going to blow your head off."

Frankie's eyes fell on another photo, more recent. It was in the grounds of a construction site. Carter wore a shiny plastic hard-hat but retained his brown leather shoes and smart jeans. The man beside him looked on, smiling as any loyal subject might, and Debbie Carter stood to one side, unsmiling. But there was something in her eyes. It wasn't hatred. It was stronger than that. It was the look of somebody who'd lost something and watched as somebody else walked away with what once could have been theirs. It was a look of jealousy.

Doors slammed upstairs again, and Nigel fired off twice. A few seconds later, he fired four more rounds. Two sets of two. Two headshots, and two chest shots to the two men he'd just dropped.

"Okay, listen to me, chum. I'm going to make this easy for you," said Frankie, conscious of time ticking by. "You can either show yourself and try to kill me. But you won't. I'll maim you, disable you and let you die a slow painful death..."

The sentence was designed to set off a new burst of fear in the boy. And it worked.

"Or," continued Frankie, "you could just put that gun of yours to your head and pull the trigger. You wouldn't feel a thing and all this will be over. Of course, you could always wait and hope the police come. But you'll spend the rest of your life in prison, and I'd bet money you've got some kind of narcotic in your pocket. Judging by the smell in here, you've got some weed, and judging by the kitchen surface, you've got a bit of coke as well. It's your choice. Now you can't say I'm being unfair, can you?"

The boy was crying now. Loud and unashamed.

"So, what will it be? One, two or three?"

There was running upstairs. A door was kicked in, and Debbie began screaming again. Nigel had cornered her.

"If you don't decide yourself, I'll decide, and it'll hurt a lot more than option two."

A tiny click of metal, its tone was sharp against the audible thrum of the boy's breathing.

Heavy boots on the stairs and the struggled complaints of a woman.

"You're running out of time, boy. You've got three seconds."

As if releasing the last of his tears in one final almighty burst of sobbing, the boy broke.

Nigel stepped from the stairs with one arm around Debbie Carter's neck and his hand across her mouth to stop her screaming. He stopped, gave Frankie an inquisitive look, and held a set of car keys in the air. Frankie replied in silence by holding up three fingers. Then he stared at a very frightened Debbie Carter, holding her gaze while the last threat was eliminated.

"Three."

A shuffle of movement from the corner of the kitchen.

"Two."

One finger dropped to Frankie's fist, leaving two standing.

"One."

The single shot of a Glock Nineteen rang throughout the house. Then, as gravity worked its magic, the heavy weight of the boy's dead body slumped the floor.

Frankie turned to Nigel and his hostage.

"Good afternoon, Debbie. Let's go. We'll take your car."

CHAPTER FORTY-THREE

"This is ridiculous, Bobby," said Isaac. "Do you know what you'll get for kidnapping a minor?" He let the question hang, and watched as the edges of Carter's smile lifted even further. "Add that to my murder, and I'd be surprised if they ever let you out. Except maybe in a wooden overcoat. Of course, it wouldn't be the fine mahogany finish you might have envisaged. Oh, no. By that time, Bobby, you'd be a nobody. Just another ex-con that no-one loves or cares. There'll be no funeral. No. The state wouldn't waste money on it. When you finally die in your tiny little cell, I'll tell you what will happen. The doors will open one morning, as they do. The guard assigned to your landing will call out his headcount, as he does every morning. But he'll be one down. A man missing, Bobby."

"You paint a pretty picture, Isaac."

"But he won't run down to make sure you're okay. He'll walk. Slow enough to give you a little more opportunity to show your face. But you won't, of course. Show your face, that is. No, you'll be long gone by then. The other prisoners will be sent back to their cells, disgruntled at missing breakfast. The doors will close once more and the doctor will come and pronounce you dead. I doubt they'd even do an autopsy. You'd be taken to the infirmary, covered in a blanket and stuffed in a cooler so you don't rot and stink the place out even more. Then some poor sod in admin will be charged with finding someone that loves you enough to be told. But you know what?" Isaac let out a stab of laughter as if it might be his last. "They won't find anybody. The poor sod in admin will be calling around all known relatives, who I imagine will just hang up the phone at the mention of your name."

"You've given this a lot of thought, Isaac. I imagine it's a story where you once played the lead role."

With the fading smile still warm on Isaac's cheeks, he let the coughing fit play out. The stabs in his heart were sharper, but they no longer carried the fear of death. It was a matter of time.

He continued his story, letting Carter's words roll away into nothing.

"So, having found no-one to arrange a funeral, you'd be slung in a wooden box. And make no bones about it, Bobby, it won't be a coffin. It'll be a box that the apprentice threw together in his lunch break. Chipboard or plywood or something cheap. There won't be any brass handles, Bobby. Oh, no. There'll be a few handholds cut out with a jigsaw, so they can shift you around. There'll be a little clipboard attached to your box and each time you pass from the coroner to guard and from guard to cremator, whoever receives it will have to sign for you. Probably while they have a chat and a smoke. I imagine some young guard and some underpaid driver standing at the back of the van, leaning on your wooden overcoat like it was a bar with pints in their hands, chatting about the football or the weather or some bird one of them met the weekend before. And then, eventually, they'd drag you out of the van, dump you in a puddle on the ground and sign the clipboard. The guard will then whistle for the forklift driver to come and pick you up and, in turn, he'd dump you on a conveyor belt. The chief cremator would look at the form on your clipboard, detach it from the box, then hit the big green button. There'll be no crying relatives. No sombre poems read by your mother, father, and definitely not your brother. Do you see what I'm saying, Bobby? That fire will destroy any evidence you ever existed. Because you're scum. Society's outcast. The lowest of the low. And the sooner you get that into your ugly fat head, the better the world will be."

"Enough, Isaac. You'll give yourself a heart attack."

"I'm dying, Bobby. Let the boy go. Then go and do something useful with your life while you still can. Don't be like me."

"Be like you?" Carter laughed. "I'll never be like you, Isaac. That story you just told, as touching as it was, was just the imaginings of a man who came close. A man who could have had it all, but let the love of family betray his success."

Carter shook his head, animating his the words that followed.

"But not me, Isaac. Oh, no. You see, there's only one person in this world I care about, and he's standing right in front of you. There'll be no matters of the heart or battles of loyalty that will send me down. And that, old man, is where you and I differ. That is why I'm standing here, free as a bird, and you're sitting there with the hand of death on your shoulder."

"You always were a callous bastard, Bobby."

"Callous is a bit strong, Isaac. I prefer determined."

Carter hoisted Jake onto his arm, walked to the empty space where the balcony would be, and sat the boy on the steel tube.

"What are you doing, Bobby?"

"You see that out there?" said Carter to the boy. He swept his hand across a mass of flattened houses and construction. "That's all mine. One day, in a year or two, all that will be luxurious apartments. A place where thousands of people will call their home. And they'll be grateful for it. They'd be happy that someone like me decided to build these homes. Do you see, Jake?"

The boy nodded and clung to Carter's jacket.

"And to build something like this takes a lot of money, Jake. More money than most people can ever dream of."

"Are you rich?" asked Jake. His voice was high with the impressionable tones of naivety.

"Well, I am, Jake. But I'm not rich enough to build all this. No-one is really."

"So how can you build all this?" the boy asked.

Each word the boy spoke seemed to fuel Carter's ego. Clearly, he'd been waiting for the day he could brag about his success and be listened to with enthusiasm.

"Well, Jake, this is the lesson I'm working towards. You see, in life, there are winners and losers. Some men are born to lose and some men are born to win."

"Like football?"

"Exactly. You're a smart kid. Now, you see that man there? The man who said he was your granddad?"

Jake looked back at Isaac and nodded. There was no compassion in his eyes. No love or hate. Just indifference.

"Well, he was born to lose. He's a born loser, right?"

Jake nodded, following Carter's story.

"And well, look at me. I dress smart, don't I?"

Another nod.

"And I'm successful, Jake. I'm one of life's winners. And out there are other winners, who believe in me so much that they've invested all their money into my little project. They know I'm a winner. They know that I'll make them winners too. Do you see?"

"Kind of."

"So what do you want to be when you're older? A loser like him?" He gestured at Isaac. "Or a winner like me?"

"A winner," said Jake.

"A winner, eh? Are you listening, Isaac?"

There was no need for Isaac to respond. All he could do is sit and watch the man that he'd created destroy his own family.

"You want to be a winner, do you, Jake?" said Carter. His steely eyes peered past Jake and seemed to penetrate Isaac. Carter grinned.

The boy nodded once more.

"Just like me?"

"Just like you."

CHAPTER FORTY-FOUR

HALF EXPECTING TO SEE FRANKIE, NIGEL AND DEBBIE SCREECH to a halt beside her in the smashed up Range Rover, Penelope was caught off-guard when the silver SUV cruised around the corner and drew up to the side of the road with the unhurried manner of a mother collecting a child from school. The passenger door opened to reveal an empty front seat, but through the rear window, a single bare foot pressed on the glass. Penelope peered into the back to find Nigel holding Debbie still with one arm, and with his other hand over her mouth to stop her screaming.

"Get in," said Frankie. But Penelope was fixed by the wide, frightened eyes of Debbie Carter who lay across the back seat wrestling with Nigel. She fell still when she saw Penelope.

"Now, Penelope," said Frankie. "Let's go."

Seeing no other option, Penelope climbed in and closed the door, then snapped around to face Frankie.

"You said you wouldn't hurt her," she hissed.

"We're not hurting her, Penelope," said Nigel. "We just need to get her away from here and fast."

The growing wail of police sirens drew closer. Frankie pulled away as casually as he had parked. He kept to the speed limit, indicated, then turned and joined the traffic heading away from London. It was only when Debbie Carter began to panic again, and struggle against Nigel's iron grip, that Frankie addressed everyone in the car. He spoke with the calm professionalism of a man who had kidnapped before. His words carried an unseen power that held everyone's attention. But above all, thought Penelope, he spoke with conviction and authority.

"Penelope, I understand you've met Debbie Carter?"

"Yes, I told you I have."

"And you can confirm that the woman in the rear seat is indeed Debbie Carter, wife of Bobby Carter?"

"Yes, you know all this."

With casual indifference to Penelope's words, Frankie leaned over, checked his side mirror, then changed lanes to join the three-lane A-road that would lead them back to the Essex countryside.

"Debbie Carter," said Frankie, making it clear that he was addressing the prisoner.

Nigel released his hand and let her sit up straight.

"What do you want with me?" she said, and wiped the mouth with the back of her hand, offering Nigel a disgusted look.

"It's not what *we* want with *you*, Mrs Carter. It's what *you* want from *us*."

"I don't get it. What do you mean?"

"You came to Miss Pike here and asked for her help. Am I right?"

"Yeah, that's right. I asked for help, not to be put in the middle of a gunfight and then dragged out and kidnapped."

"That's a quiet street, where you live."

"Yeah, it's nice."

"People like it that way?"

"I guess."

"Do you think many of them will talk to the police?"

"I doubt they will. Most of them have too much to hide."

"But some will?" asked Frankie.

Debbie nodded, thinking of a few individuals with nothing better to do than to get involved in other people's business. Every street has people like that, figured Penelope.

"Yeah, probably."

"And what do you think they'll say?"

"What will they say? Have you lost your mind? You just drove a bloody car into my house and let rip with a machine gun. What do you think they'll bloody say?"

"And then what did I do?" asked Frankie. "Once I'd driven into your house and let rip with a machine gun?"

"You dragged me out, threw me in the car, and left."

"So what conclusion will the police come to? The house of a rich man is stormed by two men. A few gunshots later and the wife is dragged out and thrown into a car."

Realisation dawned on Debbie that she was now free. But her panicked breaths still relayed the need for confirmation.

"Penelope, can you please explain that we are *not* the bad guys?"

"It's okay, Debbie. You're out now," said Penelope. She reached into the back seat for Debbie's hand.

"I don't believe it," Debbie replied. "You could have warned me or something."

"If we'd have told you we were coming, you might have given the game away. It was better this way."

"But my things, I haven't had time to-"

"We can arrange for your belongings to be sent later, Mrs Carter," said Nigel.

"So where are you taking me?"

Cool as can be, Frankie indicated, cut through the traffic and pulled the car to a stop in a lay-by on the side of the busy road. He put the car in park and turned to face the rear seat.

"Mrs Carter, there's something you need to know. So I need you to listen very carefully, okay?"

"Okay," she said. Her eyes flicked between the three of them and the door.

"Before you get any ideas, the door is locked, and Nigel here is faster than any of us."

Debbie seemed to relax a little, knowing that trying to escape would be futile.

"This is not a one-way transaction, Mrs Carter."

"Not a what?" she said, screwing her face up.

"This isn't entirely about getting you out of an abusive relationship."

"So what is it then? Penelope? What is this?" She edged into the corner of the seat and tried the door handle anyway, only to find it was indeed locked.

"Calm down, Mrs Carter. I need you to be calm," said Frankie. "Are you calm?"

Debbie peered around the car again. Then nodded once.

"Okay," continued Frankie. "I need your help with something. So you can make this hard on yourself, or you can make it easy. But either way, in return for me getting you out of there, you're going to help me get my son back."

CHAPTER FORTY-FIVE

"It's there," said Debbie. "The two towers at the end of the road."

The towers Debbie was referring to were unfinished apartment blocks at the end of a long road that a hundred years before would have been lined with dockside warehouses. The warehouses had long since given way to post-war housing, and now one side of the road was completely demolished to make way for the new apartment blocks. It left a sorry-looking row of houses on the opposite side of the road still standing. Most had been abandoned and were either boarded up or wide open, providing temporary homes for the homeless or a place for the junkies to get out of the rain and get their fix. The rows of doomed houses sat in the shadow of the huge towers like ranks of subordinate infantrymen beside an army of tanks.

"Does he have an office here?" asked Nigel. "The place looks deserted."

"The project was going under up until six months ago."

"And your husband took over a dying project? He's a brave man. Why was it going under?"

"Cash flow," replied Debbie. "The investors were pulling out."

"Pulling out or being pushed out?" said Frankie. "Let me guess, your husband happened to be in the right place at the right time with a bunch of new investors?"

"Something like that," said Debbie. "He wanted the development. He got the development. That's the way it works with Bobby."

"So he has an office here?" asked Nigel.

"No, he just likes to come here. Work starts in a few weeks as far as I can tell from overhearing his phone calls."

"So it's an empty construction site?" said Nigel.

"It's the perfect place to make some noise, and lose a few bodies if he needs to," said Frankie.

"What are you going to do?" asked Debbie. "How will you find him?"

Frankie let the question settle while his mind formulated an answer. He pulled the car to a stop before the entrance to the site. Wooden boarding fenced off the area to his left and right. In front of him was a large iron gate that had been left open. To the left was the smaller of the buildings, perhaps twenty to thirty floors, with a Mercedes van parked in a small dry car park. Two-hundred yards into the site, the taller of the two towers loomed above. An old bright yellow bulldozer sat waiting at the entrance. To the right of both buildings, a steep bank led down to the River Thames.

"Do you see that Nigel?" said Frankie, gesturing at the taller of the buildings.

"I do," replied Nigel. "Are you thinking what I'm thinking?"

"If you owned all this. Where would you go?"

"To the top. The view must be incredible."

"He does go there," said Debbie. "I remember him saying about the views, and how the penthouse apartments will have balconies and en-suite bathrooms."

"So how do we get up there without him seeing us?" asked Penelope.

"First of all, Penelope, you don't get up there at all." Frankie caught her eye in a sideways glance and gave her a look to soften the harshness of his words. "It's going to be dangerous."

"So you leave the weak and feeble girls here?" replied Penelope. "Is that it?"

Frankie turned in his seat to face her, and so that he could see Debbie.

"I've got a plan, but I need to say something..." All three passengers waited to hear his idea. "I'll be going in alone," continued Frankie. "He wants me. I want Jake."

"But what about-" Penelope began to protest.

Frankie cut her off with a glare, then shifted his gaze to Nigel.

"Here's what we're going to do."

CHAPTER FORTY-SIX

"Your dad is a brave man," said Carter to Jake. "Do you see him down there?"

"Is that my dad?" said Jake, his voice high with excitement. He sucked in a breath of air, preparing to call down to his father. But Carter foresaw it and slipped his hand across the boy's mouth to stifle his shout.

"No you don't," said Carter. He pulled Jake from the scaffold and set him down on the floor, flicking a nod to the man who stood behind Isaac's chair. The goon stepped forward, placed a hand on Jake's shoulder and steered him through to another room.

When the boy was out of sight, Carter turned his attention back to Isaac.

"I hope you're ready for this, Isaac. I've waited a long time to see you die."

"So just kill me. Let the boy go and be done with it."

Carter laughed. It was as if he'd practised his cruel, mocking cackle before a mirror, as an actor might rehearse a line.

"Too easy," he said. "Too quick."

A numbness had spread across Isaac's chest. Like a weed

might consume a garden flower, the loss of feeling advanced into the very core of his limbs with ferocious speed.

"I'm dying anyway. I keep telling you."

"You just hang in there, Isaac. You might just get to see your son again. You do want to say goodbye, don't you?"

A sudden cough was the only response Isaac could muster. A drool of bloodied spit ran across his chin and he leaned back trying to control the harrowing, short, sharp breaths that were growing shorter with each minute as blood seeped into his lungs. With nothing but the occasional whistle of wind through the open doorways and the clatter of chains that hung from the dormant cranes outside, Isaac's racing pulse fired dull, irregular beats that filled the audible void.

Isaac closed his eyes to block the stain of Bobby Carter from his mind's eye. Instead, he allowed the memories of his past to play one final time. The joy of Frankie being born. His wedding to Frankie's mother. Amid the reel of his past, a scene on a beach in Cornwall kept finding its way to the front. He'd done a job in South London and had taken the family away for a holiday in St Ives in Cornwall. For some reason, Frankie's mother was missing from the memory, but Frankie was young and carefree. He hadn't yet developed the serious frown that had carved permanent lines into his forehead, which the army had given him.

Isaac lifted Frankie from the sea, tossing him high into the air. Sometimes, the boy would spin into a somersault. Sometimes, he would curl into a ball and then splash back into the water, only to emerge a few seconds later erupting in wild laughter with seawater streaming from his nose.

That was the Frankie he would choose to remember. The boy had been fearless. Calculated, not careless. But once he set his mind on something, nothing would stop him. It was a trait Isaac had admired so much in Bobby and Billy. But the Carter brothers had that something else that Frankie's sense of right and wrong wouldn't bend to. There was no limit to what the boys wouldn't do to get what they wanted.

An all-embracing sense of betrayal swept through Isaac as Frankie's smiling face faded to accommodate the evil stares of two young boys who would do anything to rise through the ranks.

"I remember the first job you did for me," said Isaac. His eyes remained closed. "Your first real job."

Although Carter offered no response, Isaac felt him close by. The sweet smell of his expensive aftershave was unmistakable.

"I remember the look in your eye when you shot that man. You were so calm. So unmovable. And that you did it to protect me, well, actions speak louder than words, Bobby. Right there and then, I knew you'd do well."

"It's a bit late to blow smoke up my arse, Isaac." His voice came from beside Isaac, precisely where he felt him standing. Isaac kept his eyes closed and continued to enjoy his memories.

"You handled it well, your first job, Bobby. Yeah, you did well. I half expected you to be a little over-enthusiastic and shoot someone unnecessarily. But you didn't. You kept your cool. A lot of the men admired you, you know? They respected the way you carried yourself, and Billy too, of course. Both of you. But Billy was a little wider, less controlled."

"You don't mention his name, Isaac. You don't even think his name."

"Who? Billy? Behave, Bobby. I haven't served all those years inside to come out and be worried about Billy's name. I paid my penance."

"Not yet you haven't."

"I paid my penance with the law, I repaid my debt to society, and in the eyes of God, I'm a free man, Bobby."

The sweet scent of Bobby's aftershave was strong in Isaac's hampered breaths. His face was close, inches perhaps. But Isaac refused to open his eyes.

"Forget about the law, Isaac, and society. Even God. They've got nothing on me. And it's me you need to concern yourself with right now. It's me you owe. And it's me you'll pay. I'm going to break you into tiny pieces and parade around with your head on a stick, and anyone who's anyone will know that Isaac Black didn't get away with it after all. Bobby Carter got him. Bobby Carter was the one to take him down, the almighty Isaac Black."

A faint wash of air suggested that Bobby had stood. A single exhale in disgust confirmed it.

"You're nobody, Isaac, and the whole world is going to see how weak you were."

Isaac smiled and held his breath waiting for death to take him. But then a voice cut through the tension. It was familiar and full of the strength that Isaac had always admired.

"Not if I have anything to do with it, Carter."

CHAPTER FORTY-SEVEN

Armed with just his Sig, aimed at Carter's forehead, Frankie stood with his feet shoulder-width apart, his finger on the trigger, and his breathing calm and controlled.

"The legendary Frankie Black," said Carter. "You don't mind if I call you that, do you?"

"It doesn't matter what you call me. You're going to die anyway."

Carter feigned a saddened expression, but couldn't retain the grin that emerged, crinkling his face and deepening the lines around his eyes.

"So you found me," said Carter. "I knew you would. It is, after all, your forte. Finding people. Am I right?"

"We all have different skills, Carter. I'm struggling to see what yours are though if I'm honest."

"And being that you're so good at finding people," said Carter, ignoring Frankie's jibe, "it makes you quite difficult to find. Am I right?"

"Did you ever find me?"

"Did I ever look?" Carter returned as if a battle of words and wit would gain the upper hand.

"Where's Jake?"

"He's safe."

"I've come for him. Bring him here."

"Haven't you come to collect your daddy?" asked Carter. "After so many years, I imagine you two have a lot of catching up to do."

"Bring me my son, Carter."

But Carter, not fazed in the slightest by the gun that was aimed at his head, began to pace the room. He walked slowly with his hands behind his back in an open invitation to shoot him. Carter stopped at a gap in the wall where a balcony might one day be. But as a temporary safety measure, a scaffold tube ran across it. The way Carter stood and peered out across London reminded Frankie of a movie where a king surveyed his land from the walls of his castle.

"It doesn't work like that, Frankie. I would have thought you'd be a little more intelligent than that."

"I'm the one with the gun. It works how I say it works."

"But I'm the one with your boy, Frankie. And if you shoot me, who is going to give the order to release him?"

"Have you brought me here for a game, Bobby? I don't have time for games. Show me he's alive."

"Oh, he's alive, Frankie. He's alive and kicking. We had a nice little chat, Jake and me."

"Is that right?"

"He's a smart boy. He wants to be a winner."

"Just get him."

"He wants to be like me, Frankie. Can you imagine that? Your little boy following in the footsteps of your old man. It has a certain cyclical feel, doesn't it?"

"Just get him."

"A friend of mine is looking after him, but I gave instructions not to hurt the boy," said Carter. "Unless, of course, you try anything stupid."

"You've got everything you asked for. Just hand him over."

"There is one more thing that would please me, Frankie. It's a little thing. A matter of honour really. But it would mean a lot to me."

Unwilling to satisfy Carter's appetite for power and control, Frankie remained silent and re-aimed his gun.

"Get Jake here now."

"Harry?" called Carter.

"Yes, boss." The response from somewhere in the bare concrete apartment, behind the block walls.

"Bring me the boy." Carter then quietened and spoke directly to Frankie. "You want to see your boy? You want your family back? You've got two options, which is damn well more than your father gave me and my family."

Over Carter's shoulder, with his head hung low, Jake appeared from the back room. There were two goons behind him, each with a hand on Jake's shoulders.

"Jake?" said Frankie. "Jake, I'm here. It's dad."

Jake's face erupted into a smile. But as the boy started to run, Harry held him back by the collar until the momentum was lost, and Jake fell back into the man's legs.

"Dad," cried Jake. "Dad, where were you?"

"That's far enough," said Carter.

His smile grew even wider. He stepped closer to Frankie, staring into his eyes, and stopped with the barrel of the gun touching his forehead. Then, with a single outstretched finger, Carter redirected the weapon to point at Isaac, all the while holding Frankie's gaze.

"Now," he continued, content that his plan was in play. "As I said, Frankie, you've got two options." He clicked his fingers in the air. "Harry, show him we mean business."

The larger of the goons scooped Jake up with ease and raised him above the single scaffold tube. He held him out over forty floors of nothing.

"Dad," Jake cried again. His voice pierced the air, bouncing from the hard, concrete walls. He began to cry.

"Carter, get him down. Now."

"Two options, Frankie. No compromise."

Frankie made a start towards the balcony, but the goon held Jake out further. His weight was nothing for the huge man to hold.

"Two options, Frankie. One of them dies, and you get to choose who."

"Okay, okay," said Frankie. "Whatever you want. But bring him inside."

"Son, it's okay. You don't have to worry," said Isaac.

"Shut up, Dad," said Frankie, cutting his father off above the petrified squeals of his son. He raised the gun once more. "Bring him in, Carter, and I'll do it."

"Dad," called Jake.

"I'm coming, Jake. It's okay. You're not going to fall," said Frankie. Then, quieter and below Jake's shrill screams, he hissed at Carter, "Get him in, and I'll do it." He placed the gun to Isaac's temple.

A loud and shrill whistle from Carter's pursed lips was all it took for Harry the goon to bring Jake back in. But he held the boy tight, three feet from the ground, ready to throw him on Carter's command. He nodded at the other goon who stood behind Frankie and pressed the muzzle of a handgun into the back of Frankie's head.

"What will it be, Frankie?" said Carter. His cruel tone echoed off the bare concrete apartment walls and seemed to Frankie, that it would echo for eternity. "It's time to decide who dies."

The handgun was heavy in Frankie's hand and burdensome on his heart.

Despite the lies, the deceit, and that the man who was sitting in the chair besides where he stood was nothing but an old criminal, full of evil greed, and hatred, still, deep inside, Frankie felt the blood connection and the lost time.

The regret.

The muzzle of his own gun touched his father's temple.

A dizzying haze of emotions, memories, and bitterness sang through his mind in a swirl of anger, tears, and love. One day the apartment would have smooth plastered walls painted white, expensive wooden floors and soft furnishing that made the place a home. Frankie imagined the owners toasting themselves with fine wine on the balcony, looking down at the River Thames as if they'd just bought a slice of heaven.

For Frankie, it was anything but heaven. It was just a dusty, concrete shell and the next time his feet touched the earth, his world would be a very different place.

"Do it now," Carter shouted. His voice was deep and commanding above the high-pitched squeals and cries of Frankie's son. "Do it now or the boy dies."

"Dad," cried Jake from the shadows. "Dad, he's hurting me."

The boy's plea for help was cut short with a whimper.

At the sound of his son's anguished cries, Frankie exhaled as if he'd taken a blow to his gut. Then he sucked a deep breath of warm stale air. He panted as if it were the first breath he'd ever taken, or maybe the last he'd ever take. Heavy footsteps rumbled in the shadows at the edge of his blurred vision. Carter approached, dragging Jake by the scruff of his neck. The boy's feet scrambled for purchase on the bare, concrete floor. Frankie startled, blinked away the tears, then turned to face Carter as the man raised his son into the air and held him with one hand over two-hundred metres of nothing but biting cold air.

"All you have to do is pull the trigger," said Carter. His voice boomed like a drum in the empty space.

A wave of pressure pulsed through Frankie. He hung his head, and let his eyes refocus on the bare and broken feet of his father who sat, stripped to the waist, on a small wooden chair beside him, with his arms bound and with a smear of dark red blood across his torso. Angry blue bruises lay beneath the blood from the brutal beatings the men had delivered.

Frankie met his father's eyes, but the man who had raised him cast his head down, shame weighing heavily on his mind.

"I'm sorry, Dad," he said, his voice thick with emotion.

"Don't be sorry, Son," came his father's broken reply. He raised his head to meet Frankie's sorrowful stare. "It's your turn for life now. So live." A sudden passion grew in his tone, unfamiliar yet endearing. It would be the last words Frankie heard from his father, they had to count. "Just promise me you won't make the same mistakes I did. Be there for Jake. Watch him grow. Be a father, Frankie. Be a better father than I ever was."

"But, Dad–"

"Don't," said his father. "Just don't say it."

A silence fell, thick and impenetrable like being lost in a fog.

Jake struggled. Carter tightened his grip, holding him further out above the drop. The biting wind seemed to suck at Jake's hair and clothes. The rain that fell in sheets washed away his tears. But that face, that tortured expression could never be washed away. He stared at his father with hope, and with fright; his eyes pleading for help.

"Pull the trigger, Son," Frankie's father whispered. "Pull the trigger and start over."

"This is all most touching," said Carter. "You've said your goodbyes. Now get on with it."

Through the haze of Frankie's muddled mind, he held Jake's eyes. Carter's fat hands held the boy tight.

"Don't look, Jake," called Frankie. "Close your eyes."

Frankie raised the gun once more and returned his gaze to his father.

"I love you, Dad."

His father tore his eyes away ashamed of the tears that ran free. His face contorted as he fought the battle inside him to remain strong for his son, and grandson. The choices he had made so long ago had finally come full circle.

"I love you too, Son," he croaked.

"Finish him," Carter screamed.

"On three, Dad," said Frankie and he raised his left hand, extending three fingers.

His father closed his eyes, braced himself and nodded once in confirmation.

"Three," said Frankie. His voice wavered.

His father's head rocked forward once as if counting along in silence.

"Two."

His father took a deep breath through his nose, leaned his head back and, for the briefest of seconds, seemed at peace with the world. Frankie withdrew a single digit.

"One."

CHAPTER FORTY-EIGHT

THE SOUND OF THE BULLET PIERCING A SKULL WAS PERCUSSIVE. A spray of warm blood cast a red hue over the scene. But instead of feeling the split second of agonising pain as the bullet tore open his skull, Isaac's consciousness remained.

Is this death? He thought. *Is death painless?*

During the few moments of bliss that Isaac enjoyed, where even the claws of the demon in his heart subsided and peace fell upon him, he felt as if his journey to heaven had begun.

But around him, all hell had broken loose. Isaac's odyssey was cut short by the short, sharp blasts of Frankie's gun.

The man behind Frankie slumped to the floor.

A second shot found Harry's arm and knocked him to the ground. Jake rolled free and searched for his father.

"Run, Jake. Run," cried Frankie. He fired his gun empty at Carter, who was hot on Jake's heels.

Harry the goon was stumbling to his feet clutching his arm. He swung a wild punch and as Frankie sprinted after Carter, he connected with Frankie's jaw, sending him reeling to the floor.

Harry loomed high above him and reached down to grab hold of Frankie's collar. Then, with the force of a sledgehammer, Harry slammed backwards. A spurt of red blood burst from his shoulder and the big man stumbled and fell.

Seizing the reprise in the attack, Frankie jumped to his feet.

"Delta-two. Copy?" said Frankie, with his finger to his ear. He stepped over to where Harry lay still on the hard, concrete floor.

The turbulent events had woken Isaac's demon. But instead of the sharp stabs of pain that had felt as if they penetrated the flesh his heart, the demon dozed from a state of quiescence and ran its sharp talons across the surface of Isaac's erratic heart. A reminder of its presence. A cool sweat formed once more across Isaac's brow. The heat inside him felt as if the demon was dragging him closer to the fires of hell.

Whoever Frankie was talking to must have replied because Frankie stared through the opening and began to gesture to the ground level. Isaac stared at him with the love of a father and admired everything his son had become. For everything that Isaac wasn't, somehow something good had come from him.

"Delta-two, this is Delta-one," said Frankie. "The target is moving." He listened for a response, then dropped the formalities. "Keep your eyes out for Jake. Nigel. He's on his own."

Frankie gave the thumbs up to the sniper, then turned to face Isaac.

"Dad, I have to go after Jake. I'll come back for you," said Frankie. And for the first time in as long as Isaac could remember, there was compassion in his voice. He untied the ropes that bound Isaac to the chair. Though free from his bindings, Isaac still lacked the control over his arms; they were numb and cold.

"You go," said Isaac. "I'm done here anyway."

"Dad?"

"I'm dying, son. I can feel it."

"No, Dad. Wait. Hang on. At least try. You owe me that much."

But the demon heard Frankie's plea and thrust the first of his talons into Isaac's heart.

Each breath grew shorter. Each exhale grew weaker.

"Dad?" It was Frankie's voice, somewhere far off.

Give me one last look at him, thought Isaac. The message was aimed at his demon. *Please, let me see him one last time.*

But something held his eyes closed. The same foreign being that had hijacked his limbs now held his face in contortion.

"One last time," said Isaac out loud. "You can't take that from me."

In response, the demon dug harder and deeper than ever before. He coughed and a spray of pink shot from Isaac's mouth. But Isaac held fast and whether, by sheer will or fortune, his eyes opened wide, offering him one last glance at the world and his son.

The scene that greeted Isaac induced yet another stab of pain.

Frankie leaned over him, his face was worried but calm.

And a figure rose from behind him.

Isaac tried to speak but no words came.

Harry the goon had managed to stand and although the wounded man hobbled in pain, his determination was clear. He reached down and grabbed Frankie by his throat, wrenching him back. Frankie fought back, but his blows found only solid muscle with little reaction.

Harry slammed Frankie face-first against the wall out of the line of the sniper's fire. He hit him twice in the kidneys, then dragged him to the floor. He raised his leg and stamped down on Frankie's head.

Frankie rolled just in time. He got to his hands and knees and spat, staring up at Harry with bitter hatred. He glanced at the exit then back at Harry.

Harry moved to stand opposite Frankie, blocking his escape to catch up with Carter. Frankie rose to his feet and sized the man up.

And the battle commenced.

Each man held a defensive stance. The much smaller Frankie

stood his ground, blocking punch after punch but the force behind each attack powered through Frankie's defences. When the goon paused for breath, Frankie seized his chance and delivered a series of blows, perfectly timed and placed, but with insufficient power to knock the much broader and taller Harry to the floor.

Calling on every morsel of energy he had, Isaac pushed himself to his feet. His legs trembled beneath his weight. He held onto the chair for balance as his son fought for his life.

But it was too much. Isaac crashed back onto the old wooden chair.

Frankie connected with a hook and stunned Harry enough for a series of follow up jabs to the big man's throat, the last of which had him doubled him over gasping for breath through his crushed windpipe. Harry stumbled and swayed as Frankie, tenacious in his efforts, delivered blow after relentless blow, sending Harry closer and closer to the balcony.

But, with a sudden fight for life and a burst of immense energy, Harry lashed out with the back of his hand, catching Frankie off-guard. Frankie staggered back and fell to the floor and watched as Harry then gripped the scaffold tube that was bolted to the wall with heavy steel clamps. With all his weight, the huge man wrenched one end from the wall.

Seeing the new weapon being brought into play, Isaac tried to scream out. But his feeble lungs were fighting their own battle and his heart was being crushed by the fierce claws of that demon.

Dazed and groggy, Frankie rolled to his knees as Harry wrenched the final bolts from the wall and wielded the three-meter scaffold tube in both hands.

Once more, Isaac summoned the strength to stand. With one leg out straight and the other bent to take his weight, he filled the remains of his lungs and pushed.

The first swing of the scaffold tube fell short of Frankie's face by mere inches but sent him owling away. He scrambled to his feet as the second swing began and he ducked in time for the breeze to brush past his hair.

Then Frankie stood and squared up to the big man. Isaac had never been so proud to call him his son.

He lunged at Harry, but the big man was ready. He jabbed with the pole then lined up for the third swing of the steel pole. It connected with Frankie's gut with a loud, dull, sickening thud.

Isaac straightened his second leg and held fast to the back of the chair. He raised his head slowly, feeling the blood drain from his face as the spinning began.

Harry's next swing was wild and short. The momentum carried the tube far to his side leaving enough room for Frankie to charge at him. There were no punches thrown. No feet kicked out. Just Frankie's shoulder connecting hard and deep into the goon's gut and his strong legs powering them both towards the balcony.

It took a few seconds for the big man to realise what Frankie was doing. As the edge of the building drew closer, Harry pulled the tube horizontal, catching the wall on both sides and bringing the surge to a stop. He responded by slamming his forehead into Frankie's nose and delivering a kick to his side. But Frankie was fast. He saw the move and caught the huge thick leg in the crook of his arm. Then, with lightning speed, Frankie delivered a hard kick of his own into the goons knee.

A loud crack shattered the space, and Harry dropped to the ground. But there was no sign of pain on his face. Instead, Harry spun the tube and jabbed at Frankie's mid-rift. Frankie blocked the first jab, but the second connected, and Frankie doubled over to his knees.

Isaac pushed from the safety of the chair, held his hand to his chest as if it might somehow alleviate the steely grip of the demon. He took a cautious, shaky step towards Harry.

Frankie began his final charge.

The goon dropped to his knee. He raised the tube above his head and readied himself to deliver the final blow.

Isaac pushed from the wall that steadied him and grabbed hold of the tube with all his remaining strength. He felt the pull as Harry tried to swing with both arms, but Isaac's weight was too great for the man to swing above his head.

Frankie delivered a blow to Harry's face, followed by two more. Harry staggered back to move away from Frankie, but Frankie didn't let up. He gripped the man by his throat forcing him back to the void. The two men were locked in a battle of strength and will to live as they edged closer to the drop.

"Dad, get out of here," said Frankie.

But there was only one way out for Isaac Black.

Frankie watched him stagger closer to the fight, but his momentary lapse of concentration was all Harry needed. The big man hit out hard and sent Isaac to the floor. Frankie reacted but it was too late. He dragged Frankie to the floor by his throat and pulled him across the concrete until his short hair blew in the wind.

Isaac spat blood.

Every bone in his tired body ached. Every muscle moaned, and every memory stung like wildfire.

Harry stood over his son and beyond him was a wonderful city that had been Isaac's birthplace, his playground and his prison.

Harry dragged Frankie further out over the ledge so that his head hung clear of the concrete.

"Frankie," called Isaac, but no sound came.

"Frankie," he called again, as he rolled to his knees. He clawed his way across the concrete floor like the demon inside him that clawed his way through his body. He dug his fingers into the rough floor. He dragged his body on with only hate and love fuelling every dying movement.

Until he reached them and he stood.

"Frankie," he called, and he heard his own words, though it was no longer his own voice.

"Get out, dad," said Frankie.

Isaac collected the scaffold tube from the ground and held it the way a man might rely on a cane.

"I'm sorry, son," he said, and he edged closer.

Harry pulled Frankie further and until Frankie's hands gripping the concrete wall were all that stopped him falling.

"I love you, son," said Isaac. "And he let the demon inside him, feast."

CHAPTER FORTY-NINE

THE URGE TO JUST TURN THE CAR AROUND AND LEAVE WAS strong. This was serious. In my Penelope's mind, the situation had gone from bad to worse.

Someone was going to die.

In contrast to her instincts, she had a mind to call in the media team to capture the events. It would be the scoop of the year for her. But, there were moral elements to it. Jake's life was at stake, and Frankie's too. Frankie's huge shift in persona, along with how he had taken on the Carter house, had instilled in Penelope an unwavering confidence in his abilities. But it also raised new doubts.

She reached out a finger and hit the auto-lock button on the dashboard. The car doors all locked in unison in a synchronised series of reassuring thuds.

There was another thud. It wasn't the sound of a door locking, but Penelope remembered it well.

It was a rifle shot.

She found Debbie wide-eyed in the rear-view mirror.

"How long have you known Frankie?" asked Debbie.

Craning her neck to see the smaller of the two buildings, she spotted Nigel on the top floor. He was positioned on the roof with his rifle peering over the side of the building. But who he was shooting at, Penelope couldn't be sure.

"Long enough," she replied.

"He seems like a good man," said Debbie. A sadness in her voice conveyed her disappointment in her own choice of husband.

Then a flash of colour caught Penelope's eye. There was movement on the top floor of the taller building. She followed Nigel's aim, tracing it across the expanse of air to a large opening on the top floor of the opposite building.

"What was that?" she said. "There, at the top of the big building."

She heard Debbie shift in the back seat.

"I can't see anything."

"This is so frustrating," said Penelope. "I can't wait here like this." Her hand poised above the door handle.

"No," shouted Debbie. "Don't leave me here."

Then, two more rifle shots thundered in the air and echoed off the empty buildings.

Penelope moved her hand away from the door handle.

More guns burst into life. They were single shots and lighter in sound. The construction site became an audible war zone, with the cracks of gunfire loud in the valley of concrete and mud. For Penelope, sitting in the car away from all the danger wasn't so terrible. But the not knowing what was happening invoked tremendous anxiety.

The firing stopped as suddenly as it had begun.

"Do you think Frankie is okay?" asked Penelope.

She glanced up at Nigel, who was now aiming his rifle at the ground, sweeping across the entrance to the taller building. The sound of gunfire ceased, leaving an eerie sense of foreboding. Penelope shifted across to the driver's side and adjusted the seat. The engine was running, but it had been years since she had driven a car, always preferring to ride her little motorcycle through the city traffic.

"Look," said Debbie, and she pointed from the back seat. "A boy. It must be Jake."

"It is," said Penelope.

Jake emerged from the stairwell and ran into the open area of mud.

Seconds later, a man appeared. He paused to catch his breath, then gave chase.

Both women gasped.

"That's not Frankie," said Penelope.

"That's Bobby," replied Debbie.

"So where is Frankie?" said Penelope and of the first time heard the fear in her own voice.

Images of Frankie laying on a cold concrete floor, bleeding to death, ran through her mind.

"You don't know what's happened yet," said Debbie.

But without thinking, Penelope let her emotions run amok. She crunched the car into drive and slammed the throttle to the floor. The rear wheels spun, spraying mud into the air, the huge car bucked and twisted as it fought for grip in the sludge. But Penelope countered the steering, keeping the nose pointed at Jake. Carter was right behind him.

Penelope slammed her hand on the horn, guiding the car to one side of the little boy. He ran with everything he had. Tears streamed from his wide eyes. His mouth hung open in terror and his little arms and legs pumped like tiny pistons.

She tore past Jake, judging the turn, the momentum and the speed. Then she wrenched the wheel hard to the right.

"Look out," screamed Debbie, as Carter grew larger and closer in the windscreen.

There was no sickening crunch of bones. No gut-twisting feeling of dread or guilt. Just the sound of denting metal panels and shattering glass as Bobby Carter's body rolled up the bonnet of the car. His head shattered the windscreen, and he bounced over the car out of sight.

The car slewed in the slick mud and twisted from Penelope's control. It spun around one hundred and eighty degrees and then slammed into the side of a bright yellow bulldozer.

Jake stood frozen to the spot in the centre of the huge expanse of mud.

Penelope gripped the wheel with petrified hands. The shock sent her heart racing. A cool sweat formed on her body as the adrenaline worked through her veins.

Carter lay face down in the mud.

The rear door opened behind her, and Debbie rolled out.

Penelope tried her door, but the hard yellow frame of the dozer blocked it. She turned in her seat to see if Debbie was okay. But before she could speak, and with an ear-splitting crunch of bones, shattering glass and twisted steel, the car roof caved in. The windows shattered around her and the airbags fired harmlessly into life.

Penelope was trapped. The buckled roof hung so low it touched the steering wheel. The only refuge for Penelope was to squeeze through the gap into the passenger foot-well.

She peered through the gap in the wheel for Carter, for anybody. But all she saw was a thick trail of fresh blood trickle through the jagged criss-cross of glass in the shattered windscreen. Penelope tried the door handle, but the damage had wedged the door closed.

Twisting her body around, with her feet to the door, Penelope began to pound on the leather door trim with the heels of her feet. But it wouldn't budge.

Jake cried out for his dad somewhere nearby. She wanted to go to him. A maternal instinct inside her just wanted to hold him, but she was trapped.

Penelope kicked at the door again, frustrated and imprisoned.

But the movement rocked the car, and something shifted on the roof.

Was it Carter?

She froze and something above her settled.

There was a sliding sound. She cocked her head, trying to work out what the sound was. Then from the crushed roof above her, a hand slid into view.

She gasped and edged away as far as she could.

The arm followed and as more of the body teased into view, she waited for the face, praying it wasn't Frankie.

And then the deathly stare of Isaac Black slid into view.

CHAPTER FIFTY

No screams of anguished fury left Frankie's mouth. No tears of loss fell from his eyes. But as he lay on the cold, hard concrete staring down at his father's body, intertwined with Harry's twisted corpse on the roof of his SUV, he could feel only a harsh pang of resent.

Then Jake caught his eye. He was standing alone in the middle of the construction site. Frankie called down to him, but his voice wouldn't carry the distance. Instead, Jake looked lost and turned a full circle looking for someone to help him.

Carter's body lay face down in the mud just twenty-feet away.

By the time Frankie reached the ground floor, Jake had stopped in the centre of the track, scared to go forwards and scared to go back. Frankie burst from the building at full speed.

"Jake," he called.

His eyes filled as he ran, and streamed along the side of his face. Jake turned and saw him. His little face lit up. Jake raised his arms and, as Frankie reached him, he scooped the boy up, holding him tight to his body. He gazed down at Carter's unmoving body.

"I'm so sorry, Jake," he said quietly. "I'm so sorry."

Jake buried his face into his father's neck. Warm tears found their way down Frankie's chest.

"I love you, Jake. You know that right?" He pulled his son away to look at his face. The boy was red-faced with tears and fear, but he sniffed and nodded.

"Are you hurt?" asked Frankie. "Did they hurt you?"

Jake shook his head.

"Okay. Let's get you home," said Frankie. "You're going to sleep a thousand sleeps tonight."

Jake lay his head back on Frankie's shoulder and Frankie walked toward Nigel, who had smashed the window of the silver Mercedes van and was climbing into the driver's seat. Frankie sat Jake in the back, pulled the seat belt across, then climbed in beside him. He slid his arm around the boy and spoke to Nigel.

"Let's go get the girls, Nigel. Then get the hell out of here."

"Roger that," he replied, as he eased the van onto the slick, muddy track.

The tyres slipped and spun, but Nigel kept the accelerator hard down and spun the wheel from left to right, expertly seeking the higher and dryer spots of the track.

Frankie distracted Jake with promises of dinners in front of the TV and late nights. He was surprised at the boy's resilience. He'd been through a lot, and on the surface, at least, he appeared to have come out the other side unscathed. Just tired and ready for a bath and bed.

Nigel stopped the van beside the ruined SUV and gave the area a glance. He nodded at Frankie. Penelope's beaming face smiled helplessly at them from the window. She gestured that the door was stuck.

"Okay, Jake. I'm just going to be a moment, okay? I'm going to get Penelope," said Frankie, then leaned forward to whisper to Nigel. "Keep your eyes open. He could be anywhere."

A few moments later, Frankie was standing in the pouring rain at the side of SUV. Harry the goon's massive weight had crushed the roof down to the tops of the seats and the steering wheel. He tried the driver's door, but it was jammed. His fingers slipped from the wet handles and the door refused to budge. Rain dripped from Harry's bloodied body and had formed a pool of red in the dented roof, which spilt over the edge onto Frankie's hands.

Frankie forced himself not to look at his father. He leaned into the open rear door and reclined the front seat. He reached out a hand to Penelope and his father stared back at him through the shattered windscreen.

For a moment, Frankie was transfixed. A thousand memories flashed through across his mind in a blur of sunny beaches, family dinners and then the flash of the shotgun that had torn their family apart.

"Frankie?" called Penelope. "Frankie, help me."

He snapped to the memory of the judge's hammer that condemned his father to prison.

"Frankie?" she called again.

He reached out once more and helped Penelope squeeze through the gap. They fell to the mud together and for a moment they just laid there. Penelope wrapped her arms around Frankie's neck, and just as Jake had, she let her head fall onto his shoulder.

The rain continued to soak them both. He pulled her away and looked at her face, shiny and wet in the dark.

"Thank you," he whispered.

Her lower lip trembled. Then with surprising force, she pulled him tight and buried her face into him once more.

Nigel honked the van's horn.

"Come on," he said. "Let's get you into the van."

Moments later, she was stood at the sliding door. She smiled up at Jake.

"Hello, Jake," she said.

It was as if she was somehow asking his permission to enter the van. A few tense moments passed as Jake studied her face. Then he smiled back at her.

"Hello, Penelope," he said.

"Do you mind if I join you here in the back?"

Jake laughed. It was a beautiful laugh that crushed Frankie's heart.

"Of course, silly." Then he scooted across as far as his belt would allow.

Nigel, who had been silent until now, turned his head from Jake to the smashed driver's window where Frankie was standing.

"Where's the other one?" he asked.

"Other one?" Frankie replied.

Then he realised Debbie was missing.

"She was in the car with me," said Penelope. "But she got out when we crashed."

Frankie spun around, searching the rain for movement.

"Debbie?" he called.

"Frankie," said Nigel. His voice carried a warning tone.

"Debbie?" Frankie continued to shout.

"Frankie," said Nigel. This time, his voice was authoritative.

Frankie stopped and looked at him, then followed his gaze to the empty muddy track.

"Carter's gone."

CHAPTER FIFTY-ONE

THE FEW MOMENTS OF ELATION THE GROUP HAD SHARED AND the wonderful joy that Penelope had felt when Jake had invited her to sit beside him in the van, was sucked away in a heartbeat.

With one hand on the sliding door and one foot on the step, Frankie was clearly in two minds. Stay and find Debbie. Or get his family out of there.

"What do you think, Nigel?" asked Frankie, nearly shouting to be heard above the rain on the roof of the van.

"I think she's a big girl and you should get Jake somewhere safe," the red-headed man replied. "We'll come back for her. But let's get these two out of here first."

With reluctance, Frankie agreed and climbed in. He left the sliding door open and hung from the van, searching for Debbie as Nigel coaxed onto the muddy track. The window wipers were on full, and the powerful headlights lit the path ahead, leaving eerie darkness and shadows to each side. The engine roared as Nigel forced the big van through the thick mud. The tyres slipped and squirmed as Nigel carved a route from side to side, avoiding the deep tracks left by heavy machinery.

"Stop," shouted Frankie. He was peering into the darkness to one side of the track. "I thought I saw something."

Nigel eased the van to a stop at the next patch of high ground. Frankie stared into the darkness.

"Kill the motor," said Frankie, offering his ear to the outside, trying to place a sound.

The van shuddered to a stop, leaving the drumming rain on the roof to fill the empty space. But another sound was growing louder. A chugging rumble. Then a throaty roaring sound.

"Frankie?" What's that?" Penelope asked, and pulled Jake in close to her, searching through the windows all around, but seeing nothing.

"Move," shouted Frankie. "Go, go, go."

The van's engine roared to life, and Nigel pushed hard down on the accelerator, but the van didn't move. The tail end began to slide from side to side, slipping in the thick mud. Nigel fought for purchase, but the wheels sank lower and lower.

"Nigel, move," shouted Frankie.

"We're stuck, Frankie."

"Right. Everyone out," said Frankie and pulled open the sliding door. He jumped down into the mud and reached in to help Penelope and Jake.

But it was too late. From nowhere, two bright spotlights lit the side of the van, growing bigger like the bright eyes of a dragon; its roar growing louder every second.

"Too late," shouted, Nigel.

Just as Frankie pulled himself inside and put his arm across Penelope and Jake, the huge, steel blade of the bulldozer slammed into the side of the van. The force sent Frankie tumbling into the back of the seats. With one arm around Jake, Penelope held Jake tight, telling him everything was going to be okay.

But, deep down, she knew otherwise.

The van rocked as the bulldozer smashed into the side for a

second time. Nigel's head crashed into the door, knocking him out cold. His head rolled to one side.

"Hold on," shouted Frankie and he climbed to his feet to put his arms around Penelope and Jake.

The noise of the big diesel engine was deafening. The van was being forced sideways.

"We're going over," called Frankie, as the van tipped onto its side. The sound of twisting metal was loud in the confines of what was essentially a large steel box. The sliding door was torn off with the weight of the van on top of it. Muddied earth scraped past below them, and Frankie hung from the seats, his feet danced across the ground as it rushed by until he pulled himself up and planted his feet either side of the open doorway.

"It's Carter," he called, as he searched through whatever window he could. "He's pushing us into the river. Get your seat belts off and get to the back door."

"But, Frankie-" Penelope protested.

"Just get out of the bloody van, Penelope," Frankie snapped. "Go, now. I'll pass Jake to you, and you both jump."

Penelope looked up at him, frozen in shock and horror at what he was asking her to do.

"Penelope, go now," he shouted. "I'll get Nigel out."

Her hands trembled with uncontrollable fear as she fumbled with the belt. When it eventually released, she fell into Frankie's arms and her feet hung above the ground that was rushing past below. Holding on with one hand, Frankie pushed her up into the back of the van.

"Quickly, Penelope, climb over and open the doors. I'll pass Jake to you."

With the van on its side, Penelope was disoriented. She stumbled between the roof and the seats, felt for the door handle, and shoved it open. The ground outside caught the edge of the door. In seconds, it was torn from the van with an angry screech of twisting metal.

A wide-eyed and visibly-frightened Jake hung from Frankie's strong-arm when she turned back. Penelope reached for the boy and helped him through to the rear of the van, where she stood with her feet planted on the seats.

"Do you trust me, Jake?"

Jake glanced outside then back at his dad, who had climbed into the front to help Nigel. He looked back, and the two shared a moment; a paternal, unspoken message was being conveyed.

Without warning, the van came to an abrupt stop. Both Penelope and Jake stumbled forwards and fell outside into the mud. Penelope looked behind, and the huge steel scoop of the bulldozer loomed above. The van had hit the barrier that ran between the edge of the site and the river.

"Move," said Frankie. "Get out of here."

"Crawl, Jake," she said, spotting a patch of heavy, wild grass and bushes that were growing on the bank of the river. "Over there."

From the relative safety of the riverbank, Penelope pulled Jake in close to her, burying his head into her chest. She glanced over the tip off the bank. Frankie had kicked the windscreen out and was wrestling with Nigel's limp body. The bulldozer gears crunched like huge metallic teeth. The throttle roared and in the gloom of the rain, thick smoke belched from the upstanding exhaust. The huge spotlights were like evil, piercing eyes. The huge machine gave everything it had to force the van over the edge.

The driver was hidden in the dark shadows, but Penelope could easily imagine Carter's wild eyes and evil grin as he worked the machine to its limits.

Steel screeched, engines roared, and the mud sucked. Then, against all odds, Frankie appeared at the front of the van with his arms around Nigel's chest. Penelope saw him preparing for one final push when the van was forced over the edge.

"Frankie," she called, but her voice was lost to the angry diesel engine and twisting steel.

Words failed her. She was helpless. She turned Jake away as the van crashed down the riverbank, where it rolled onto its roof, slid a little, then bounced down the forty feet of steep mud.

It hit with the water with an almighty splash and turned upside down, leaving Penelope staring at the underside of the van.

CHAPTER FIFTY-TWO

Freezing cold water filled the van in a few short seconds.

Frankie gasped the last of his air, then submerged into the murky, gloom of the River Thames.

The undertow tugged at his legs, threatening to pull him from the van. He held onto Nigel with everything he had. Frankie's lungs screamed for air. The bright lights of the bulldozer above them, grew dimmer and dimmer as the van sank lower and lower to the depths of the river.

He plunged himself back inside the upturned van and found the passenger foot-well where a final pocket of air offered him a few more critical seconds of life. In the murky water, Nigel's limp body rocked to and fro with the ebb and flow of the water. Frankie's best friend would have seconds before his body surrendered to the frigid water.

Frankie pulled his body around, hooked his feet behind the passenger seat, and grabbed hold of Nigel's torso. The time for being careful had long passed. Frankie wrenched his friend from the seat, but his foot that was tucked behind the brake pedal. Frankie pulled even harder but to no avail.

He pinched Nigel's nose and breathed into his mouth, but there was no reaction.

Only the fortuitous jolt of the van hitting the river bed was enough the rock Nigel in just the right way. Nigel's body rose from the seat.

Frankie pulled himself into the foot-well one last time, found that tiny pocket of air then prepared to surface. He squeezed Nigel's nose, breathed air into his lungs, feeling his chest rise as he did, and then pushed him out through the empty windscreen.

Frankie pushed off, just catching hold of Nigel's body as the current took hold of him. He kicked as hard as he could. The military training courses on such incidents had been set in controlled circumstances, often in deep, indoor specialist pools. They were nothing compared to the real thing. Frankie kicked and kicked, holding Nigel in the hook of one arm.

As the surface grew closer, and the light of the bulldozer's spots began to grow stronger, Frankie kicked even harder.

With a massive intake of air, the two men broke through the surface of the water. Frankie held Nigel's face upturned and breathed clean air into his body.

They were caught on the outer bend of the river, where the water ran fast and wild. Frankie caught hold of an overhanging tree. The bough bent with the weight of the men and the force of the current. But still, Frankie held Nigel's head out of the water. Screaming with the effort for his frozen hands to hold on, he scrambled for a foothold, finding nothing but soft mud below him. But then there was a rock. It large enough to place his foot on. Frankie dug deeper than ever before, and with one final surge of energy, he heaved Nigel close the water's edge where there were roots and plants for him to grab.

One step at a time, he pulled Nigel from the freezing water and dropped him onto the river bank. Then, with a final heave, and as the remains of his energy drained away, he fell down beside him.

But his work wasn't over. He forced himself to his knees, tipped Nigel's head back and checked his throat for a swallowed tongue or debris. Then, pinching his nose, Frankie breathed two breaths into his body. He gripped one frozen hand with the other and began to pound on Nigel's chest.

The years of training had worked. Instinct took over. But no amount of training could match the sheer will of a man trying to pull his friend back from the brink of death.

After thirty compressions, Frankie breathed twice into Nigel. He watched as his friend's chest rose, then sank.

"Come on, you bastard," he shouted. "Breathe for God's sake."

But Nigel remained still.

Frankie returned to the compressions.

"You can lay there all you bloody want, Nigel. But you're going to breathe if you like it or bloody not."

Talking to his lifeless friend somehow kept Nigel alive in Frankie's mind. His body may have stopped working, but Nigel's spirit was strong, and Frankie clung to that thought as he finished the round of compressions and gave him two more breaths of air.

"Nigel, wake up. Don't do this."

Lowering his cheek to Nigel's mouth, Frankie waited to feel the faintest lick of warm breath.

But nothing came.

"You selfish bastard," he shouted, unaware of the tears that rolled down his face. The emotions of the day, the anger at his father and Carter, the fear and relief of losing and finding Jake, and now losing his best friend, ploughed through Frankie's mind and stabbed at his heart.

He sat back on his haunches, looked up at the sky, the frustration tearing him all directions, and screamed. He screamed until his throat rasped and stung, and then he screamed some more, pushing through the pain, and feeling the veins on his temples pulse with the rapid beat of his heart.

And with a final vent of anger, he slammed his clenched fist down on Nigel's chest.

Once.

"You bastard, Nigel."

Twice.

"Breathe, you son of a bitch."

Three times.

"You selfish wanker."

But the fourth punch fell away mid-swing.

Water spewed from Nigel's mouth.

He sat up as if electrified, puked onto himself, and sucked in air like it was the first breath he'd ever taken.

Frankie watched on with shock as Nigel then rolled to his side, and puked up the river water that had flooded his body. A few moments passed before Nigel was able to comprehend his surroundings. He clutched his chest and winced at the pain until his eyes fell on Frankie and his breathing calmed.

"I was hoping for an angel," said Nigel, as he buried his face into the mud and worked his limbs. He flexed his toes, straightened his legs and arms, and clenched and unclenched his fists then fell back onto the mud.

The shivers kicked in.

"The day you wake up to find an angel, buddy, I'll be right beside you."

Nigel raised an eyebrow as if it were the only muscle he had the energy to move.

"I bet you I'd get her number before you."

Frankie smiled. The urge to laugh was strong, but the energy required had long since been spent.

"I think you broke a rib," said Nigel, his breathing short and sharp. He clutched his chest and gingerly felt for a break.

"I'd have broken them all if it would have woken you up, you selfish bastard."

But Frankie's elation was short-lived.

At the top of the riverbank, silhouetted against the lights of the bulldozer, Carter's form stood in the pouring rain. He leaned on a short length of wood he was using as a crutch. He balanced on his good leg, clapped three loud claps, then lifted the rifle and aimed at the two men.

"What a touching scene," Carter called down to them. "You two should be in the movies."

"You should try it," said Frankie. "The water's lovely."

"We're screwed," said Nigel under his breath. "Are you carrying?"

Frankie shook his head, not taking his eyes off Carter.

"I found something of yours," said Carter. He turned and gestured for Penelope and Jake, who emerged from the darkness, to join Frankie and Nigel.

A crushing feeling of failure sucked whatever energy remained in Frankie's body as his son and the girl he'd grown to love, made their way down through the bulrushes and weeds and across the muddy bank to stand by his side. Defeated and broken, Frankie could barely look Jake in the eye as he ran the final few steps and threw his little arms around him. But there was no time for sentiment. Penelope's face was fearful. Her body was rigid and shaking with the cold, and the fright of what was about to happen.

"Why Carter?" shouted Frankie. "You got my father. He's dead. That's what you wanted, wasn't it?"

Carter's laugh cut through the shower of rain on the river's surface. It carved its way through the heavy wind that tore along the riverbank and rustled the weeds and rippled the water.

"Your father was just the beginning, Frankie. But how can I let *you* go? How can I ever live in peace knowing that you're out there somewhere? A tiny piece of Isaac Black lives inside you, and as much as you hate it, you are your father's son, Frankie."

"So kill me then," shouted Frankie. "Let the others go."

"Your boy," said Carter. "There's Black blood in him, too."

"He's just a child, Bobby."

Raindrops fell from Frankie's face, and hope drained from his body. It was all he could do to stay upright, kneeling beside Nigel with Jake in his arms and Penelope behind him.

"You die together. All of you," Carter called. "That way I'll know."

"You're a coward, Bobby. You always were."

"Is that right? Is that why I'm the one standing up here with the gun, and you're the one down there, crying and pleading for your life?"

"Your brother would be alive if you weren't such a coward."

Carter strengthened his aim.

"You just signed the deal, Frankie."

"If you hadn't insisted we drop you with the money, you'd have been there when Billy died."

"You better watch what you say, Frankie."

"Why? You're going to kill us anyway. You might as well know the truth."

"If you hadn't got such a big mouth, the argument would never have happened."

"My dad asked me to pick him and his mates up from the high street, Bobby," said Frankie. "I was on leave from serving my country. How was I supposed to know I was picking him and his mates up from a bloody robbery?"

"Not my problem, Frankie."

"Well, it was your brother's problem. At least he had the balls to stand up for himself, face his battles like a man, and not hide away with the money."

"And look where that got him," said Carter.

"You sick bastard, Carter. He wanted to be like you, you know. It was written on his face. He looked up to you. And what did you do? You left him high and dry, knowing full well that the police were on our tails."

"Survival, Frankie," said Carter. "Some of us have an instinct.

Some of us don't. Which leads me nicely to the point I was going to make."

Carter aimed the gun at each of them in turn.

"Who's first?" he said.

Never before had Frankie felt his heart pounding so hard. How could he make such a choice?

"I'll go," shouted Nigel. He rolled onto his side and sat up on his knees. "Me. I'm first. But you better be ready for me, Carter. I'm going to haunt you."

It was all going wrong. Everything Frankie had done. Everything he'd worked for in the space of a single day was slipping away. It was his fault. It wasn't Nigel's, it wasn't Jake's and it sure as hell wasn't Penelope's.

"Wait," he called out. "Stop."

Carter's cruel smile was visible even from the top of the bank.

"It's me who should die first. This is *my* fault. It's *my* fault my dad's dead. It's *my* fault we're here. And it's my fault we're in this bloody mess. I should have shot you when I shot your brother."

Carter's head cocked to one side. His gun lowered a fraction as Carter digested the statement.

"That's right, Bobby," said Frankie, pushing himself to his feet and passing Jake to Penelope. It was me that killed your low-life brother. My dad just took the hit. Do you want to know what I felt when I shot him in the face and saw his head explode?"

Carter seemed to rock on his feet. The two-by-four he leaned on barely supported his body and the news knocked him.

"It felt like I was stamping on a bug," continued Frankie. "A no good, dirty, thieving-"

"Say goodbye to your family, Frankie," said Carter. He raised his gun with trembling hands, aimed at Frankie, and a flash of wild gunfire split the night.

CHAPTER FIFTY-THREE

Bobby Carter's last words would haunt Penelope for as long as she lived. The look in his eye and the sheer cold-blooded nature of the man sent a repulsive shiver through her body.

She pulled Jake away and held him close, burying his head in her body. But the terror that gripped her as she expected Frankie to fall at her feet turned to confusion, as Bobby's lifeless corpse balanced for few moments before gravity sent him tumbling to the muddy bank. He rolled harmlessly down the steep riverbank and stopped with his face turned up to the wind and rain.

A feeling of disbelief ran through her, and by the look of shock on Frankie's face, he too felt it.

Nigel sat back on his knees and heels, let his head fall back and allowed the rain to wash over his face.

But Frankie remained poised, his feet planted. He was ready to take the hit as Debbie Carter emerged from the darkness; her silhouette replacing that of her dead husband's.

Penelope saw the shape of Frankie's handgun hanging from her grip. She dropped it to the mud, fell to her knees and let her face fall into her open hands.

Frankie turned in an instant and scooped Jake up into his arms.

Penelope stepped forward slowly, feeling lost. But something inside told her to go to Debbie.

"It's over," she said, and she rested her hand on Debbie's head. "It's all over, Debbie."

Debbie's body seemed to convulse beneath Penelope's hand. The tears that had been suppressed for so many years came flooding out, bringing with them every ounce of hate, fury and disgust that poisoned her life.

"I've just killed my husband," she said, as if in disbelief.

Debbie's arms unfurled and wrapped around Penelope's legs. Then, as the convulsions grew stronger, and the hug grew tighter, Debbie openly wailed. Frankie stared up from the riverbank, but Penelope waved him away and then slid to the ground to hold Debbie.

They stayed like that for over an hour. They shivered in the rain together. They held each other for warmth, comfort and strength. As the inevitable came, and the construction site was awash with flashing blue lights, an EMT placed a red blanket around their shoulders.

"Come and sit in the ambulance," she said. She was a middle-aged woman with natural beauty. She knew the two of them needed to be alone by what Penelope could only describe as maternal instinct. "I'll be here when you're ready, okay?" said the EMT, and she moved away leaving Penelope with a warm smile.

No more words passed between Debbie and Penelope, but they sat on the riverbank watching the inky water flow by in a shared moment of utter fear and helplessness. At first, Penelope had held Debbie to let her know that she was there. If she wanted to talk, Penelope was there to listen. If she wanted to squeeze tight, Penelope would squeeze back. But only a few minutes had passed when Penelope, reflecting on the day, needed Debbie just as much. The shock of being held at gunpoint in an execution tent. The horror of the near-rape that Frankie had saved her from. And the terrible events that had taken place in that God-awful construction site.

It was then that she realised they needed each other. The two women were sitting side by side, arm in arm and together they wept.

Bobby Carter's blanket-covered corpse lay just a few feet in front of them, but neither mentioned him. Neither tried to move him or moved further along the bank away from his lifeless body. They ignored him because, for both of them, they were entering a new chapter in their lives.

For Penelope, who stared beyond Bobby Carter at the doting father she had grown to love, the future was uncertain.

For Debbie, uncertainty was not the problem. She had survived an abusive marriage. She had escaped the beatings and rapes and in any other circumstances, would have been free to do as she pleased; if it wasn't for the two police officers who waited for her just a few steps away.

For Debbie Carter, the future was grim and bright. The future was safe yet insecure.

For Debbie Carter, the future was certain.

CHAPTER FIFTY-FOUR

"Are you ready, Jake?" called Frankie.

He put his coffee down on the kitchen work surface and took a final look at the double-page spread of the newspaper. Penelope's article told a story so very different from the one she had been planning. The article was appealing for the release of Debbie Carter who was being held on remand for the murder of her husband. There was also mention of a single father who had rescued his son but had lost his own dad as the tragedy played out.

There was no mention of the military or special forces of any kind. For that, Frankie was grateful.

"But you haven't told me where we're going," Jake called back. He appeared at the top of the stairs. "I'm not coming down until you tell me where we're going."

Frankie gave a sideways glance at Penelope, who stood in the living room admiring the photo of Jacqui in the rain in London. She smiled back at him and took a sip of her coffee.

"Well, I guess you don't want to see the lions and tigers then?" said Frankie. "That's a shame. We were looking forward to the zoo."

Jake thundered down the stairs and burst into the kitchen.

"We're going to the zoo?" he said, his voice full of excitement.

Frankie gave a little laugh. "Yes, we are. So you better go and get dressed, or the animals will all be asleep by the time we get there."

Jake thundered back up the stairs and into his room. Frankie took the opportunity to sidle up behind Penelope, but she moved away, turned and offered him a weak smile.

"Have you made your mind up?" he asked.

She nodded.

"I'm sorry," she said. "There's just too much-"

"Don't say a thing," said Frankie.

"What will you do?"

"I'll go on doing what I do best," said Frankie.

"So, if ever I need to find somebody."

"You should call the police," said Frankie.

She laughed once then stopped. "Maybe. Unless I need an secretive ex-special forces operative-"

Frankie raised an eyebrow.

"That I know nothing about," she finished.

"And never will."

She shook her head. No more words were needed.

Aside from Jake's heavy footsteps thumping on the floor above them, another familiar sound caught Frankie's ear.

Penelope smiled up at him.

"Is that-" he began. But his question fell redundant when a flash of green passed by outside and the rumble of the old V6 engine pulled onto his drive. "No," said Frankie. "It can't be."

He pulled away from Penelope to peer through the window.

"Is this you?" he asked as he strode to the front door and pulled it open. "It was you, wasn't it?"

He stepped down to his driveway to find Nigel climbing from the driver's seat of Frankie's nineteen fifty-three Aston Martin DB3.

"I don't believe it," he said.

Frankie walked around the car and admired the repaired body-work. He ran his hand across the new windshield, which must have cost a small fortune to find and replace.

"How did you do it?" said Frankie to Nigel.

"I had to use another body shop, and their work might not be as good as yours, but here she is," said Nigel, failing to hide his smile.

Penelope stepped out and welcomed Nigel with a hug and kiss on his cheek.

"Thank you," she said under her breath. But Frankie heard and knew she'd arranged it with him.

"My way of saying thank you," said Penelope.

"She's as good as new," said Frankie. "I'm totally shocked." He peeled his eyes from the car and looked across the bonnet at the two of them as they stood there mischievously. "Thank you. Thank you both. You've no idea how much this means to me."

"Ah, come on, Frankie," said Nigel. He gave Penelope a side-ways wink. "You did save both our lives, after all."

"Yeah," said Penelope, "we figured we had to say thanks some-how. Besides, it was *my* head that smashed the windscreen."

"Guys, this is incredible," replied Frankie, as Jake ran through the door.

"Uncle Nigel," he cried and jumped up for Nigel to catch him. "We're going to the zoo."

"You're going where?" replied Nigel, his voice full of enthu-siasm for the boy.

"We're going to the zoo. Are you coming too?"

"Oh, Jake, I'd love to go to the zoo, but I have work to do," said Nigel. "I have a few unexpected meetings to attend." He offered Frankie a sideways glance.

"Oh," said Jake.

"Maybe some other time, yeah?"

Frankie always marvelled at how natural Nigel was with Jake, even with no children of his own.

"Yeah, I guess," said Jake. "Are we going soon, Dad?"

"Well, as soon as you get yourself strapped in."

While Jake made himself comfortable in the tiny rear seat and Penelope helped him with the seat belt, Frankie shook Nigel's hand.

"Thanks, mate. I really appreciate it. How's the rib?"

"Broken," replied Nigel. "Broken and very painful."

"Good," said Frankie. "You need a reminder of who was the better soldier." He winked at his friend.

"Go have fun at the zoo," said Nigel. He leaned in close one more time. "I left a little something for you in the glove compartment." It was Nigel's turn to wink. He slapped the bonnet twice in farewell, then turned and headed up the road towards a waiting black SUV.

"Come on, Dad," said Jake.

"I've locked the house," said Penelope, and she handed him a single key. "Go have fun."

"I'm not used to taking orders from you, Miss Pike," he said as he climbed into the driver's seat and shut the door. He ran his hand across the leather steering wheel, and then the dashboard, feeling it all as if for the first time. "But I could get used to it."

"Maybe one day," she said, and she pulled her helmet on.

He fired up the car and couldn't hide his grin at the sound of the old engine, running as smoothly as she ever did.

Penelope leaned over the car door and gave Frankie a peck on the cheek.

"Take good care of that little boy, Frankie Black."

Her hair smelled good and her skin was soft and smooth. He closed his eyes and breathed her in for the last time.

By the time he opened his eyes, the little Vespa engine was starting up.

Frankie swallowed his thoughts.

"Are you okay, Daddy?"

He found Jake in the little rear-view mirror.

"Yeah," he said, and he smiled. "Yeah, we're good mate."

She blew him a kiss as she pulled off the drive and Frankie watched her grow smaller as she left his life. He wondered if their paths would cross again.

Before setting off, he reached across to the glove compartment, pulled the little hatch open and found a cassette tape that Nigel had planted there.

He slid the cassette into the old tape player.

"Are you ready for this Jake?" he said as he reversed off the drive, knowing exactly what song would play.

"I'm ready, Dad," came Jake's excited reply.

The opening bars of Led Zeppelin's, Black Dog fired out from the car's speakers. It was the song that Nigel and the guys had played when they returned from their first tour as a unit with Frankie in command.

Frankie turned the volume to full, found first, and pulled away from his house. And with his son in the back seat, he turned right, away from London, and into the great British countryside.

The End

Also by J.D. Weston

Award-winning author and creator of Harvey Stone and Frankie Black, J.D. Weston was born in London, England, and after more than a decade in the Middle East, now enjoys a tranquil life in Lincolnshire with his wife.

The Harvey Stone series is the prequel series set ten years before The Stone Cold Thriller series.

With more than twenty novels to J.D. Weston's name, the Harvey Stone series is the result of many years of storytelling, and is his finest work to date. You can find more about J.D. Weston at www.jdweston.com.

Turn the page to see his other books.

THE HARVEY STONE SERIES

Free Novella

A terrible moment in time, captured in blood.

See *www.jdweston.com for details.*

The Silent Man

To catch the shadow he must break all the rules...

See www.jdweston.com for details.

The Spider's Web

The harder you struggle the tighter his web becomes...

See www.jdweston.com for details.

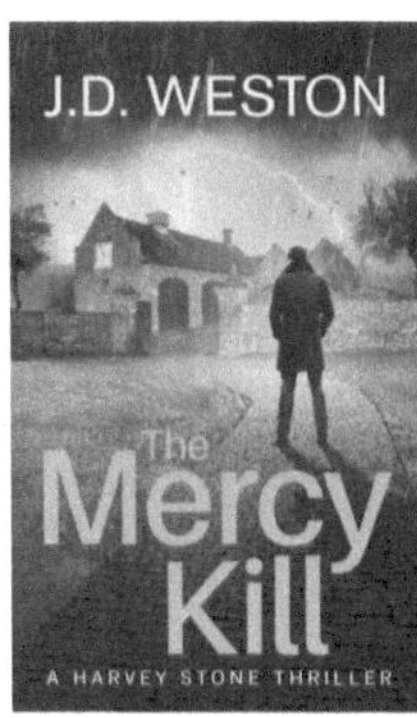

The Mercy Kill

To light the way, he must burn his past...

See www.jdweston.com for details.

The Savage Few

Coming October 2021

Join the J.D. Weston Reader Group to stay up to date on new releases, receive discounts, and get three free eBooks.

See www.jdweston.com for details.

THE STONE COLD THRILLER SERIES

The Stone Cold Thriller Series

Stone Cold

Stone Fury

Stone Fall

Stone Rage

Stone Free

Stone Rush

Stone Game

Stone Raid

Stone Deep

Stone Fist

Stone Army

Stone Face

The Stone Cold Box Sets

Boxset One

Boxset Two

Boxset Three

Boxset Four

Visit www.jdweston.com for details.

THE FRANKIE BLACK FILES

Visit www.jdweston.com for details.